The Heart's Own Truth

ALICE BONTHRON

The Heart's Own Truth
Copyright © 2019 by Alice Bonthron

ISBN: 978-1-0830-5383-1

This is a work of fiction. Names, characters, businesses, places, events, and incidents are either the products of the author's imagination or used in a fictitious manner. Any resemblance to actual persons, living or dead, or actual events is purely coincidental.

DEDICATION

To Betty Ferguson

Thanks for the Final Push

And

The Fallston Commons Community

ACKNOWLEDGMENTS

Thanks to my critique partners – Laurie Claypole, Sara Thorn, Mary Blain, Julie Rief, Leah Chrest and my porch pal, Nikki Coffman.

To Tom Yingling for his eagle eyes and for being our Computer Guru and to Susan Thomey for sharing her grandfather's surgical kit from the mid-1800s with me.

CHAPTER 1

New York City – 1880

Bernice removed a packet from her purse and handed it to her mother. "This should relieve your sea sickness. Have Sally mix it in some hot water. You can chew on the ginger root if you need immediate relief."

"I will not be requiring any of your silly herbal remedies. They have a well-respected physician on board to attend the passengers. Would that you spent as much energy as you do with your weeds on more important things." Her mother waved a hand in a royal dismissal, or perhaps it was an imperial decree. Either way meant that the subject matter was going to turn in the direction of marriage, a subject that Bernice wished to avoid discussing with her mother yet again.

In an effort to keep the conversation on herbs, she addressed her mother's maid. "I provided enough for you also, should you need it, Sally. Infuse the horehound powder in hot water, and make sure you let it sit for about five minutes before you drink it." The maid took the packet, gave Bernice a sympathetic smile, and said, "Thank you, Miss Bernice."

Coming to the rescue, her father rose from a chair in

the corner of the cabin. "If we don't get off this ship, we'll be making the trip with them."

Father and daughter bestowed a farewell kiss on the traveler's raised cheek, and Bernice thought maybe she might be able to disembark without a lecture. However, her mother was not going to cross the Atlantic Ocean and be away for six months without issuing instructions.

"I expect to be planning your wedding when I return from Europe. That is the only reason I agreed to leave you behind. It is your duty to secure a proper husband and take your place in society. Ambrose Kingsley will make a fine son-in-law. Perhaps not quite as fine as Theodora Delacourte's, but we could not aspire to such a match. Amelia far surpasses you in grace, poise, and beauty. It is no surprise that she has made her mother the envy of all of Baltimore society by marrying into the Astor family. Still, Ambrose Kingsley is more than suitable. It is a miracle he has shown any interest in you at all after that scandal with the farmer's son."

The farmer's son that her mother spoke of with such disdain was Doctor Peter Schmidt, and the phantom scandal took place at the Reilly New Year's Ball. He had waltzed her out into the hallway behind a large arrangement of white and red roses where they were hidden from view to save her from the unwanted attentions of a potential suitor sent by her mother.

She was surprised by his response to her expression of gratitude. "He does not deserve you. You should have someone who appreciates you for yourself and not your family's fortune - someone who will unlock the woman hiding behind that prim and proper exterior."

"And where might I find such a suitor?" She had found herself flirting shamelessly, which was uncharacteristic for her.

He leaned in and brushed her neck with his lips as he whispered, "He may be closer than you think."

She turned and looked up at him. He lowered his face

until his lips were so close she could feel his breath on her own. She thought he was about to kiss her. She hoped he was about to kiss her, but the spell was broken by the sound of a loud gasp. Bernice whirled around to see Amelia Delacourte. Amelia said nothing, but stood in silent condemnation with a smirk on her face.

In an attempt to save her reputation, Peter said, "Miss Peterson was feeling faint. I thought it best to get her out of the crowded ballroom."

That was the end of anything that might have happened between them. Peter was polite and distant after that. Most likely he came to his senses when he saw the sparkling, beautiful Amelia in comparison to plain, dull Bernice Peterson.

Bernice felt a twinge of anger at her mother's denigrating reference to Peter. "That farmer's son happens to be a doctor, and he was simply concerned for my welfare. Amelia Delacourte has a vicious imagination." It was a partial truth. Peter had been concerned for her welfare, just not in the manner she just described.

Her mother gave her a disapproving frown. "It is of little importance now. The entire incident will all be forgotten once you are married to Ambrose."

Bernice gave a weary sigh. "Ambrose and I are not in love."

"Love has nothing to do with it. A successful marriage is based on one's breeding and class. Look at your father and me. We have taken our proper places in society and established a good home for you and your sister."

At last her mother had provided her a way out of the conversation. "Please give my love to Emma and Aunt Harriet."

Her mother nodded, and then took one last opportunity to remind Bernice of her inadequacies as she looked up and down her daughter's slim figure. "You lack the physical attributes and style of your sister and the other young ladies in our social circle. Be grateful Ambrose has shown you so much attention. Perhaps he feels comfortable with you because you have known one another since you were children. Whatever the reason, he has given his mother cause to believe there is the possibility of a marriage. She insinuated as much to me at Mrs. Ridgley's luncheon last month. That is the only reason I am allowing you to remain home with your father."

The ship's whistle blew one long blast warning for all visitors to disembark. Bernice's father held out his arm. "Come along, we must take our leave." She took the offered arm gladly, walking at a rapid pace until they stepped onto the dock.

"We are off the ship now. You can slow the pace a bit. No need to worry about taking the trip to Europe," her father teased.

Bernice looked back at the large ocean liner as the ship's crewmembers pulled the lines and the gangway was raised. "Am I that obvious?"

"I doubt your mother noticed. She is too busy with her own plans for you." Her father pulled her out of the way of a dockworker pushing a cart loaded with boxes. "The years have taught me to be more observant."

She gave his arm a squeeze. "I could never hide my true feelings from you."

"How would you like to have dinner at Delmonico's this evening? I think a special treat would do us both good."

"That sounds wonderful."

*****

Bernice popped the last of her Lobster Newberg into her mouth. "That was delicious."

Her father rested his knife and fork next to the plate that had once been filled with the famous Delmonico's steak and said, "We can't leave Delmonico's without having some of their Baked Alaska."

"I really can't eat a full desert, but would enjoy some

coffee and perhaps a bite or two of yours."

"All right then – one Baked Alaska and two coffees," her father instructed their waiter.

While they waited for their desert to be served, Bernice looked about the room. It was richly decorated in gold and green, and was even more ornate than the lobby's grand staircase they had ascended to reach the main dining room. Delmonico's was the establishment where visitors wanted to dine when they were in New York. Samuel Clemens, who wrote under the name of Mark Twain, dined at Delmonico's, as had the famous opera singer Jenny Lind, and the American actress, Lillian Russell. Presidents and politicians were also known to frequent the establishment.

A short time later, the waiter returned with their dessert and two cups of coffee. Bernice swirled her spoon around in the coffee, watching the cream lighten it.

"Father, was mother right? Did you marry out of duty and not love?"

He reached across the table and took her hand. "What I did is of little importance now. What will you do? Will you marry out of duty, or for love?

She gave a little sigh. "Love, but I fear no one will ever fall in love with me. Mother's right, I'm not attractive."

Her father banged his coffee cup onto the saucer. "She has fed you that nonsense since you became a young woman, but she is wrong. You are a lovely, vibrant woman, and I'm sure Ambrose is attracted to you for that reason."

"Well, mother is right about one thing. Ambrose isn't attracted by my physical attributes."

Her father emptied his cup and then motioned for the waiter to bring him another. After the man left their table, he asked, "How would you like to stay in New York for a few weeks?"

"Do you have business to attend?" She was used to his frequent trips to New York.

"I have some business, but I was thinking we might have ourselves a vacation. What do you say?"

Bernice patted his hand across the table. "I would like that very much."

*****

The next afternoon they took a carriage ride through Central Park, New York's playground for the wealthy, where the paths were crowded with luxurious carriages. Bernice couldn't help but think how impressed her mother would be with such status symbols, but she was more interested in observing the landscape. When they reached the Mall's doubled allées of elms, they decided to stroll a bit. They walked until they came to the Bethesda Terrace, and then took one of the grand staircases that led to the fountain, stopping to admire it. An eight-foot bronze statue of a female winged angel touching down upon the top of the fountain stood in its center, where water spouted and cascaded into the upper basin and into the surrounding pool. Beneath her were four-foot high cherubs representing Temperance, Purity, Health, and Peace. Also called the Angel of the Waters, the statue represented the angel blessing the Pool of Bethesda, giving it healing powers. The sculpture was designed by Emma Stebbins, the first woman to receive a public commission for major work in New York City.

An attractive woman sat nearby sketching the view beyond the lake and woodland. She raised her head and a cascade of dark curls streaked with silver, fell over her shoulders. Bernice could just imagine what her mother would have to say about a woman in public without her hair pinned up. The woman smiled as if she were expecting them. Bernice smiled back, not quite understanding why she felt drawn to this stranger. Her father waved and steered her toward the woman. "I thought I'd find you here this afternoon."

She put her art supplies in a carrying case that sat next to her and reached out her hands to him. "Am I so predictable?"

Her father took the woman's hands, giving them a gentle squeeze. "Only to your friends."

Bernice studied the two of them and realized her father had never spoken in such a relaxed manner to her mother. Her parents' speech with one another was stilted and formal when they conversed, which was as little as possible.

Her father gave a nervous cough, upon noticing her scrutiny. "Bernice, may I present Mrs. Boughers. Mrs. Boughers, my daughter, Bernice."

The woman took her hand and said, "Julie, to my friends."

Bernice liked the woman. There was warmth and familiarity about her. "Have we met before?"

Her father looked at the woman and smiled. "Julie is Matthew's mother. That is why you recognize the name."

Bernice nodded. "Father says he would be lost without Matthew."

"I'm happy to hear that." Julie's dark eyes shone warmly when they met her father's. "He's much more suited to business than art, I'm afraid."

Matthew had come to work for her father as his assistant a few years back and had been invited to their home for various occasions, much to her mother's chagrin. Since Matthew was her father's employee, her mother saw no reason why he should be treated as a guest in their home, but her father insisted. It was the only time Bernice had ever seen her father argue with her mother, and even then, her mother had sent her from the parlor and closed the doors, but she had stood outside listening.

Looking out over the landscape, Bernice suddenly remembered something else. "You're J. Boughers. I've seen your paintings in several homes and galleries. They are beautiful."

"Thank you." Julie bent and picked up her art case. "May I invite the two of you to dinner?"

"What do you say, Bernice?" Her father reminded her of an eager schoolboy.

"That would be lovely." She wanted to get to know this woman who made her father smile.

As Bernice and her father chatted with Julie, she saw a couple walking on a nearby pathway. The woman wore a stylish navy blue walking suit with gold trim at the neck and down the bodice. She had one gloved hand hooked in the crook of her companion's arm, while the other twirled a blue striped parasol. A Bird of Paradise bobbled among the feathers in a hat that sat atop the most stunning red hair Bernice had ever seen. It wasn't bright red or dark red, but a combination of both and when she held her parasol back so the sun shone on it, it looked as if it had spun gold in it. She walked alongside the gentleman with an air of confidence, and why wouldn't she? This woman with her looks and shapely figure could command the attention of any man in her presence. It was at that moment that Bernice took notice of the young woman's suitor.

No, it could not possibly be him. What was he doing in New York? He leaned down and said something to the young woman causing her to laugh. She removed her hand and patted his arm as they walked toward another man waiting at the end of the path. Just then, he looked over and his eyes caught hers making it impossible to pretend she hadn't noticed them. Before Bernice could look away, he broke away from the young woman and the other gentleman and strode purposely toward her.

Her father recognized him at once. "Doctor Schmidt, what brings you to New York?"

"I am attending a medical conference. And you, sir?"

"We are having a little vacation. Allow me to introduce our good friend, Mrs. Boughers." Bernice's father gave Julie that special smile once more. "Julie, this is Doctor Peter Schmidt, a very prominent doctor in Baltimore."

Peter bowed and said, "Mrs. Boughers, it is an honor to meet you."

"Please, call me Julie," she said just as she had done when introduced to Bernice. "Our society is far too formal."

"I could not agree with you more," he gave her a charming smile.

Bernice remained silent. What could she say? That he had left her in a state of confusion and hurt? That even now when she should care less about him, her heart beat faster and the same vulnerable feeling took hold of her when he scrutinized her face with those amber eyes.

There was a moment of awkward silence before her father said, "I hear congratulations are in order. Doctor Hawkins is a good friend of mine, and he tells me he decided upon you as his replacement as Director of the City Dispensary."

"I have not accepted the position." Peter's brows slanted in a frown.

"I'm sure they will be very lucky if you do," Julie interjected before spontaneously adding, "Bernice and her father are joining me for dinner this evening; perhaps you might also join us."

He gave her a regretful smile. "Thank you for the invitation, but I will be spending this evening preparing a presentation I have to give tomorrow." Then noticing that his attractive friend and the other gentleman were up ahead a little ways waiting for him, he excused himself.

After Peter had left and Bernice's father was taking down Julie's easel, Julie whispered to Bernice, "I feel sorry for Peter. He is a very lonely young man."

Caught by surprise once more, Bernice asked, "Why do you say that?" He didn't seem to be lonely to her, not with a gorgeous woman attached to his arm.

"My dear, you can tell by looking at him. It is right there in his eyes. There is sadness there, even when he smiles. How well do you know him?"

"We have mutual friends." Bernice felt as if Julie knew there was more, but the older woman refrained from further inquiry.

Julie sighed. "Something has happened in his life that has left deep scars."

"And you could tell that by being in his presence for so brief a period of time?" Bernice laughed lightly, but in the depths of her heart she knew Julie was right.

"You forget that I look with the eyes of an artist. I see more than just what appears on the surface." Julie took Bernice's hands in hers and looked into her eyes intently. "For instance, in you I see doubt and uncertainty, but also passion, kindness, and generosity of spirit. I see a woman who is not yet aware of her own beauty and power. That young man needs someone like you in his life."

The conversation was taking an uncomfortable direction for Bernice. "So tell me, how you would paint said subjects?"

Julie was kind enough to follow the change in conversation. "I would have to give great care to the eyes and facial expression, for that is where a person's story is written."

Bernice wondered how she would keep her secrets safe from this woman, or if she even wanted to, for that matter.

*****

Peter stared out his hotel bedroom window. It was long after midnight, and yet the noise from the traffic below reminded him that New York's streets were never quiet or empty. The carriages and hacks were taking their passengers from the theaters to other late night entertainments. Soon there would be less traffic as the likes of the Vanderbilts, Astors, and other prominent society members would depart to their mansions in Newport for the summer season. One of the carriages stopped in front of the hotel across the street where a gentleman in formal attire alighted and then assisted a woman in an evening gown from the vehicle. The woman was tall and slender, reminding him of Bernice. Not that he needed reminding. She was the reason he was staring out the window in the first place.

He should have pretended not to see her today in the park, but he could not have done that even if his life depended upon it. His eyes had been drawn to her like a magnet. He saw the hurt and confusion in her gaze before she masked it with a deceptive nonchalance. He cursed himself for being the one to put it there.

Last year he had been attracted to her, but fortunately, his survival instincts prevented him from going down a path that would have been the wrong one for both of them. Anyone with a beaker of sense could see that there was more to Bernice Peterson than just physical beauty. If he allowed her, she would ensnare his emotions, and that was an affliction to be avoided at all costs. Jenny had taught him that lesson long ago. So he had done the best thing for Bernice and broke all contact with her and buried himself in his work at the City Dispensary.

Now he would be forced to deal with his attraction to her, thanks to Dugan. There was no way he could accept the position as Director, no matter how much Doctor Hawkins wanted him. In order to avoid any scandal to the Dispensary, he would have to remove himself from the city. It would be best for him to return to North County and practice medicine there. Besides, it was an idea he had been contemplating seriously before Bernice entered his life. North County needed a doctor, and he would be able to not only practice medicine there, but do some research and occasionally travel and give lectures. The only reason he had abandoned the plan was his growing attachment to her. Now he had no choice. Dugan had sealed his fate. He was returning to North County.

There would be no avoiding Bernice. She was

Rasheen's best friend and Rasheen was now family to him, since she had married Connor Reilly. Peter was closer to Connor than any of his own brothers. The two men had come to live at Sara's Glen when they were in their early teens. Connor had been orphaned and become the ward of his uncle who bought Sara's Glen in hopes that it would remind the boy of his life on a horse-breeding farm in his native Ireland. Connor's uncle was married to Peter's mother's cousin Elaine, and so Peter and his parents had come to Sara's Glen to live so his parents could run the estate for the Reillys. The Reillys only liked to come to Sara's Glen during the summer because they preferred the city. Peter would return to the city with them during the winter months where he and Connor attended Loyola Boy's School. From there Peter went onto college, and then Medical School thanks to the generosity of Patrick Reilly.

Connor was the only one in whom he had confided the reason behind his plans to return to North County to practice medicine. In fact, Peter had entrusted him the task of getting a home and office ready for him when he returned, and Connor had insisted he take the original Stone House on his estate. It was perfect since it was at the edge of the estate and nearer to town. At least with his own home, he would not see Bernice as much as if he were actually living at Sara's Glen, but he would be spending time there visiting and she was sure to be there. It was not going to be easy, but somehow he would have to manage.

Seeing her today had reminded him of the spell she was capable of casting. His blood heated at the sight of her and the memory of the way she had looked the night of the Reilly ball when he had been about to kiss her. Kissing her would have been a mistake, and yet he could not banish the memory of that moment, or how her lips would feel touched to his own. Time seemed to go backwards when he was in her company, as if there had been no absence at all. He was grateful her father brought him back to the present by inquiring about the Directorship of the Dispensary.

Bernice had so much to give a man, the right man. Unfortunately, he was not that man.   He was not capable of any kind of love, unless it was purely physical with no emotional ensnarement. A solitary existence kept one free from the threat of pain and loss

CHAPTER 2

Bernice and Rasheen Reilly sat on a blanket spread on the porch floor while baby Clare crawled from one to the other. When the infant changed direction and headed toward Finn, the large brown family dog sleeping on the other side of the blanket, her mother reached down and plucked her up. "Little Missy, you leave poor Finn have his rest now. You wore him out this morning, and considering the amount of energy he has, that was quite an accomplishment." Clare responded with a burst of baby giggles.

"I can't believe she started to crawl while I was away," Bernice said, shaking her head in disbelief.

"You were gone over a month. Babies grow fast, too fast." Rasheen kissed Clare and put her down on the blanket with a sock toy that Martha made. "We were surprised that you stayed in New York after your mother left, but it must have been nice to have a vacation with just you and your father."

"It was wonderful. We dined at Delmonico's, took several carriage rides and strolls in Central Park, and ran into an old friend of father's. Actually, Mrs. Boughers, Julie, is Matthew's mother."

Rasheen raised an eyebrow. "And just who is

Matthew? Someone you met in New York? Is he a recent conquest?"

"Stop teasing me. Matthew is father's assistant. Father says he would be lost without him, and you would like his mother. I enjoyed the time we spent together. She took me on several shopping trips when father had business to attend to. That reminds me, I almost forgot that I bought a special gift for Clare." Bernice reached into her skirt pocket and produced a small gold box with a red velvet ribbon around it and handed it to Rasheen.

Carefully untying the ribbon, Rasheen removed the lid and lifted a tiny gold cross which dangled from a thin chain. "It's lovely."

"She won't be able to wear it for a bit, but I just could not resist when I saw it," Bernice said as she glanced down at the baby who had tired of playing with the sock toy and crawled over to her.

"She wants you to help her sit up. Take her hands and sit her up against you," said Rasheen.

Bernice took the child's hands and helped her move to a sitting position. "All these changes while I was away. My goodness!"

Martha came through the screen door with a tray holding a pitcher of lemonade and some glasses. "There have been more changes than Clare sitting up while you were away." She sat the tray on a nearby table and filled three glasses with lemonade, handing one to each of the young women before taking her own and plopping down in a nearby rocking chair. "Did you tell her the good news?"

Rasheen shook her head. "I left that for you."

Bernice looked at the excited expressions on her friends' faces and wondered what their good news could be? It had to be something to do with Sara's Glen or maybe North County, or maybe Connor was going to run for Governor. His uncle had been after him to run for public office for some time now, but he preferred the quiet

life of Sara's Glen. Her speculation was brought to an
abrupt halt when Martha said, "Peter has left the city and
set up his practice here. North County has a doctor, and I
have my son home."

Bernice forced a smile. So that was the reason Peter
told her father he had not made a decision about the
Directorship of the City Dispensary. He had already made
plans to move back to North County. Connor was seeing
to things in North County even as they were chatting with
Peter about the Directorship, yet he had said nothing.
What of the woman she had seen him with? Well, it
wasn't any of her business what he did, but there would be
no avoiding him now. Good heavens, suppose he came
up the porch steps right now? Her heart skittered at the
thought, even as a feeling of hopelessness filled her chest,
but she forced a neutral expression. "You must be very
happy. Will he be living here at Sara's Glen?"

"No. He has had additions put on the little stone
house and a separate building put up on the property for
his office. Connor oversaw the work while Peter was still
in the city," Martha answered.

Rasheen laughed. "I think Connor was as excited
about the project as Peter. He would ride out to the train
station every morning to check on deliveries of building
materials, and then oversee the delivery to the workers and
make sure they understood just what was to be done and
how it was to be done. He was so proud when Peter
expressed his appreciation and approval."

Bernice tried not to let her relief show, but let out the
breath she had been holding. She wouldn't run into him.
"Is he settled in the stone house?"

Martha nodded. "He still needs some furniture, but the
house is habitable, and the office is ready for business.
But then knowing him, you would expect his medicine
would come first. You should drop by on your way home
and say hello. Come to think of it, I can't believe you
didn't notice the additions when you drove by on your way

in."

"I'm afraid I was probably not paying much attention. I had to make some social calls this morning on my mother's behalf. Tuesday mornings are reserved for calls, and she left the task for me to see that her cards are left all over the county in the proper homes." Bernice rolled her eyes.

Rasheen let out a sigh. "Bless my dear husband for freeing me from that tedious duty. If I didn't love Connor Reilly for so many other reasons, that one alone would have won my heart."

"After this morning's visits, I envy you. Perhaps I'll find my hero someday." Bernice stood and sat her empty glass on the tray.

Martha got up and took Rasheen's empty glass from her and sat it on the tray along with her own. "Well, you make sure you stop by and see Peter on your way out." She took the tray into the house.

When the two young women were alone with the baby again, Rasheen remarked, "I doubt that marriage to Ambrose will take you away from the madness."

"Ambrose is a good friend and nothing more, but he does help to keep my mother from trying to match me up with others like that horrible Mr. Hilliard. She still chastises me for not encouraging his attentions."

"Martha will be happy to hear that. She still has hopes that she might play matchmaker for you and Peter."

"Please discourage her. Her intentions, though they are meant well, will only cause me embarrassment. He never showed me any attention other than when you and I attended Connor's Aunt's New Year's ball. I think he was just being polite to the plain girl."

"Why do you keep saying that? You are not plain. You have a lovely face with a delicate bone structure, like a Grecian goddess."

"And no figure."

"You are slender and graceful. Now that we have

you in the right colors and not those awful styles your mother picked, you outshine any woman in your presence. More than one man's head turned at that ball. And as I recall, your dance card was filled."

"I think it's more a matter of the Peterson fortune and not my attractiveness. My mother keeps me grounded in that reality."

Rasheen threw her hands up. "I give up!"

"That's good, because I think Peter may have formed an attachment. We saw him walking with a very attractive woman when we were in Central Park."

Shaking her head, Rasheen said, "It was probably nothing serious. If it were, Connor would know, and he has not said anything. Peter did have a woman he was seeing off and on in New York a few years back, but Connor said it was nothing serious. She was a wealthy young widow and the arrangement worked well for both of them as neither desired marriage, but she moved to Europe and they parted company."

Bernice fished in her pocket for her watch. The hunter pocket watch with its black enamel star motifs set with seed pearls and rose-cut diamonds was a gift from her father for her 24th birthday which had just passed. She checked the time and said, "I have to be on my way. There are a few things I need to attend to before father comes home."

Bernice stuck her head inside the screen door to say goodbye to Martha, happy that she had managed to avoid seeing Peter.

"I'm sure Peter will want to see you. He hasn't had much time since his return, but he does join us for dinner. Perhaps you could also join us this evening?" Martha asked.

"Father is home this evening, and I want to spend time with him." Bernice did want to spend the time with her father, but more than that, she wasn't ready to see Peter Schmidt, not when her heart still raced at the mention of his name.

"We will make it tomorrow then," Martha insisted.

Bernice bit her lower lip. There would be no escaping. Besides, she reasoned, sooner or later she would have to see him again. "Tomorrow will be fine."

*****

Peter signed the papers set before him, pushed them back across the desk toward Connor, and leaned his chair back as he raised his arms stretching them above his head. The two men had been holed up in the library which also acted as Connor's office for over two hours. "I expect these investments will make as good a return as the others."

"We have been fortunate in our expansions of our own business, and Uncle Patrick seems to have a keen sense when it comes to outside investing. You have to admit he has done well for the two of us, and our investments with your cousin's firm have been lucrative as well." Connor took the papers and stacked them on the side of the desk before rising and going over to a side table to pour himself and Peter a glass of brandy.

"Violet appreciates our faith in her. Most of her clients think that Gilbert is the only head of their firm." Peter swirled the brandy around in his glass. "I saw her recently, and she advised that maybe you might consider direct trade with China instead of going through the English?"

"The European countries already have the established trade routes. We're lagging behind them when it comes to the manufacture of modern steamboats." Connor swallowed some of the amber liquid in his glass before continuing. "But Uncle Patrick has just purchased another steamship for the Reilly line from an English firm. The ship is fairly new and should be faster than our current ones."

"From what I read in the papers when I was in New York, it should prove profitable. The consensus of opinion among the bankers is that the recession is ending and trade with Europe will be picking up." Peter finished the last of his drink just as Rasheen swept into the room with baby Clare resting on her hip.

"Your daughter wanted to say goodnight to her da," she said as she kissed Connor and handed him the baby.

Connor took the baby, held her high over his head amid a burst of baby giggles, and promptly was scolded by his wife. He lowered her and gently rocked her in his arms before kissing her cheek. "Isn't it a little early for her to be going to sleep?"

"Oh, she isn't going to sleep just yet, but since Bernice is having dinner with us tonight, we asked Bertie to stay and play with her until bed time so Martha and I could enjoy dinner uninterrupted. I think Bernice is a little disappointed, but she got to spend most of yesterday afternoon with the little darling." Rasheen took the baby from Connor, and as she was going out of the room, said over her shoulder, "Dinner will be in about half an hour."

Conner walked over to the doorway and watched his wife and daughter, a tender smile on his face, before he closed the door and returned to sink down into the soft leather sofa.

"Wedded bliss has made you a love sick school boy," Peter mocked.

"There is nothing wrong with wedded bliss. You should try it."

"I'll take your word for it. Though I am happy for you, I like my solitude. Few women would be willing to put up with the life of a doctor's wife," Peter said.

Connor studied him closely before speaking. "Jenny was a long time ago. It is time for you to move on."

Peter's expression became that of the professional, completely unreadable, but there was a tinge of warning in his words. "I have moved on. My life consists of my work. I can't become emotionally entangled. It would be too distracting."

Connor heeded the challenge and changed the subject. "I suppose you should be warned then."

"About?" Peter raised a questioning brow.

"Martha hasn't given up on her matchmaking, and now she has an ally in Rasheen. Why do you think they insisted Bernice stay for dinner?"

"I think I can manage, but it was easier when I had you on my side." Peter's voice held a hint of laughter, now that the discussion had drifted from the past.

Connor got up and slapped him on the shoulder. "I am on your side. Why do you think I warned you? However, I cannot promise to remain so if my wife pressures me otherwise. She has remarkable powers of persuasion."

*****

Just as Connor had predicted, Martha and Rasheen were aligned in their matchmaking. Peter found himself seated next to Bernice at dinner. Connor was seated at the head of the table as usual, with Peter's father, John, at the other end and Martha and Rasheen on one side with Jack, Connor and Rasheen's adopted son, between them. Bernice sat next to Peter on the other. It didn't mean anything, he told himself, even though normally Jack sat next to him. His mother and Rasheen were just keeping the seating arrangement even between male and female, he assured himself.

That illusion soon passed when during the dinner conversation, Rasheen brought up the subject of the new school in the county and asked Jack how his friends liked it. Jack no longer attended the county school with his friends because he attended Loyola Boy's School in Baltimore; the same school Connor and Peter had attended in their teenage years. "They like it fine, but we all miss being together with you and Miss Peterson. It's nice to be home for the summer so I can spend some time with my old friends," Jack said as he stuffed a spoonful of mashed potatoes into his mouth.

Martha gave him a frown. "Don't talk with your mouth full."

Jack nodded as he continued to cram food into his mouth.

Rasheen patted his shoulder. "We miss being with you too. In fact, Miss Peterson was just saying that she misses having something useful to occupy her time."

Peter glanced sideways at Bernice. "I would think you are busy with many social commitments given your family's standing in the community." What he really meant was her family's leadership of the beau monde.

"My mother is the social queen. I prefer to put my time to better use."

Martha jumped into the conversation. "Speaking of putting your time to better use, why don't you help Peter?"

"I doubt I have any skills that would be of use in a doctor's office," Bernice protested.

"Nonsense," Martha insisted, "you know a lot about herbal cures and you could help keep the office in order and free his time for patients."

"I'm sure Peter isn't interested in herbal cures. Most doctors today consider them next to witchcraft," Bernice laughed.

"Actually, I think there is a great deal of merit to using herbs for a cure rather than chemical compounds if possible," Peter found himself saying even though he knew where the statement would lead.

"Good. Then it's settled. Bernice will start working with you, and I won't have to worry about you. I'll know you will have someone to see that you don't work yourself into an early grave." Martha looked every bit the concerned mother. Peter looked over at Connor who gave him a knowing look. Martha's concern had less to do with an early grave than making Bernice her daughter-in-law.

Bernice gave him an apologetic smile. "I really don't think you want someone like me in your way."

Peter felt his lonely heart bask in the warmth of her

smile. "I could use the help and would be willing to incorporate the use of herbal cures in my practice, if you would consider working with me." Peter couldn't believe he had let his mother set him up and given her his full cooperation. He looked over at Connor's surprised expression and gave a slight shrug. He was just as surprised at his next question. "Can you start tomorrow?"

"I suppose I could, if you are sure you really want my help and you're not being bullied into this by Martha."

Bernice's pale blue eyes searched his, and he felt a surge of heat run through his veins. This was a mistake, but one that he couldn't prevent himself from making.

Peter shook his head. "Not at all. I need help, and I am interested in anything that will improve the care of my patients."

CHAPTER 3

Bernice shook her head and gave herself a good mental scolding. She had to stop being such a silly goose. Just because Peter had been courteous to her during his visit to Sara's Glen last year and paid attention to her at the New Year's ball given by Connor's uncle, didn't mean he was interested in forming an attachment. He had invited her to come and work with him, and she intended to learn everything she could about the practice of medicine. Perhaps he would allow her to use her skills in herbal healing although she realized most doctors frowned on such practices. None of it would matter until they had an honest discussion as to whether he had really wanted her help, or had simply been bullied into it by Martha. She would insist he be truthful with her without the presence of his mother to intervene, and if he said he didn't require her assistance, she would understand. She may not like it, but she wouldn't blame him.

She was well aware that Martha was trying to make a match between Peter and herself, just as she had done with Rasheen and Connor. But there was a difference between the two couples, Connor was in love with Rasheen and needed little encouragement from Martha. Peter would never fall in love with someone who was plain, dull, odd, and completely lacking in grace and charm. She had heard that description so often from her mother's lips, and seen the reflection in her mother's eyes, that the image was ever before her. She could no more escape it than the shadow the sun cast before her when it was at her back. It burned away any illusions of her own beauty she might have possessed.

She wouldn't be forced on anyone. If the good Doctor Schmidt didn't want her assistance, then she would just.... She never finished the thought because as she pulled the buggy in front of Peter's office, she noticed a woman pulling a screaming boy by the ear trying to get him through the gate to the dispensary's front yard. Upon coming closer, she saw that the boy was Tommy Leichter, one of the students she and Rasheen had taught at the schoolhouse Connor provided for the local children before the county built their own school and hired a teacher.

Bernice stopped the buggy and jumped down, gathering her skirts in one hand so as not to catch them on anything, while holding the side of the vehicle with the other for support.

"What on earth is going on?" she asked.

Mrs. Leichter, still pulling on Tommy's ear, had one hand on the gate. "He has a fish hook in his hand, and we need to get Doctor Schmidt to take it out."

"No, ma. He'll cut off my hand. The fellows said so." Tommy tried to break free of his mother's hold on his ear.

From the way she was pulling, Bernice thought Doctor Schmidt may have to attend to the ear, too. "Tommy, would you go into see Doctor Schmidt with me? I promise not let him cut off your hand."

Tommy stopped screaming for a minute and contemplated her offer. "You promise?"

"You have my word." Bernice reached out her hand and the boy took it. The mother let go of the ear and followed them inside.

Bernice gave a quick rap on the door which was immediately opened by Peter. Her heart skipped a beat at the sight of his tall well-built form filling the doorframe, but she managed to stay focused on the matter at hand. "Tommy has a fish hook caught in his hand."

Peter stepped aside so the two women and the boy could enter. He motioned for Tommy's mother to sit in one of the four wooden chairs lining the wall of the small room inside. "And you can come with me, young man," he said as he opened another door leading to the examining room. He motioned for Bernice to follow.

Tommy pulled back. Bernice put her hand on Tommy's shoulder and gently nudged him toward Peter. "The other boys told him you were going to cut off his hand."

"Oh, I see. Well, perhaps you can assure him otherwise, Miss Peterson." The boy walked past Peter looking like someone going to the gallows. Bernice bit her lower lip to keep from smiling and followed silently.

Peter left the door to the examining room open so the boy could see his mother sitting nearby. "All right, Tommy, climb up on the table and let's get that hook out."

Tommy looked toward the open door, and for a minute, Bernice thought he might try and bolt for it, but he jumped up on the table using his good hand for balance. Once he was up on the table, Peter turned his back to them and began to get some instruments from the shelves on the other side of the room. He came back with something that looked like a heavy pair of pliers which he set on the small metal table next to the examining table and then went out into another room returning with two bottles of liquid. He went to the sink and poured liquid from one of the bottles over his hands and called Bernice over and instructed her to wash her hands with soap and water. This came as no surprise since Peter had followed the work of Doctor Lister in regard to his surgery. It had taken awhile, but the idea of using antiseptics was finally catching on in America and saving many lives that would have previously been lost after surgery. Peter was a surgeon and would naturally follow the cleaning ritual even for a small procedure such as the one about to occur. What surprised Bernice was that he had a sink with running water in his examining room.

Tommy's eyes grew rounder when he saw the instruments. Bernice took his free hand and began talking to him. "How did you manage to get the fish hook in your hand?"

"It was Ben's fault. I was trying to bait my hook and he tripped over the line."

"Did you catch anything before you got yourself caught?"

"Yes ma'am. I caught a nice size rockfish. Ma's gonna fry 'em up for dinner."

While she was talking, Bernice kept her eye on Peter. He had already cut the hook's barb end and was about to pull it out. She squeezed Tommy's hand hard.

"Ouch! Why'd you do that Miss Peterson?"

"She wanted to distract you while I removed your fish hook." Peter swabbed the tiny wound with some of the liquid from the bottle. "This will sting a bit."

"Ouch!" Tommy let out the breath he had been holding and studied his wounded hand.

"You will need to keep a bandage on it for a few days. Think you can handle that?" Peter wrapped the wound in a bandage and then went to the shelf and came back with a jar of candy sticks. "Pick your favorite flavor."

The boy took a cinnamon stick and said, "That wasn't so bad. Thanks, Doc."

Peter than held the jar out to Bernice. "No thank you, perhaps later. It is a bit early for me to eat candy."

Tommy squirmed off the table. "Can I go now?"

Peter nodded and then followed the boy into the waiting room where he handed Mrs. Leichter some bandages and a small bottle. "Remove the bandage at night to let the wound get some air and then apply a fresh one in the morning for about three or four days. Make sure to put the tincture of iodine on it, and he will fine."

Tommy's mother thanked Peter and inquired about the bill.

"Since he was my first patient, this one is on me, but maybe Tommy could spread the word that I'm not such a bad guy." Peter gave Tommy a questioning look.

"Yes sir," the boy said in between licks of his candy stick.

"And Tommy, please try not to get that hand dirty for the next few days or else we'll have a more serious problem." Peter ruffled the boy's hair as mother and son walked past him out the door.

Bernice remained in the examining room, but watched Peter through the open door. He stood at the outside door for a few minutes as Tommy and his mother left, giving Bernice an opportunity to study him while he was otherwise occupied. He was a tall, rather muscular man for a doctor, she thought, but then he had grown up on a farm and was used to physical labor. Though his hands may have once worked the land, now they were the hands of a skilled surgeon. She, along with the rest of North County, was grateful he had brought those hands home to take care of his friends and neighbors. Still, it was difficult to be around him and control the unsteady beat of her heart, or the carousel that seemed to be going round and round in her stomach.

She let her eyes wander about the examining room and noticed there were opened doors leading into other rooms. One lead to the waiting or reception room, and another opened to his office. Inside the office doorway, an open book rested on his desk, and on the wall behind it hung his medical degree. There were other framed documents, but she couldn't make them out. On the other side of the room, a door stood open to what appeared to be some sort of laboratory. She took a step forward and was about to go peer inside when he called her out to the reception room.

The afternoon sun shone on the lighter streaks of his

close-cropped brown hair and cast the rest of his body in shadow until he stepped inside and shut the door. "Thanks for getting him inside and keeping him distracted."

"I am certain you would have handled him." But still she was pleased that he appreciated her efforts. "His poor mother was the one needing help."

He took her by the arm and led her through the examining room and into the laboratory. "Perhaps, but your distraction made things go much faster than if I were attempting to both treat him and relieve his fears."

She racked her brain for something more to say. "Are you settled in?" Of course he was settled in. Hadn't he just taken care of his first patient? Now he would think her an addled-brained female for certain.

"As you can see, the office is set up. My house is still in chaos, but mother and Rasheen have offered to set it to rights."

Bernice glanced in the direction of a window facing the stone house where Peter would be living. "The new construction compliments the little stone house."

He gave her a satisfied smile. "The stone house was too small, but I didn't want it destroyed since it was the home of the original owners of Sara's Glen, Sara and James Bartlett. Adding the second story and the wings on either side gave me the room I need for now and in the future."

"Rasheen has told me the story of Sara and James. From what I hear, their spirits make periodic visits. Have you seen them since you've taken up residence in their home?"

"I only saw James once and that was when I was a boy. He warned me to stay away from one of the outbuildings where a rabid raccoon was lurking. Apparently, the Bartlett's only appear when someone needs their help."

"Speaking of help, perhaps you can show me where to put the bottle you used and what to do with the instruments. I assume they need to be cleaned and stored away," she said as she held up the brown bottle she had unconsciously picked up.

He walked over to a wall of shelves and pointed to the second one which was filled with various shapes and sizes and colors of bottles. There were brown glass bottles, some cobalt blue ones, and even a few of the older ceramic type. All of them were labeled. He stepped out to the examining room and returned with the bromide he had used to clean his hands. "This goes here," he said as he placed it on a shelf with bottles marked creosote, zinc chloride, and nitric acid. He explained that all of those were used for washing before surgery. The other shelves contained chemical compounds she had never heard of except for a bottle of laudanum which was commonly used for pain and also to calm nerves.

Bernice thought she could use something to calm her nerves since they were a bit on edge at the moment, but she would never take laudanum. Too many people became dependent on it. She preferred to use lavender to sooth and calm.

On another wall there were mostly empty shelves except for a few small jugs marked with herbal names. There was some lavender, feverfew, rosemary, anise hyssop, and goldenseal. When she looked back at him, he smiled apologetically. "My mother has given me some herbs, but I need to fill the shelves with the more exotic ones that she doesn't grow in her garden. If you tell me what you require, I will be happy to get them for you."

She gave him a surprised smile. "Then you have no objection to herbal cures?"

"Not if they work." He led her back into his office. "Anything you need, I can get. I have friends in Europe and in various parts of this country. Give me your list and we will begin to fill these shelves. I had the table put in here so you can mix your herbs and make your tinctures. I may use it occasionally to make some chemical compounds, but I prefer to order my medicines from the pharmaceutical company the City Dispensary uses."

For the remainder of the morning, there were no patients so Peter read the medical book on his desk, occasionally making notes on a sheet of paper, and Bernice sat at the table in the lab, working on her list of herbs. She also studied the shelves, trying to memorize the different bottles and where they were located so she would be able to locate them quickly when he asked for them. A sharp whiff of alcohol floated through the air every now and then, but it didn't bother her. Rather, it served as a reminder of where she was and what she was doing – something she found interesting and at the same time worthwhile

At the end of the day Peter surprised her by asking if she would like to see the house. "I'm afraid I must decline. I have another engagement." In an effort to look convincing, she fished in her pocket for her watch. And the engagement she was using as an excuse was a dinner at home with her father.

As much as she wanted to enjoy Peter's company, being in his home alone with him wouldn't be proper and if anyone found out, there would be the devil to pay with her mother. It was definitely something of which her mother would disapprove, but thankfully there was an ocean between them for now.

He opened the door and stepped outside, disappointment apparent in his amber eyes. "Perhaps another time?"

She took the arm he offered her, let him lead her down the steps, and help her up into the buggy. Giving what she hoped was her sincerest smile, she said, "I look forward to it."

CHAPTER 4

Bernice had left the dispensary over an hour ago, but Peter still couldn't concentrate on the papers in front of him. Memories of the day they had just spent together filled his brain, leaving little room for anything else. In only one morning, his decision to go along with his mother's suggestion of asking Bernice to help in the surgery had proven to be a good one. If his mother wanted to believe she was succeeding in her matchmaking that would be fine with him, as long as she didn't push any harder.

His experience with the Sisters of Mercy and their work at the City Dispensary had taught him the importance of cleanliness when treating the sick. Bernice would be responsible for seeing that his examining room was scrubbed and spotless. She had already begun that task when she put on an apron and wiped down the table with alcohol after they finished with Tommy. She not only didn't complain about such menial tasks, but actually hummed while doing them.

In some ways, she reminded him of the nuns as she went about her tasks with quiet competency, except that he never had to control lustful thoughts creeping into his mind where the nuns were concerned. Bernice was another case entirely, he mused to himself. And yet, even with the challenge, he found himself more than pleased to have her in his employee. She was easy on the eye, a hard worker, and good company.

Several times he found himself looking up from his reading to watch her as she moved about the lab or sat at the table working on her list of herbs. Watching her made his blood simmer as it flowed through his veins, heating to the point where he had to get up and walk over to the bookcase as a pretense to getting another book. He shook his head. Bernice Peterson was not the woman for him, no matter how much effort his mother put into her matchmaking.

Last year he had considered a future with her, and had begun to show an interest until her mother's friend, Mrs. Delacourte had warned him off. Mrs. Delacourte's daughter, Amelia, had found Bernice and him in what could have been a compromising position at the Reilly ball. At that time, he disregarded the woman's insistence that Bernice was attracted to Reginald Hilliard. In fact, he would have relished taking her away from Reg, as he and Connor referred to Hilliard, much to the man's annoyance.

When Connor and Peter were youths, they came across Hilliard and another boy bullying a much smaller, younger boy. Connor and Peter pulled the bullies off the smaller boy, giving them a dose of their own medicine. Reg Hilliard ran away rather than help his friend, spreading the word that Connor and Peter were the bullies.

Amelia had spread vicious gossip about her encounter with them; to the point that he thought he might at least offer Bernice a proposal of marriage. He could never give her the love she deserved, but he would be a faithful husband and give her a good life. Soon after the incident, however, Connor's aunt had pointed out an article in the Baltimore Sun's society section about the soon-to-be announced engagement of Ambrose Kingsley and Bernice Peterson. After that, he dropped his idea of pursuing her. Protecting her from Hilliard was one thing, but Kingsley was a decent chap and would have her mother's approval; something that would never happen if she chose Peter. He had no ties to high society other than his friendship with Connor Reilly. Even Connor, being an Irish immigrant who just happened to have an acceptable aunt, was on the sidelines of that elite group.

He pushed the papers aside. It was in the best interest of everyone for him to keep his relationship with the lovely Miss Peterson on a professional level. Which reminded him – there was the matter of salary. He would have to discuss that with her tomorrow. No doubt she would say it wasn't necessary given her station in life, but he would insist that if she wanted to be considered in a professional capacity, it was necessary.

The rumbling of his stomach reminded him it must be getting close to dinnertime. He slid his chair back and stood up knocking a small stack of papers from the corner of the desk. Bending over to retrieve them, he noticed the herb list Bernice worked on all afternoon.

He sat down again and read the list. She had not only listed the herbs, but also shown what their uses were and how she would prepare them – some would be in tincture form, others powders or infusions. She had even listed the types of bottles and jars she would require. Many of the herbs and their cures were familiar, like Comfrey for cough, lung conditions, burns and insect bites, Parsley for fevers and arthritis, and Yarrow for measles, chicken pox, and smallpox. There were quite a few unfamiliar ones like Squaw Vine or Partridge Berry to be used for childbirth, dysentery, and rheumatism, Lobelia for blood poisoning, boils and bruises, or White Poplar for cholera, flu, and gangrene.

Sitting the papers down, he mused that their partnership was going to be unconventional to say the least, as most of his colleagues frowned upon the old methods of curing the sick, but then it had taken him years to get them to realize the benefits of keeping the operating area sterile. More complaints from his stomach reminded him that it was time to start for Sara's Glen.

When he first moved into the Stone House, his mother made him agree to take his dinner at Sara's Glen with his parents, Rasheen and Connor, their adopted son, Jack, and baby Clare. It made more sense to have his evening meal with the family rather than have someone go to the trouble of cooking for one person. And he was grateful for the opportunity to be with people he cared about. His mother made sure something was sent to him at the stone house in the event he was unable to make dinner due to an unexpected medical emergency.

*****

"We were just about to start without you," his mother said as he came through the dining room door.

Peter apologized to his mother and the other family members. "I was doing some research for a colleague and lost track of the time."

"I hope you didn't keep Bernice this late," Martha said.

Peter unfolded his napkin laying it in his lap. "No. She left hours ago."

"Don't hesitate to ask her to stay should you need her," Rasheen chimed in. "She was such a help to me when I was teaching, and even took over the class at times. I think you will find her a fast learner."

Peter nodded, but didn't give the description of the day that both his mother and Rasheen were waiting for.

"You might as well tell them how the day went or they will keep dropping hints all through dinner," Connor said between spoonfuls of soup.

"Be thankful you are sitting on the other side of the table where I can't box your ears," Martha said.

Rasheen reached up as if to do so, but her hand was quickly caught and kissed by Connor. "Now, now, love, you know I'm only trying to help. Peter, in the interest of my poor ears, please share the events of your day."

"It wasn't that momentous. We had to remove a

fishhook from Tommy's hand and Bernice handled the situation very well for someone with no experience."

"Is he all right?" Jack asked before swallowing the food he had just shoveled into his mouth.

"He will have to wear a bandage for a bit and keep it clean, but it isn't serious," Peter reassured.

"Though Bernice was an excellent teacher, I think she is more suited to the healing arts. She has always been interested in herbal cures, and her herbs certainly helped me with my headaches," Rasheen said.

Connor gave his wife a wolfish grin. "I thought I was the reason your headaches were gone."

Rasheen blushed. "Don't flatter yourself so."

Peter felt the emptiness in his chest as he listened to the two them. He was happy that Connor had found someone to share his life, but also a little envious. "I'm going to utilize her knowledge of herbal cures and incorporate them into my practice. She has already begun a list of herbs she'll need besides the ones I have from mother's garden. I can get anything she needs from my friends here and abroad."

"That's wonderful," Rasheen said. "No one has ever taken her interest in herbs seriously. You know she has read every book and paper there is on herbal cures and she learned a lot from one of the cooks at a boarding school she attended. When she found out my uncle's wife out west was raised using ancient Indian cures, she began a correspondence to learn all she could from her."

"Bernice is a beautiful, kind, intelligent and remarkable young woman. She is going to make someone a wonderful wife some day," Martha sighed.

Connor looked over at Peter with a raised eyebrow. Both men knew her implications.

Mercifully, Peter's father who had been his usual quiet self during dinner changed the subject. "We need to begin planning for the summer picnic."

After that the conversation switched to the upcoming

social event.

Peter had forgotten about the annual summer barbecue Connor hosted each year for his workers and the townspeople. He had missed most of them the last few years since he was living in Baltimore, but now he was home again, and Connor was throwing this year's picnic in his honor to welcome him as the town's new physician.

*****

Bernice and Rasheen sat on a blanket near the makeshift ball field and watched as Ambrose Kingsley hit the ball into the left field where Connor scrambled to retrieve it.

"It looks as if your Mr. Kingsley may tie up the ball game," Rasheen said as Ambrose ran past first and second base.

Shielding her eyes from the sun with her hand, Bernice looked over just in time to see Connor throw the ball to the infielder who caught it with a surprised look and then throw it to Peter who was the third baseman. "I've told you he isn't my Mr. Kingsley."

Peter tagged Kingsley as he rounded onto third base.

"You're out!" Mr. Hutchins, the local butcher and acting umpire, shouted. "This year's victory goes to the Reilly workers." The two teams shook hands, dispersed and returned to their families.

Connor Reilly had started the tradition of hosting a summer picnic at Sara's Glen a few years back for his workers and anyone else in the town who wished to attend. The ball game between the farm workers and the men from town had become a tradition. "Looks like everyone is having a good time," he said as he bent down to kiss his wife.

"What's that smell?" Rasheen asked.

Peter took an onion from his pocket and threw it back over toward the onion field.

Rasheen lifted an eyebrow.

Grinning sheepishly, Connor said, "I didn't know it

was an onion until after I had thrown it. The ball was next to it and I grabbed it by mistake."

"Well, you might have said something."

"About what?" Peter asked as he strolled over to the blanket where Bernice and Rasheen sat.

"About the onion that you substituted for a ball," Rasheen admonished. "I wondered why young Billie looked so surprised when he caught it. You two should be ashamed of yourselves - setting such a poor example for that boy."

"I didn't know it wasn't a ball until I had it in my hands and touched Kingsley," Peter responded, shrugging and holding his hands out palms up. "I didn't want to look ridiculous thanks to your husband. It's his fault, not mine."

"Your failure to make the truth known to the umpire makes you just as guilty as Connor," Rasheen said.

Bernice drew her lips in to keep from smiling. The two grown men were fighting a losing battle. Rasheen's expression was the same as when she stood at the head of the classroom addressing an errant student.

"It was just a friendly game," Peter insisted. "It isn't like we committed some great conspiracy."

Connor grinned at Rasheen. "An onion and a ball are both round and they look a lot alike, so what's the harm?"

"You are impossible," Rasheen said holding her hands out for Connor to help her up. "I need to go see if Clare is awake from her nap yet. Martha stayed up at the house to watch out for her so I could come see you cheat at baseball, but I think it's time she joined the festivities."

So, this errant schoolboy knew how to get around the teacher, Bernice thought as she watched Connor bend down and whisper something in his wife's ear that made her laugh. They shared a quick kiss as they walked arm in arm to the big house that sat in the midst of all the festivities. Forgetting that Peter was standing behind her, she was startled out of her musings.

"May I join you?" He gestured toward the empty place on the blanket.

"Please do." She moved a little to allow him more room and felt her heart beat a bit faster at his nearness.

He plopped down next to her, taking up the remainder of the blanket. "Why didn't you join Rasheen in her chastisement?"

"She didn't need any assistance from me, and I have more patience with mischief than she does. I didn't grow up with two brothers, and a large number of male cousins to torment me."

Leaning back on his elbows, he gave her a skeptical look. "And that gives you more patience? I would think it would be just the opposite."

"I think it would be fun to grow up in a large family with lots of noise and activity. Our house was always so quiet." If she wanted her mother's approval, she had to be a perfectly mannered child when the nanny presented her to her parents for a few minutes each evening. Her mother never came to the nursery to play as her father did when he had time to spare. It wasn't until she was much older and had been away at school that her mother began to show an interest, and even then, it was only to attempt to groom her to become the wife of a socially prominent individual and express her disappointment at the results.

"But you have a sister, haven't you? I'm sure the two of you must have had a few adventures."

Bernice shook her head. "My sister is much younger."

"My brothers were older than me, but they acted as surrogate parents when they weren't torturing me. I would have missed them when we moved here from our old farm, had it not been for Connor. He became my best friend and another brother. We had similar interests since we were the same age. We also got into a lot of mischief." Peter gestured toward the house, "I am willing to guess that my mother has told you a few stories."

Bernice laughed. "Martha has often said how she

wished she had a daughter to help balance things out."

"Now she has five. So, I guess that makes up for all the difficulties Connor and I caused."

Bernice gave him a puzzled look. "Five?"

"Both my brothers are married, and one of them had a little girl. She considers Rasheen as a daughter, and now she has baby Clare. So now the females outnumber the males."

Bernice realized this was the first time they had discussed family even though they had been working together for a few weeks. At the dispensary, it was all work. The unguarded way he spoke of his family warmed her heart. She could sit with him talking like this all afternoon, but the moment was broken when Ambrose Kingsley came strolling over to the blanket.

"Good game, Schmidt." Ambrose extended his hand to Peter.

Peter clasped it. "Better luck next time."

"Smells like onions around here," Ambrose said as he sniffed the air around him.

Bernice felt her shoulders shake as she tried to restrain herself from dissolving into a fit of giggles when Peter winked at her. "Sorry, it must be me. I had onions on my hot dog."

Ambrose had been her escort to the picnic. He studied her carefully for a few seconds before asking, "I am going to have to leave in a few minutes. My assistant has just informed me there are some business affairs I must attend to. If you would like to stay longer, I'm sure I could have someone else take you home."

She knew what he was up to and was having no part of it. "That's all right. I'm tired anyway." Peter stood and helped her up. "I have a patient I need to look in on as well, so I will take my leave of the two of you."

"My mother is having a small dinner party on Saturday, and we would be honored if you would attend since you are the new physician, after all." Ambrose all but blurted out the invitation to Peter. Bernice wondered what on earth he was up to now.

To Bernice's surprise, Peter faltered in his answer and looked uncertain. She had only seen the confident, professional doctor. Why was he hesitating? Surely, he must have attended many such events in the city and during his time in Europe. After all, he was not only a highly respected doctor, but also a teacher and leader in the medical profession.

Ambrose cut in before he could decline the invitation. "We will look forward to seeing you there. I will see that the invitation is personally delivered to you tomorrow." Ambrose offered his arm to Bernice.

They walked away leaving Peter standing next to the blanket with a scowl on his face.

"And just what was all that about?" Bernice asked.

"I was just trying to be hospitable." Ambrose lifted her up into the buggy.

"Hospitable? I think not. Why are you doing this?"

He jumped in beside her, and placed a kiss on her forehead. "Because I love you, darling."

Bernice rapped him on the arm with her closed fan. "Leave things be."

*****

Peter fumbled with the silver scrolled cuff link until the spring caught and then proceeded to secure its partner on his other wrist cuff. Next came the white bowtie, waistcoat, and finally the tailcoat. Surveying himself in the standing oval mirror, he thought he at least looked like someone who belonged at a society dinner party, and not some country bumpkin. Although the country bumpkin in him said he would enjoy his food a lot more if he were dressed more comfortably.

There was still time. He could get one of the local boys to deliver a note expressing his regrets to Kingsley. No, it was too late. Unless someone came knocking on his door with a serious medical problem in the next half hour, there was no escape. He told Kingsley he would attend, and to back out now would not only be rude, but cowardly.

Why did it bother him attending a local society dinner party? He had attended dozens of such events during his stay abroad and even before that he had been a guest at many social events and balls given by Connor's Aunt Elaine. Elaine had seen to it that he and Connor knew how to dress for such events, how to behave, and how to converse properly, so why the anxiety attack? Because the people at all the other events didn't know him as the son of the Reilly estate manager, he reasoned.

The other guests at the Kingsley dinner this evening would certainly question his presence among them, even if he were a renowned member of the medical profession. Such a standing didn't make him their equal. It didn't matter, he reminded himself. He respected his father far more than any stranger, whatever their social status. He doubted that any of these people had ever worked at anything other than their own self-promotion. And there was the other question eating at him, why did Kingsley invite him? They barely knew one another.

If all that was not enough to make him uneasy, there was Bernice. His thoughts drifted back to the first time he had seen her as a fully-grown woman. It was during a visit home to Sara's Glen after being away for a long time. She had been riding with Rasheen, and her blond hair was tumbling down her back where it was loosely tied with a blue ribbon that matched her riding outfit. Her eyes sparkled with excitement, yet her smile was calm and angelic.

In spite of his attraction, he had managed to brush off his mother's matchmaking attempts during his visit, because the time wasn't right. There were too many things in his life needing his attention for him to begin a romantic attachment. Getting involved with Bernice Peterson would be a mistake. It wasn't just the timing.

The memory of Jenny's loss still haunted him, the pain as fresh as if she had died yesterday and not over ten years ago.

He had returned to his work at the City Dispensary and managed to work himself into exhaustion whenever thoughts of Bernice surfaced. Finally, he had settled into his normal routine with his mind occupied with all things medical. Life would have continued on his charted course, had it not been for Dugan. Dugan sent his life in a different direction, just as Jenny had many years earlier.

Seeing Bernice every day, working with her, was no problem, he assured himself. He managed to control any attraction he might have toward her --- until he saw her at the picnic. The urge to touch her had been so strong; he had to shove his hands in his pockets. At the Dispensary, he admired her work, and if his thoughts wandered down a forbidden path, he could busy himself with his patients or lose himself in some medical journal.

The picnic was an entirely different situation. Though she was dressed in a simple green dress with few frills and a wide straw bonnet with matching ribbons, she still reminded him of the Grecian Goddess he had held in his arms the night of the Reilly New Year's ball. The memory of his hand encircling her tiny waist as they swirled around the dance floor made his heart beat a little faster. Seeing her with Kingsley at the picnic brought out a jealous streak he was unaware of and made him uncomfortable. He was a scientist, after all, and dealt in logic, not emotion.

Bernice belonged with someone who could give her the life to which she was accustomed. True, he could provide her the same level of financial security thanks to the counseling and advice he had received from Connor's uncle over the years. If he wanted, he could buy her a fancy home with all the things that went with it, but he could never be part of the social sphere in which she traveled, nor would he wish to, even it were possible. Kingsley belonged to that world. Their attitudes and way of interacting with the world had been drummed into them since birth. Peter wanted none of that, nor did he want the feelings that went along with an emotional attachment – feelings that upset his sphere.

*****

Peter timed his arrival for ten minutes past eight o'clock. This was one of the many times he was thankful for Aunt Elaine's insistence that he learn the rules of etiquette. It was considered inconsiderate of one's hostess to arrive exactly on time, but rude to arrive more than fifteen minutes late. Her instruction, though bemoaned when he was a young man, had helped him fit in the social circles he had traveled in during his time in Europe.

The butler showed him into the drawing room where the widowed Mrs. Kingsley stood receiving her guests. He paid his respects to his hostess, and then looked about the room for a familiar face, one in particular. She was on the other side of the room speaking to an older woman. Ambrose Kingsley was a few feet away speaking to another gentleman. Kingsley excused himself and walked across the room. "Doctor Schmidt, I'm so happy you could attend. Let me introduce you to our other guests."

After the introductions were made, the butler announced that dinner was ready to be served. Just before they lined up to enter the dining room, Mrs. Kingsley changed the seating arrangements. "Doctor Schmidt, I hope you won't mind escorting me into dinner, and Mr. Peterson will escort Miss Bosley." Bernice's father gave her a puzzled look, but offered his arm to Miss Bosley nevertheless. Mrs. Kingsley waited for the astonished Peter to offer his arm, which he did after a moment's hesitation.

Once he had seated his hostess, everyone took their seats. There were twenty people at the table. Peter took a quick look around and made sure he remembered all the names. He complimented Mrs. Kingsley on the floral arrangement, and remarked that the colors reminded him of a painting he had recently seen at Mr. Walter's home in Mount Vernon. This led to the usual dinner conversation, and he found himself chatting with Mrs. Kingsley and then turning to his left to carry on a short conversation with Mrs. Barsett. Things were going well until he looked down the table. There, on the opposite side, sat Ambrose with Bernice on his right, a vision of loveliness in her violet gown. She smiled at something amusing her dinner partner had said. Peter felt a pang of jealously wishing he were the recipient of her favor.

"They make an amiable couple," Mrs. Kingsley followed his gaze. "Her mother desires a match between them, but I wouldn't want to see…."

"Excuse me, Mrs. Kingsley," Peter bolted from his seat and rounded the table. Mr. Trost, the gentleman seated on the other side of Bernice had begun to move his arms wildly, all the while making no sound. Peter stood him up, turned him away from the table, bent him over and thumped him on the back soundly. "Cough, cough, cough, whoosh." The piece of meat that was lodged in the man's throat flew across the room and under the buffet server, where one of the servants discretely scooped it up and removed it. Peter said a silent prayer of thanks that he had turned the man. Mrs. Kingsley wouldn't have wanted her guests to witness such a vulgar display. It would have ruined her dinner party. But then so would a man choking to death at her table. Oh God, now he was beginning to think like these people.

"Easy, take slow deep breaths. You had something lodged in your throat. Better?" Peter helped the older man back into his seat and handed him his water glass. "Take a slow sip."

Mr. Trost did as requested and took another deep breath. "You saved my life."

Peter ignored the praise and instead apologized to their hostess for the disruption.

"Thank goodness you were here." Mrs. Kingsley gave him an appreciative smile.

Not comfortable with the attention, Peter returned to his seat. "Everything seems to be fine now. Shall we continue with dinner?"

Mrs. Kingsley nodded to her servants to begin serving the next course, and the dinner conversation continued as if there had been no interruption. She made no further mention of Bernice and Ambrose, even though Peter's attention drifted in their direction several times. He supposed she thought he was keeping an eye on Mr. Trost, but that gentleman was doing just fine. The choking incident hadn't dulled his appetite.

What was she going to say about Bernice before the interruption? Whatever it was, she apparently had changed her mind. "We are fortunate you decided to return to North County to set up your practice. I've read about your research and your involvement with Doctor Lister. It is quite impressive."

A society matron keeping abreast of his work? Well that was a surprise

Apparently, she noted his astonishment. "My maternal grandfather was an apothecary. I spent many an afternoon watching his hands fly as he mixed his potions. I think I inherited his interest in healing arts. What is your opinion of herbal cures?"

"Their use wasn't encouraged in my studies, or in the hospitals where I practiced medicine, but my mother has used herbs quite effectively for some illnesses."

Mrs. Kingsley looked down the table to where Bernice sat. "You should consult with Miss Peterson. She has a wealth of knowledge in that area."

"Miss Peterson has agreed to instruct me in the art of herbal cures." Kingsley must have told his mother of Bernice's work in the dispensary, but she did not bring it up for discussion. The other dinner guests would surely voice their disproval of such an arrangement.

"You could not have a more qualified instructor." Mrs. Kingsley gave Bernice an approving nod.

After dinner, the ladies retired to the parlor, while the gentlemen remained seated at the dinner table to discuss politics and business while enjoying their cigars and brandy. Peter did more listening than talking. Over the years, he learned a lot of what was happening in the business world, and where a wise investment might be made by being attentive during such conversations.

Eventually the men joined the ladies in the parlor, and Mrs. Kingsley coached Bernice to play for them. Since Kingsley had somehow managed to skirt off to the corner and was busy chatting with Miss Bosley's escort, Peter was the nearest gentleman and it fell to him to aide Bernice. She handed him her fan while she removed her gloves and then gave them to him. He wasn't quite sure what to do, but she whispered, "Put them on top of the piano and help me turn the music pages."

It was a pleasure to stand there and turn the pages while she played. Her upper body, arms, and hands moved in tempo with the music as her slender fingers danced over the keys, coaching the notes from them. Thoughts of those fingers gliding over his body ambushed him. Forget it. He looked up and stole a glance at her face which reflected the celestial mood of the music. For the moment, she was taking everyone in the room to her magical realm. Time seemed to cease as did his breath. All too soon the music ended and he was brought back to reality by the sound of clapping.

Reluctantly, he handed her the gloves and waited until she tugged them on before placing the fan in her hand. He wanted to say something, but couldn't find the words to start a conversation as he escorted her back to her seat. It was probably for the best, he reminded himself.

A short time later, the party ended and he found himself once more in his buggy headed home. It hadn't been a bad evening. Much to his surprise, he discovered that he genuinely liked Kingsley and his mother, though he still wondered what she had been about to say concerning Bernice before Mr. Trost's choking incident. Probably just wanted to warn me off, he thought

CHAPTER 5

Peter watched Connor playing with the baby, but his mind was on the invitation in his pocket. Going to the Kingsley dinner party had been one thing, but now he had been invited to an operatic performance at Hampton, the Ridgely estate. This invitation no doubt stemmed from the former. It would seem Mrs. Kingsley was using her influence to have him included in North County's high society, but why? He liked Ambrose Kingsley's mother, but that didn't mean he wanted to be part of the beau monde.

Connor raised little Clare high above his head much to the baby's delight. "The child is just like her mother. She has no fear."

"And why should she when she is safe in her father's capable hands?" Rasheen rose on her toes and gently kissed his cheek before taking a seat in the wooden porch rocker.

Connor handed the baby to his wife and plopped down onto the swing where Peter was sitting causing it to move sideways in an awkward motion.

"Easy, Connor, this is a piece of furniture, not one of your race horses to be jumped on," Peter muttered.

"Beg pardon. You seem a wee bit irritable this fine

afternoon. What's got your long johns bunched up?"

Peter pulled the invitation from his breast pocket. "I received an invitation to a musical performance at Hampton, the Ridgely mansion, and I'm wondering why it was extended."

Connor hooted. "Sweet Jay…..I mean sweet Jakers. I have to attend that affair also. It will be nice to have another miserable soul to share my pain." Connor only swore in the stables out of his wife's earshot these days, but Peter remembered the many times he had heard the phrase Sweet Jaysus and all the saints above.

"Peter happens to enjoy the opera, and you well know it, Connor Reilly." Rasheen bounced the baby on her lap as she frowned over the infant's head at Connor.

"Sorry love, but it will still be nice to have Peter with us."

Peter slapped the invitation into his palm. "I never said I accepted."

"Oh, but you must. Madame Pavaleoni is to sing for us. She is performing at the Baltimore Opera House, and Mr. Ridgely hired her for a private performance at his home. They are even going to have some of the members of the Peabody Orchestra accompany her. Do come, Peter; you will enjoy it, and you can help me make Connor behave himself," Rasheen pleaded.

Connor grinned devilishly and shrugged.

Peter smiled at her. How could he say no? He had come to think of Rasheen as a younger sister since her marriage to Connor. Sometimes he envied the two of them their happiness, but not for long. They belonged together, and one couldn't be in their company and not be happy along with them. "All right, I will go, but I'm taking my own vehicle so I can leave right after the performance."

Rasheen raised her brows and dropped her chin. "Oh come now, you can stay for at least a glass of champagne afterwards."

Peter chuckled as he shook his head. "All right, I will stay long enough to drink a glass of champagne. Promise me you will not try and wheedle me into staying longer."

Rasheen shook her head. "No wheedling – I promise."

"Right, leave me to suffer through all the boring conversations," Connor moaned.

*****

The Ridgely mansion, Hampton, was ablaze with candle light on every wall of the great entrance hall, as well as the large gas lit chandeliers hanging from the high ceiling on either end of the vast room which had been pressed into service for tonight's performance. Chairs were set up so that everyone had a decent view of Madame Pavaleoni, and the orchestra was placed off to the side. The entire entertainment area was filled with flowers, potted ferns, and small lemon trees from the estate's orangery.

Madame Pavaleoni sang pieces from several operas as well as a few popular pieces and finished her performance with two compositions from her current opera as an enticement for the guests to attend her performance at the Opera House. Peter enjoyed the music, admitting to himself that Madame had just given one of the most moving performances he had ever heard. In fact, it was equal to, if not greater, than some of the operas he had attended during his stay in Europe.

His ears may have been listening to Madame Pavaleoni, but his eyes kept straying to Bernice. Her hair was swept up and a ribbon woven into it with little ringlets dripping down, just like it had been the night he had danced with her at the Reilly New Year's Ball. Memories glided through his mind of how lovely she was that night and how she had felt in his arms as they waltzed. When she leaned up and whispered something in Kingsley's ear causing her escort to smile, Peter was brought back to the present reality that Bernice was born into this social circle, whereas he was merely invited at the whim of the fashionably elite. Yet, something in his gut tightened at the sight of her sharing some small secret with Kingsley.

Finally, the music ended, Madame took her bows, and everyone was invited to partake of champagne and light refreshments. The guests broke up into small groups, some remained in the hall, others moved into the music room, parlor, or dining room, while the servants moved among them with trays of champagne glasses and finger foods.

"I wish we could see Madame Pavaleoni at the Opera House." Rasheen took a sip of champagne and then handed her glass to Connor while she took a hors d'oeuvre from one of the trays carried by a passing servant.

"If you give me a bite of that, I'll take you to the Opera House to see her performance," Connor said. "We could take a trip into Baltimore and stay with Patrick and Elaine. I am certain they would enjoy minding Clare while we have an evening to ourselves."

Peter took the glass from Connor. "Get your own food. Your aunt and uncle are coming to Sara's Glen to spend some time with their great niece."

"And just how do you know that?" Connor asked.

"Mother told me," Peter answered, his eyes unconsciously scanning the room for Bernice, until he saw Kingsley and her coming in his direction.

She bestowed a bright smile on them, and gave Rasheen a warm hug. "Wasn't Madame Pavaleoni magnificent?"

"She gave such a brilliant performance, that my wife has persuaded me to take her to the Baltimore Opera House to see her," Connor said, giving Peter a smug look. "My aunt and uncle can have two visits with Clare. Certainly they will not object to that."

"You won't be disappointed," Kingsley said, and then in a complete change of subject, asked, "Doctor Schmidt, I wonder if I might impose upon you. My business associate, Mr. St. Vincent, has requested my help in a private matter, and I am afraid I must leave. Would you mind escorting Bernice home for me?"

Bernice raised a brow in disbelief and said, "That's quite all right, Ambrose, I will be happy to have you take me home now."

"Mr. St. Vincent needs my immediate attention, dearest. There isn't time to take you home. I am sure Doctor Schmidt won't mind."

"I would be happy to escort Bernice home," Peter found himself saying before he thought better of it. This really wasn't a good idea.

Rasheen gave Kingsley a suspicious look. "If we hadn't brought Mr. & Mrs. McDaniels in our carriage, we could take you home."

"Ambrose, are you forgetting the fact that we arrived with Mr. St. Vincent and his sister?" Bernice asked.

"Miss St. Vincent is riding with Mr. & Mrs. Burton and their son. Mrs. Burton is quite happy with that arrangement." He gave everyone a wink. "One never knows what fate has in store, does one?"

Bernice heaved a sigh. "And I suppose that is why you didn't ask them to give me a ride home. Very well then, but only if Peter doesn't mind."

"It would be my pleasure." Peter noted that no one had bothered to mention the lack of a chaperone, not even Bernice. Not that it mattered. After all, they spent several hours a day alone when there were no patients.

There was no way he could leave early now. If he and Bernice were seen leaving together before the event was over, they would surely draw the gossips' attention. He would just have to endure the next hour or so. At the end of the evening, they would leave with the crowd and perhaps no one would notice them.

Surprisingly, the time passed more rapidly than he expected. He enjoyed talking with Connor and listening to snatches of Bernice and Rasheen's conversation as they discussed the performance and other female topics. Even more, he liked having Bernice at his side.

When the guests began to disperse, Bernice and he walked onto the drive with Connor, Rasheen, and the McDaniels where they waited for the Reilly coach and Peter's buggy to be brought around to the front of the mansion. He noticed a woman off to the side of the stairs glaring at him as he took Bernice's hand and assisted her into the buggy. Bernice followed his fixed gaze until she saw the woman. She smiled sweetly and waved, but the woman turned her head in the opposite direction whether by design or accident, Peter couldn't be sure.

Bernice's smile faded. "I suppose Mrs. Delacourte didn't see me."

"Was that Amelia Delacourte's mother?" Peter jumped up beside her in the buggy and shook the reins for the horses to move.

Bernice threw a worried glance in Mrs. Delacourte's direction. "Apparently Amelia has conveyed some false information to her mother regarding the two of us. I do hope it causes you no trouble."

"I am aware of how vicious Amelia can be. Based on that, I can assure you I could care less about Amelia or her mother and any gossip they may care to spread." Connor had been involved with Amelia and broken it off when he realized she had no desire to share his dream of building Sara's Glen into a successful horse breeding farm.

"Mrs. Delacourte and my mother are close friends, but I am afraid I don't share any such feelings toward her daughter." Before Bernice was able to make her opinion of Amelia Delacourte known, rain droplets began to fall.

"It looks like we are going to get wet if it rains hard." Peter reached down and grabbed a lap robe off the floor. "Hold this in front of you. It will shield you some." The lap robe was of little help since the buggy was open in the front and they were driving into the pelting rain.

*****

Bernice held the soggy lap robe over her head and tried to extend it to shield Peter when he helped her down from the buggy. "Just leave it," he shouted over the pouring rain. Throwing it back into the vehicle, she let Peter lift her out of the buggy, and once her feet hit the ground, took off running towards the house with him right behind her, both of them splashing through the puddles drenching their shoes. As she dashed up the front porch steps, one of her feet caught on the end of a step and she stumbled backward. Peter caught her with one arm behind her back and then swept her up in his arms quickly getting them beneath the shelter of the porch roof.

Once they were under cover, he set her down on her feet again. Wet strands of hair that had just a short time ago been pert ringlets fell across her face. Half of the ribbon holding them had come loose and hung over her eye. She looked like a water sprite standing there. Gently, he pushed the ribbon and hair out of her face.

She must have found the situation amusing for she burst into laughter. The sound made Peter think of wind chimes echoing amidst the rain. Droplets of water ran down her face, onto her cheeks and smiling mouth. Peter tightened his arm around her slender frame and ran his hand along her cheek feeling the cool dampness as he tilted her face up towards his own. He couldn't resist the urge to taste the drop of water on her lips. Leaning down, he ran his tongue across her lip catching the tiny bead, but that wasn't enough. He wanted to feel her lips pressed against his own, to taste the sweetness they promised. Giving into the urge, he gently touched his lips to hers in a soft kiss.

She surprised him by reaching her arms around his neck and pulling him closer, increasing the intensity of the kiss. Her skin smelled like rose soap and fresh rain. The scent invaded his senses. No longer able to control himself, he increased the pressure of his mouth and then began fervently searching with his tongue until her lips parted in sweet surrender. Her soft mouth with the faint taste of the champagne she had drunk earlier made him drunk with raw lust. He tightened his hold and pressed her against his frame as if that might satisfy the hunger gnawing inside him. Control was fast slipping away as the burning dance of her mouth against his matched his needs. And then like a bucket of ice-cold water being thrown over him, reason erupted.

Slowly, he pulled away, holding her at arm's length. "This was a mistake. I will not apologize, because I cannot say I am sorry, but it won't happen again. You will be safe with me in the future." Somehow he knew he was making a promise that would be impossible to keep, and yet there was no future for them other than a professional relationship.

Confusion clouded her eyes. "I...suppose I had better ...say good night then." She reached for the doorknob, turned it, and stepped inside saying, "Thank you," before closing it.

He was left standing there wondering whether she had thanked him for bringing her home or kissing her. She hadn't slapped him or acted offended or shocked, but what about the rumors he had heard of her soon-to-be announced engagement to Kingsley? She didn't strike him as the type of woman who would be disloyal.

A flare of light on the other side of the porch prevented him from considering the situation further. "Good evening, Doctor Schmidt."

Holy Hell! Mr. Peterson was sitting on the far side of the porch and no doubt seen what had just transpired. "Good evening, sir."

Now you've done it Schmidt. How are you going to explain almost ravishing the man's daughter? How indeed, since he had no explanation even for himself. He stood silently as the man quietly puffed on his pipe, the minute embers railing against the darkness. A simple kiss could hardly be construed as ravishing. At any rate, he was about to find out.

"How is it that my daughter left with Ambrose Kingsley and returned with you?" Mr. Peterson asked without any disproval in his tone, not mentioning the kiss.

Peter debated apologizing for what the man had just witnessed, but thought better of it. Perhaps he had not seen them, but something in his gut warned him that Mr. Peterson was well aware of what had just taken place on his front porch. Instead he simply told him about Kingsley's emergency and how he had been pressed into service.

When he had finished, Bernice's father said, "Ambrose is a nice fellow. I like him, but he isn't the one for Bernice. Do you not agree?"

Peter wanted to ask Bernice's father just what he meant, but under the circumstances he figured it would be wise to avoid further discussion. "I would not consider myself in a position to make such a judgment."

"I think you already have." There was a hint of warning in the statement, but still no admonishment for Peter's previous action. "Julie was right."

"Julie?" Peter was thrown completely off guard. He had been prepared to apologize for his earlier behavior, but what did Mrs. Boughers have to do with any of this.

"Never mind. Good evening." Mr. Peterson rose from his seat and started toward the front door.

"Good evening, sir."

*****

Bernice quietly pushed the door closed, and then rested her back against it to support herself, since her legs no longer seemed to want to do the job. Her stomach seemed to be all aflutter. Ambrose had kissed her, but his kiss had always been affectionate, like a brother. Placing her fingers to her lips, she touched them in astonishment. Whatever had possessed Peter to kiss her in such an intimate fashion? He couldn't be attracted to someone so plain. Perhaps he had drunk too much champagne. Yes, that was the reason, she thought sadly, for she had gotten lost in that kiss.

Bending over, she peeled her soaked slippers from her feet and tossed them on the bottom of the Black Forest Hall Tree umbrella rack, one of her mother's recent additions to the extensive collection of furniture in the Peterson mansion. As she straightened, she studied the ornate hand-carved walnut, and was once again struck by the oddness of the piece – ugliness really. It had a flat lined bottom for the wet umbrellas to drip, and then a narrow-carved strip that led up to the circular mirror that was surrounded by triangular shaped carving, with points on three sides. Her musings on the umbrella stand were brought to an abrupt halt when she saw her reflection. "Good Lord," she whispered, "I'm a mess. It most definitely was the champagne."

Bernice turned from the mirror image and quickly ascended the stairs to her room. Once inside, she rang for her maid to help her undress.

"My goodness, Miss, I hope you don't catch cold," the young woman said as she quickly undid the covered buttons on the back of the gown so Bernice could step out of it. The corset was unlaced next, followed by petticoats, camisole, and drawers until she was finally able to enjoy the comfort of a freshly laundered cotton gown.

Bernice sat at her vanity and began to remove the bedraggled ribbon and the few pins that were left in her sopping wet hair. "I think I'm going to need a towel for my hair."

A few seconds later the maid returned with two fluffy white towels that made quick work of drying Bernice's hair. Once the task was finished, the maid placed the wet gown over her arm and started out the door, but stopped and looked over her shoulder. "I forgot to tell you. A letter came for you from Mrs. Peterson. Would you like me to bring it up?"

"Don't bother. I will read it in the morning. Good

night, Anna."

Alone in her room, Bernice walked over to the opened window and leaned out enough to take a deep breath of the rain scented air. The shower was over and the clouds were breaking up giving the moon an opportunity to peek out from one of them. The memory of Peter's kiss was so fresh she could still feel his lips on hers. She would never get to sleep with these thoughts in her head, and there was no sense in encouraging them, because nothing would ever come of that one kiss. Turning around, she walked over to the slipper chair and picked up her robe, shrugged into it and tied the sash securely. "I know of one way to banish all pleasant things from my mind," she whispered to herself gloomily, "Mother." She tiptoed down the stairs, to the main entry hallway and retrieved her mother's letter from the silver tray. Letter in hand, she went to the small sitting room, and turned up the gas lamp.

Dear Daughter,

Since I expect to be receiving news of your engagement very soon, I may as well prepare you for a certain distasteful matter regarding marriage. Because you have been given a proper upbringing, you will be shocked at the vulgarities of the marriage bed, but it must be endured if you are to enjoy all the other benefits of matrimony. I have endeavored to write my advice in the hope that it will guide you through your wedding night and the years to follow.

Your wedding to Mr. Kingsley will be the happiest day because you, at long last, will be the center of attention. We will see that the church is filled with flowers-, lilies I think, and there will be a solemn ceremony followed by an elegant reception at Hollyhock Hall, since that will be your home. Of course we will have to completely redecorate before the wedding. Aunt Catherine would want it so. I will be so happy that you have finally secured the right husband. Ambrose Kingsley will elevate you to your proper place as a leader in society. This wedding will be the social event of the year. I feel it in the very essence of my being.

As intoxicating as all of this may by, it is my unfortunate obligation to inform you that at the end of such a glorious event comes the wedding night. All things come with a price and this day ends with the terrible experience of the marriage bed. I am writing this now as these matters are never to be spoken of by proper women.

Give your husband no encouragement in this regard. Otherwise what could have been a proper marriage could become filled with lust and indecency. I was fortunate not to have any problems setting your father on the right path in the early years of our marriage. If you heed the wisdom in this letter, you will have no difficulties.

Do not let your fears be extreme. While the experience may be revolting, it must be endured as it has been by women for centuries. Sadly, this is the only way we can bring our children into this world. While the ideal husband would be one who would approach his bride only for the purpose of begetting offspring, such unselfishness cannot be expected from the average man.

You will find that feigned illness, sleepiness, and headaches are among the wife's best friends in this matter. Arguments, nagging, scolding, and bickering also prove very effective, if used in the late evening about an hour before he would normally commence his seduction. I am certain you will devise new and better methods for discouraging his amorous overtures, and will have reduced the ordeal to once a week after your first child. Separate bedrooms are beneficial for this accomplishment. It would be most unfashionable for you to share a bedroom with Mr. Kingsley. I am certain he is well aware of this and should give you no argument, but he may insist on adjoining rooms. It would be preferable if we could arrange for his room to be at the opposite end of the hall.

If you follow my advice, your husband should be sleeping in his own room and have no further physical contact with you other than a respectful kiss on the forehead, by the time you have completed your child bearing. And I would remind you that people in our social circle have no more than two or three children. Most definitely only two if one or both are males.

It is my wish for you to have a proper marriage, just as your father and I have had all these years.

Your Devoted Mother

Bernice thought about Peter's kiss and couldn't imagine a marriage like the one her mother described. Definitely, if her mother had been successful in her attempt at matchmaking with Reginald Hilliard, she would find the advice helpful. She couldn't consider the advice in terms of Ambrose when there would never be a marriage of any kind between them. "Mother, how in the name of heaven did you become, so, so…" she spoke the words out loud to what she thought was an empty room.

"So what?" A voice asked from the open door to the hall.

Bernice turned around in the chair to face her father. "Cold hearted?"

"Is she listing the reasons you should marry Ambrose Kingsley, none of which has to do with love or respect?" Her father's tone was one of exasperation.

"Yes," Bernice lied, and then quickly folded the letter and stuck it in her pocket.

"Don't mind your mother. What are you doing up at this hour?"

"I couldn't sleep."

"How was your evening?"

"Madame Pavaleoni gave an outstanding performance."

Her father gave her a cryptic smile before asking, "Were you and Ambrose caught in the rain, or did you get home before it began?"

"Peter Schmidt brought me home, and we did get soaked."

"What happened to Ambrose?" Her father asked, not bothering to mention his earlier conversation with Peter.

"His friend had an emergency and he had to leave early. Since he and Mr. St. Vincent were taking the carriage, Mr. St. Vincent's sister went home with someone else, and Ambrose asked Peter to see that I got home safely."

Her father chuckled. "Ah, another missed opportunity for Mr. Kingsley to propose. It is a good thing your mother isn't here, or you would spend half the night listening to her lecture on the subject."

"She can lecture all she likes," Bernice said defiantly.

Her father patted her shoulder. "Now, now, I am on your side, remember? Let's go to bed and forget about Ambrose and your mother."

"I am sorry. I get so tired of mother's ambitions." She reached around and turned down the lamp before rising from the chair.

Her father waited for her to walk in front of him and then followed her up the stairs. When she got to her room, she kissed him on the cheek. "Good night."

"Good night to you, my sweet girl. I like Peter Schmidt. He would make a fine son-in-law."

Bernice tried to conceal her surprise with a nonchalant expression. "Whatever made you say that?"

"Your mother has her idea of the perfect son-in-law, and I have mine." There was a mischievous twinkle in her father's eyes she had never seen before. "Unlike your mother, I will merely voice my opinion, and let the matter rest." He didn't give Bernice an opportunity to question him further or argue, but quickly turned and walked to his own room. She was left standing wide-eyed in the doorway to her room.

CHAPTER 6

Bernice walked into Peter's office to say good morning as she did on her arrival every day. As if by some silent agreement, neither of them had mentioned the kiss they had shared after the evening at the Ridgley's. He said it had been a mistake. If that is how he felt, she was going to make sure he would never have even the slightest detection of the effect his kiss had on her, or how the memory of that night sent a delicious shiver through her. In his presence, her demeanor would be nothing but professional. Years of dealing with her mother had taught her that the road to self-preservation was to hide her emotions behind a mask of polite passivity.

Though his office door was open, he wasn't there going over papers, or reading medical journals as she normally found him. She was about to check the examining room when she saw the note propped up by a book sitting on the large walnut desk. It was addressed to her and said that he had gone to the Thurston farm to deliver Mrs. Thurston's baby and hoped to return later in the day. She picked up the note and put it in her pocket and in the process knocked another letter onto the floor. When she bent over to retrieve it, she noticed it was signed, Your Affectionate Bo Peep. Was Bo Beep the woman she had seen him with in New York? She could read the letter and find out more or she could respect his privacy. She decided on the latter. That was what she would want from him. Besides, he had told her the kiss between them was a mistake so if he received letters from a gorgeous woman who happened to call herself Bo Peep, it was no concern of hers. No concern at all, she told herself. None at all. Well, none at all save for the jealous ribbon that was twisting itself around her heart. She threw the letter onto the desk unread.

Disappointed that she had missed the opportunity to be present at a birth, Bernice decided she would work on some of the potted herbs that had arrived the other day and were sitting outside in the back of the doctor's office. Peter had dug a nice plot for her to have an herb garden of her own in addition to the list of herbs and oils he ordered for her. She would still have to use Martha's garden until her own got established, but once that happened, it would be far more convenient to simply step outside to cut what she wanted rather than having to harvest what she needed from Martha's garden. Besides, it wasn't fair to Martha to use her garden to supply the medicinal needs of North County.

Bernice grabbed a garden smock and put it over her clothes. On her way out the door, she lifted the big floppy hat from its hook, placed it on her head and tied the wide cotton green ribbons beneath her chin. As she shoved her hands into gloves that had been in the smock's pockets, she surveyed the freshly dug garden area, and began to mentally form places for the different varieties of herbs.

Peter had done a good job and even worked the soil so it was nice and loose. She smiled at the thought of the respected doctor turning the earth. Did he remove his shirt when he worked? After all, he had worked many years on the farm with his father and Connor Reilly, so she was sure he would dispense with propriety for practicality when no one was around. She could picture his back muscles rippling as he lifted the full shovel. She knew his frame would be well built because she had seen him without his coat, and he filled out his shirt nicely. A flush of heat ran through her midsection at the thought. Stop this nonsense, she reminded herself and got to work. No sense in tormenting herself with thoughts that led to nothing.

Once she had a plan, she sorted the pots with the small seedlings and began planting. She took the shovel and dug a hole for the first plant, and when it was big enough, she turned the pot over, gently dumped the plant out, turned it right side up, and stuck it in the ground. Then she got on her knees and used her hands to firm the soil around the plant. The earth was damp and easy to work from the previous evening's rainstorm. She smiled when she recognized the faint scent of horse manure. Martha must have reminded Peter to add it when he turned the soil because she swore by its power to make plants grow faster and stronger.

By the time Bernice had finished, the sun's heat was already scorching through the back of her dress. She looked over to where the watering can sat next to the hand pump, and decided that the newly planted herbs needed a thorough watering, and that she would have to keep an eye on them for the next week or so to make sure they settled in properly.

Taking her gloves off after the task was complete; she pushed them into the smock's pockets again before she noticed a small weed sticking up near the edge of her herb bed. Not wishing to be bothered with the gloves, she stooped over to pull it with her bare hands. It wasn't willing to be removed without a struggle, so she gave a good hard yank until it came loose along with several chunks of damp dirt, one of which landed on her cheek. She reached up and brushed the dirt away. "Now I will have to wash my face as well as my hands," she admonished the weed as if it were able to understand.

She tossed the offending plant on the side of her herb garden, and went back inside the surgery intending to wash up and then work on her dried herbs getting them into jars, labeled and shelved. It was nice to have her own little workspace, she thought as she went over to the sink and grabbed a bar of soap. Before she could turn on the water, the door to the outer office opened so she tossed the soap on the sink's edge and went to greet the visitor.

Mrs. Delacourte stood in the middle of the room and for a minute Bernice thought she might need a doctor, because the color had drained from her face, and her lips were drawn in a painful expression.

"I'm sorry Mrs. Delacourte, but Doctor Schmidt is on a house call at the present time. He isn't expected to return until later this afternoon," Bernice explained before she realized the expression on the woman's face wasn't one of pain, but of disgust and shock.

Mrs. Delacourte gave her a critical inspection from the top of her head to her toes. "I have not come to see Doctor Schmidt. I would never use his service. Just look at you, Bernice Peterson. What would your poor mother say? You look like some dirty farmer's wife."

Bernice tried to keep a neutral tone as she wiped her dirty hand across her cheek smearing the dirt. "I doubt she would approve of my gardening any more than you do. If you did not come to see Doctor Schmidt, then why are you here?" She knew the answer, but Mrs. Delacourte would not leave until she said her piece.

"The least you could do is offer me a seat," Mrs. Delacourte huffed.

Bernice waved her hand to one of the wooden chairs lined up against the wall. "By all means, please be seated. I would ring for tea, but I am afraid there are no servants in a doctor's office." She realized she should have skipped the sarcasm, but under the circumstances she couldn't resist.

"Don't be flippant with me young lady. I have made

two calls to your home and left my card and you have not had the good manners to return either of them. That is why I am here." The way she positioned herself in the chair as she adjusted her bustle reminded Bernice of a chicken about to lay an egg. She smiled at the thought that she would never have had such a comical image before she met Rasheen, who would definitely appreciate the humor in the comparison.

Bernice took a seat next to Mrs. Delacourte. "I have been very busy here at the surgery. I am sorry." She wasn't, but maybe placating the woman would get rid of her faster. "What is it you wish from me?"

Mrs. Delacourte placed both her hands on the handle of her closed parasol, which she had placed directly in front of her. "I will come straight to the purpose of my visit. As one of your mother's closest friends, I have to insist that you stop this nonsense at once."

Bernice raised a questioning eyebrow. "I beg your pardon?"

Mrs. Delacourte looked about the room and sniffed. "Really, Bernice, working in a common doctor's office is beneath you. If your mother were here, she would never allow such a thing. I can't believe Mr. Kingsley permits this foolishness. He should put a stop to it before you are ruined."

Once the purpose of Mrs. Delacourte's visit was made clear, Bernice felt the ire rise within her. "Mr. Kingsley has no say in what I do, and he is far more respectful of the Schmidts than you seem to be."

"Young woman, everyone knows your engagement is soon to be announced. Your mother went to great pains to have that little snippet put into the society column in order to force Ambrose Kingsley's hand. Do you want to give him an excuse to break it off? Was it not enough that you disgraced yourself with your behavior at the Reilly ball and lost any hope of a match with Mr. Hilliard? After that, we thought you would be more prudent. Peter Schmidt may have the title of doctor in front of his name, but he comes from common stock. Why his parents are nothing but farm people. I don't care if his mother is related to Elaine Reilly."

Bernice took a deep calming breath. "I fail to see how any of this concerns you."

"When you and Ambrose Kingsley are married, you will be invited into the highest social circles. It has always been your mother's ambition for you to take your proper place in those circles. Of course you won't have the same status as my Amelia who is married to Mr. Astor, but she will endeavor to see that you are invited to all the prestigious balls and luncheons." Even the beau monde found it amusing that Amelia and her mother insinuated that the former's husband was one of THE Astor's when everyone knew he was a very distant relation. "You would be cut in less than a heartbeat if they found out you had worked in a doctor's office without a chaperone, not to mention that this is little above a trade. It was bad enough when you helped at that school with children of mere field hands and tradesmen, but at least that could be excused because it was considered charitable work assisting Mrs. Langston. The Langston name carried a lot of respect, but this...this is simply unforgivable."

Bernice rose from her chair before Mrs. Delacourte could continue. "I will consider all the advice you have given me. Now if you will excuse me, I have a great deal of work to finish before the doctor returns."

Struggling to her feet, Mrs. Delacourte sputtered, "Are you dismissing me?"

Bernice walked to the door and opened it. "It would appear so."

On her way out the door, Mrs. Delacourte stopped to issue one last comment. "How can you be so unfeeling toward your poor mother's wishes? If you were my daughter, I would lock you in your room until you learned some respect."

"Perhaps my mother would do the same if she were here. Fortunately for me, she is not. Good day, Mrs. Delacourte." Bernice stood in the doorway with her arms crossed in front of her chest in order to prevent herself from giving into the urge to shove the woman along faster.

At the bottom of the porch steps Mrs. Delacourte squawked, "I warn you, I am going to inform your mother of this matter, and the fact that I saw you leave the Ridgely's with Doctor Schmidt. You, an unmarried young woman, rode in his vehicle with no one but the two of you. You are determined to create a scandal."

Just before she slammed the door, Bernice shouted, "I am a grown woman, capable of making my own decisions. My mother will be unhappy when she receives your letter, of that I have no doubt. I've always been a disappointment to her so it should come as no surprise that I'm once again not living up to her expectations."

Bernice went to her lab and began ripping off the herbal leaves. She banged jars down on the table, and felt her body tremble with anger. Even in her absence, her mother had her spies. What were she and Ambrose thinking? Mrs. Delacourte had just proven to her that they could never dupe Society's matriarchs while they came up with another plan that did not include matrimony.

****

Peter walked around to the back of the dispensary, and saw that Bernice had planted her herb garden. All in all, a productive morning for both of them, he mused to himself. Mrs. Thurston's delivery had progressed with no difficulty, resulting in a healthy baby boy. He wasn't sure how long she had been in labor before they sent for him in the early morning hours, but the labor went fast for a first baby. These were the times he loved his work more than any other. They made up for all the tragedy he had seen when he worked in the City Dispensary. Making the move to start a practice in North County had been the right decision.

When he entered the examining room through the back door, he saw Bernice working at her table in the adjoining lab. Something was bothering her. He could tell by the way she ripped the leaves off a dried plant branch and threw them in a jar. Normally, she worked in a quiet, efficient manner, but her movements were filled with a different energy this afternoon, a negative type of energy he had never seen in her.

"Did something happen while I was out?" He asked as he strolled into the room.

She threw her hand up to her chest and turned to face him. "I didn't hear you come in. No, no… there were no patients." She shoved a cork stopper into the jar.

Something was bothering her and he had no intention of letting it rest until he found out what it was. It couldn't have anything to do with him, as they had resumed their normal work routine after the performance at the Ridgely mansion. He had decided the best thing to do about his lapse of good judgment in kissing her was to not mention it. She must have thought along the same line, because when she returned to work at the dispensary the following week, she was her usual poised self. For some strange reason, her insouciant attitude annoyed him, because he knew she had felt something just as he did. But it was best for both of them if they let it be.

"You didn't answer my question," he persisted.

"I just told you there were no patients," she said, as she picked up the jar and placed it where it belonged on her shelf.

"Something has upset you, Bernice, and I want to know what." He stood in front of her now with no more than a few inches between them, lifting her chin to look into her eyes, but she turned away. "Tell me what is troubling you."

"There is nothing bothering me." *Nothing other than my mother and her spies and your Bo Peep.*

"We are not moving from this spot until you tell me

what is bothering you." And if she didn't say something soon, he was going to have another relapse. She was too close. He could smell the lavender on her clothes from the plants she had handled earlier; her hair had come loose with a strand falling on her dirt- smudged cheek. He pushed it behind her ear and wanted to kiss that ear. Not just the ear, the neck, the cheek, and the lips, definitely the lips. He was becoming dangerously distracted. "Have I done anything?"

She took a deep breath and let it out. "It doesn't concern you. Now can we just drop the matter?"

So, there was something. "Not if you are to work with me." That was an impotent threat as he had no intention of letting her go.

"It isn't your problem, but if you must know, Mrs. Delacourte came by this morning and voiced her opinion of my working here."

"Does her opinion matter to you?"

"I don't give a feather for her opinion."

"Then why are you so upset?"

"Because…it is difficult to explain."

He dropped his hand from her chin, and put both hands on her shoulders. "Try."

Her eyes began to mist, and he was about to drop the subject when she said, "She brought up my mother. You see my mother has always expected me to be like her, and I have never met those expectations. Mrs. Delacourte knows that my mother would never approve of my working for you. She is going to write to her. I was hoping to avoid my mother's interference this time. I have never been able to live up to her standards, because I want a different life than the one she has planned for me."

"If you want to leave, I will understand." He wouldn't, but felt he had to give her the opportunity.

"I most certainly do NOT want to leave. I enjoy my work here even more than I did teaching with Rasheen. I feel as if I am of some use, and that gives my life purpose."

Peter was so relieved that he felt like throwing his arms around her and having that relapse, but he dropped his hands from her shoulders instead. "Then forget Mrs. Delacourte and your mother. Your help, your knowledge are invaluable to me." He was about to suggest they stroll over to the stone house for some lunch, when the front door to the office opened and a woman came in holding a baby, with a small child holding to her skirt, while two others that couldn't be more than four or five years old followed. Mrs. Bristol was in her late twenties and she had two more children in addition to the ones with her now.

When Peter asked who his patient was going to be, Mrs. Bristol informed him that she needed some kind of tonic. "I don't have any energy, Doctor Schmidt. I can barely make it through the day."

Peter took her into the examining room with her children trailing along behind like little chicks following a mother hen. Bernice took the baby, while he examined the woman's eyes and ears, and then told her to open her mouth so he could check her tongue and throat. Next he listened to her chest, and stood back for a moment studying her before giving her his diagnosis. "I can give you a tonic that will help some, but it will not alter the fact that you have six children, and you haven't given your body time to recuperate in between pregnancies. You are still a young woman, but you cannot go on like this. I fear another child could very well end up in…" Realizing that the children were listening, and not wishing to frighten them with the possibility of their mother's death, he asked Bernice to take the children into the waiting room.

After Bernice and the children had departed the room, and the door closed behind them, Peter continued, "No more children, Mrs. Bristol."

The poor woman began to cry. "I…do not…want," she choked out the words, "but the law says …and my husband would never agree. I simply cannot use….or I would surely be damned. I would rather die than bear that shame."

Peter handed her his handkerchief, and gently put his arm around her slumped shoulders. He knew the prevailing teachings of the various religions and the attitudes of society when it came to women and children. The only acceptable method of family limitation was abstinence, and the majority of men might take the high moral ground where their wives were concerned when it came to artificial contraception, but they were unwilling to practice self-denial when it came to the marriage bed. "I am going to do an examination and then we may have the solution to your problem."

She gave him a bewildered look before blowing her nose loudly. "But..."

Peter reassured her and then asked her to wait while he left the room. He then went into the outer room and asked the children if they would sit quietly while he and Bernice left them for a minute. Bribing them with candy sticks worked wonders. Bernice kept the baby in her arms and followed him into the examination room. When they stepped inside, Mrs. Bristol was seated on the table waiting. Peter did a quick examination and then went to a cabinet and pulled two pessaries from one of the shelves. He took the one that looked about the right size and was about to insert it when Mrs. Bristol protested, "Doctor Schmidt, I told you... I cannot use any...."

He gently interrupted her. "I know, but you have a fallen womb from all your pregnancies and you need this to hold it in place. You won't be using it for contraception purposes, but it most likely will prevent you from conceiving again. Surely your church would want you to take care of your health so you can care for your children. If you don't wear this device, you could end up bedridden and who will care for your family? You will have to come to the surgery again in three months and we will see how it is working. In a year or so we may be able to remove it, if that is what you really want. For now, you have to wear it by order of your doctor."

Bernice stood close to the examining table and held the baby who was content to play with her loose strand of hair. She patted Mrs. Bristol's shoulder with her free hand and leaned down close to her ear to whisper, "Trust the doctor. You have nothing to be ashamed of, and you are not committing any sin. This little babe needs you as do those beautiful children in the other room. You have a duty to be the best mother you can for them."

Mrs. Bristol gave her a grateful nod and allowed Peter to finish the procedure. His first choice was a correct fit. Once he was finished, he instructed her to dress while he replaced the unused device and retrieved a bottle from another shelf. After she was dressed again, he handed her the bottle with instructions to use the contents whenever she had relations with her husband.

"Why is that necessary?" She asked.

"To keep the device sterile so you do not risk getting an infection," he lied. The contents of the bottle would further help to prevent conception.

She gave him a grateful nod. "Thank you, Doctor Schmidt."

"See that you follow my instructions and make sure you take the tonic," he said as he opened the door to the outer room and saw the other children happily licking their candy sticks. The woman paid him for her visit, and then he gave each child another candy stick before they left.

When he came back to the examining room, Bernice was putting things in order. She stopped and looked at him with the same look his mother gave him and Connor when they were caught misbehaving. "What?" he asked innocently.

"Did she really need a pessary?"

"You disapprove?" He was ready for a discussion of the Comstock Laws, knowing that she would be well informed. The laws prohibited the sale and use of contraceptives. If a doctor was found guilty of distributing any form of birth control, he would forfeit his medical license and end up in jail.

"Not at all. I think you handled the matter very well. Why should a woman be forced to have more children than she is financially, physically, or emotionally able to care for? I don't doubt that Mr. Comstock's motives were honest when he began his crusade to stop the pornographic trade, but he has become a zealot in the last few years, and women are suffering for it. When my father and I were in New York, I read an article in the Ledger that said during the last two decades thousands of dead newborns have been found in alleys, ash heaps, privies, rivers and so on – tiny ghosts of women's shame. Society sits in moral condemnation, but no one will do a thing to help. If women were allowed to have the means to prevent pregnancies until they were able to care for their children properly, this rampant infanticide could be prevented."

Bernice raised a questioning eyebrow, "The upper-class male might preach abstinence, but I would wager a good many of those men who are so considerate of their wives after they have their desired number of children are seeking physical pleasures with their mistresses or perhaps prostitutes. Yet, will they be the ones to be prosecuted? No, it will be the poor woman who is fighting for survival, and has been forced to do that which the sainted wife finds so distasteful. She will be the one to risk getting diseased, pregnant, or sent to prison."

Peter rubbed his chin thoughtfully with the back of his fingers. "My dear Miss Peterson, I certainly did not expect such an opinion from you." It was true, but he knew she approved of his actions by the encouraging words she had whispered to Mrs. Bristol.

"I have several opinions that no doubt would surprise you."

CHAPTER 7

Rasheen handed baby Clare to Bernice before buttoning the front of her dress. "This child has an appetite like her father. It seems like I am always nursing her." The kiss she planted on the baby's forehead and her soft maternal expression when she looked at the baby belied the complaint.

"Does it hurt when you nurse her?" Bernice put the baby over her own shoulder and rubbed her back the way that Rasheen had instructed her. She was rewarded by a soft burp and a happy gurgle.

"It did at first, but Martha had a balm that helped. I rather like the time we share during her feedings. I am filled with peace and contentment then and all is right with the world."

"My mother would die if she heard me having this conversation with you," Bernice whispered over the sleeping baby in her arms.

"No need to whisper, she's a sound sleeper." Rasheen motioned for Bernice to put Clare in the crib. "I imagine your mother would be upset with a great deal of the topics we discuss."

Bernice nodded agreement as both women laughed at the thought of Bernice's mother being privy to any of their conversations, which sometimes ran a bit risqué. At least her mother would think that of them. To Bernice's way of thinking, they were informative. How else would she ever know what some of life's experiences were? Surely, not from her mother or any of the society matrons. For some reason, her father's friend, Julie, came to mind. She could picture herself having this type of conversation with Julie.

The two women left the nursery and went downstairs. A few minutes later when they were sitting on the porch, the new housemaid Connor had recently hired came out to inquire if they would like something cool to drink.

"That would be lovely. Thank you, Bertie."

The young girl gave a slight curtsy and disappeared.

"How is Martha adjusting to the new maid?" Bernice asked.

"She threw a fit at first, but Connor eventually convinced her we needed her to help with the baby, and that soothed things over – that and the fact that we had a girl. I think she enjoys having the extra time with Clare. And Martha and John are family after all."

"Just because I'm family doesn't mean I want to sit around like the Queen of Sheba all day." Martha joined them on the porch with a tray laden with cookies and lemonade.

"Now you know you enjoy spending time with Clare, and I really do need your help," Rasheen cajoled.

"Hmmmph!" Martha plopped her plump frame down in the rocking chair near the swing where the other two were happily munching the cookies she had sat on a nearby table.

"And who does all the cooking around here, not to mention the fact that you keep Jack out of mischief?" Rasheen raised a questioning brow. "Furthermore, I could have never have kept the school opened while I was carrying Clare without your support, and Bernice's help too, of course."

"I enjoyed the time I spent with you and the children.

It was nice to be of some use," Bernice said as she reached down to pet a black cat with white markings on his feet. When the cat was a kitten, Connor had given it to her and agreed that it would be kept at Sara's Glen since her mother would never have allowed the feline to take up residence in her home. Bernice had named him Boots, and he had formed an attachment to her from the beginning. Whenever Bernice came to Sara's Glen, Boots came out of hiding and ran to her, jumping in her lap if she was seated.

"It's a good thing you aren't living here. You would spoil that cat so bad that he would be useless as a mouser." Martha leaned over and stroked the cat behind the ears despite the complaint. "Speaking of being of use, how are things working out at the dispensary? Peter seems pleased to have you there. He was just saying the other day how knowledgeable you are in herbal cures and that he hopes to learn from you. Coming from him, that is high praise."

Bernice felt a surge of pleasure at the compliment. "I am learning a lot from him, too."

"I knew it would be a good match." Martha gave Bernice a satisfied smile. "Now if you will excuse me, I'm going inside. The two of you need to have a visit without an old woman hanging about. I would imagine there are things you want to discuss that concern young folk. I will have plenty of time to talk to Bernice later at dinner."

Catching the screen door with her hip so it wouldn't slam, Martha looked over her shoulder and said, "Bernice, now that Rasheen is married, I am willing to bet that some lucky fellow is going to snap you up. Perhaps it might even be someone right under our noses."

Rasheen shook her head at the closed door. "You know she wasn't referring to Ambrose Kingsley. And speaking of which, what is happening with you and Ambrose? For only being a friend, you seem to spend an awful lot of time with him."

"Not so much since Mother has left," Bernice argued.

"Ambrose is still my escort when we have to attend social functions. Before you came into my life, he was the only person I could confide in, and as much as I appreciate him, there are some things that simply cannot be discussed with a gentleman."

Rasheen crooked her head to one side. "Do tell?"

"You know - things that only a woman would understand." Bernice took a deep breath and then blurted out the question that was burning inside her. "What's it like to have a man make love to you?"

"Goodness gracious, that certainly isn't something you would discuss with Mr. Kingsley, now is it?" A soft pink flush shadowed Rasheen's cheeks, causing Bernice to regret trying to satisfy her curiosity.

"I'm sorry. That was too personal. Forget I asked. My mother wrote me a letter full of advice for what she thinks is my upcoming wedding night and she described the experience as a horrible ordeal to be borne by a woman in payment for securing a husband."

"Don't be a silly goose. You just surprised me, and you know how easily I blush. Don't pay any heed to whatever your mother has told you. It is a wonderful experience if it's with the right man. There may be a bit of pain the first time, but after that it is the most glorious feeling in the world. How can I describe what it is like to share your body and your very soul with someone you love, and to know that he loves you above all others, even himself, because your feelings mirror his? When the time comes that you fall in love, I promise you that you will eagerly anticipate your wedding night."

"I suspected your marriage was quite different than the one mother described," Bernice gave a sigh of relief.

Rasheen put her arm around Bernice's shoulder and gave her a gentle hug. "I would much prefer you come to me with any concerns, rather than burden yourself with needless fear. The physical love between a man and woman is a miracle to be treasured and enjoyed, not treated like a curse. Unfortunately, a lot of women feel as your mother does." She shook her head. "How sad for your father, for both of them, really."

Now Bernice understood why her father took so many business trips to New York and why his absences lasted so long. "Let's not dwell on it anymore. There is another matter I need to discuss with you."

Rasheen leaned back in the porch swing. "We have all afternoon to discuss whatever you like, my dear."

"For some reason, my mother's Aunt Catherine has left her entire estate to me. She married a very wealthy man and they had no children. I don't remember that much about her except that we visited her at her home, Hollyhock, a few times when I was very young. Apparently, I made a favorable impression. I need Connor's legal advice as I have no intention of living there."

"I am sure Connor will be happy to help you, but what about your family solicitor?"

Bernice frowned. "I will need advice concerning Aunt Catherine's investments, and I'm not sure what I'll do with all the jewelry, and if I decide to sell the house, I can't depend upon the family solicitor to be discreet. He would feel obliged to speak to mother. That's why I want things settled before mother returns from Europe, or at the very least, have the papers drawn up. She thinks Ambrose and I will be moving into the place and take our proper position in society. There is not a chance in Hades that is going to transpire." Bernice grimaced at the thought of living in the somber mansion that had been her aunt's home for decades.

Rasheen gave a sarcastic laugh. "Isn't it every woman's dream to be a society matron?"

"Which you managed to escape by marrying Connor," Bernice reminded her.

"That is only one of the many advantages of being married to Mr. Reilly," Rasheen sighed.

"Would our previous conversation have anything to do with the rest?" Bernice teased.

A deep scarlet colored Rasheen's cheeks. "We seem to have strayed from the subject. I believe we were discussing your inheritance and what you will do with it."

"I suppose that means you are not going to share your thoughts on the matter." Bernice gently nudged Boots off of her lap and stood up and walked to the porch rail. "I will meet with your husband and then make some decisions, but for now we will keep it as our secret."

Rasheen nodded. "Agreed."

Bernice reached out her hand. "Shall we take a stroll through the garden before dinner?"

*****

Peter bounded up the porch steps, and was just about to open the screen door when the sound of women's laughter coming from his mother's herb garden caught his attention. Connor had designed the gardens so that one could view them from the porch. Herbs and flowers perfumed the occasional warm summer breeze with their scent as it drifted over the railings. The herb garden was the first garden making it closest to the house which gave him a clear view of the two women. Rasheen and Bernice strolled through the garden with Boots hiding in the lavender bushes, and then pouncing onto their shadows. The feline's adoration for Bernice was obvious, unlike its animosity toward Peter due to the fact that he had accidentally stepped on its tail. To seal his fate, he had taken a dead mouse from the cat when it presented the catch to Martha while she was working on a batch of cookies in the kitchen. Even though he had tried to make amends by replacing the mouse with a chicken wing, the cantankerous animal declared war, and now whenever he came near, it hissed at him.

Peter stood there watching them; his attention focused on Bernice as she stooped and plucked a long strand of lavender to tickle the cat's nose. Boots batted at the lavender in a playful manner. The woman fascinated him with her knowledge of herbal remedies, as well as her ability to hold an intelligent, informed conversation regarding things outside her own sphere. Most of the women he had encountered in the upper classes knew nothing of the world's misery, and cared even less. Yet, she had been keenly interested when he described the plight of the children who became maimed while working in the factories in Baltimore. He could see why she and Rasheen had become such close friends. Few women of his acquaintance matched the two of them in their compassion, wit, or thirst for knowledge.

Though he couldn't see her features from this distance, he knew them well enough to see them in his mind's eye: her soft translucent skin, sky-blue eyes that were a mixture of intelligence, gentleness, and dignity. His mind wondered back to the night he kissed her. She hadn't seemed offended by his lapse in good judgment, but it was a mistake. He didn't regret it, not in the least, but it should not have happened. He would control himself in the future. She had returned to work with him and acted as if his kiss had no effect on her, but he knew that she felt the same reaction as he did when he kissed her. She could remain silent, and choose to act as if nothing had occurred, but her response spoke for her. He should be grateful that she was making things easier for him, but for some reason, it bothered him.

"What are you looking at?" Martha stood just inside the screen door watching him watch Bernice

"Nothing," he lied.

"Hmmmm."

"What?" He asked, knowing he should have just ignored the remark.

She opened the door and stood next to him, and observed the two women in the gardens below. "Peter, the heart speaks the truth in a way that cannot be ignored; listen to your heart."

"Mother, I have not the faintest idea what you are talking about," he lied again.

"I've seen the way you steal quick glances of her when you think she isn't looking, heard the way your voice changes to a softer tone when you speak about her. She has brought you back to life. You smile more whenever she is around. Those smiles reveal your secret. It is as clear as a summer sky that the two of you belong together. Bernice acts the same as you do. Her face is turned in your direction whenever you're near, but then she quickly looks away when you sense her watching. Why are you denying yourself love? Surely it isn't because you doubt her feelings toward you, because all of that talk about her and Mr. Kingsley is nonsense. She cares for you."

Peter felt a tightening in his chest, and he wasn't sure whether it was apprehension or pleasure. "Has she said as much to you?"

"Of course not. She is as cautious as you are and every bit as private. I doubt she would even say anything about her feelings to Rasheen. Her head turns in your direction when you enter a room, even before you speak, as if she senses your presence."

Bernice had not spoken to his mother. He should be relieved that nothing would change, and yet, he felt a slight disappointment. "You are trying to play matchmaker again." Martha had played a small role in Rasheen and Connor's romance. "You see things that do not exist."

Martha reached up and touched his cheek. "Your heart knows what it wants. It does not wish to be buried in the past."

She was making him uncomfortable speaking of such things. His work at the City Dispensary, teaching, and his patients had helped him forget the past of which she spoke. Though he was just as busy since his return to North County, it was becoming more difficult to submerge the memories that would bubble to the surface from time to time, and the feelings that he experienced with Bernice;

feelings that he would not permit to interfere with his well-ordered life.

"I am content in my work. North County needs me, and Bernice or any other woman would not want an attachment with someone like me. Her life would be a lonely one since my work is my mistress." Playfully, in an attempt to lighten the mood, he reached around and tugged at his mother's apron strings until they came undone making her reach down to catch it as it fell away.

She pulled the apron in front of her, reached around and tied the strings once more. Shaking her head sadly, she said, "You haven't enough sense to know when you are starving."

"So, when is dinner to be served?" He opened the door for her to go inside.

Before she stepped inside, she put her hand on his heart. "A broken heart can heal and love stronger and better. That's the heart's own truth."

CHAPTER 8

Bernice arranged the roses in the blue and white toile porcelain china vase, one of her mother's favorites. No doubt the flowers, a thoughtful gesture on Ambrose's part, would have pleased her mother, if she had been home to witness it. Bernice was happy to merely have Ambrose visit her. "You don't have to bring me flowers, you know."

He stretched his legs out in front of himself, and leaned back against the parlor's blue velvet settee. "I have missed you. I never get to see you anymore since you started working at the good doctor's office."

Bernice came and sat next to him. "Why Ambrose Kingsley, if I didn't know better, I would swear you are jealous."

"I suppose I am a little envious. After all, we did spend a good amount of time together once your mother decided I was the better choice over Hilliard." Heaving an exaggerated sigh, he said, "Now that she is away, you have tossed me aside. Women are such fickle creatures."

"You know that I love you. You are one of my dearest friends, and I will never abandon you. It doesn't matter rather mother is here or not," she said sincerely.

"Speaking of Towson's Mrs. Astor, how is your

mother enjoying Europe?" Ambrose asked, though they both knew he wasn't really interested in her mother's trip abroad.

"She seems to be enjoying herself, but I got another letter from her asking when she is going to get word about a certain engagement."

"Oh good heavens, I thought we might enjoy some peace while the old girl was away."

Bernice giggled. "We are speaking of my mother."

"True enough. Anything else of interest?"

"As a matter of fact, there is. I have asked Connor Reilly to handle the matter of my aunt's estate. I am not sure what to do about it yet."

He got down on one knee and took her hand. "Does that mean you don't want to live there with me?"

She slapped his hand away playfully. "You said you would never want to live there. Do you have any ideas as to best use it?"

"Hmmm, you could sell it and give the money to charity or perhaps donate the mansion to an orphanage," he said as he got to his feet and dropped into a nearby chair.

Bernice tapped her fingers against her lips as she thought about his suggestion. "I like the idea of it serving a useful purpose."

"You do realize your mother is not going to be happy. She expects us to take up residence there and become the king and queen of Baltimore Society," he mused.

Bernice raised her brows. "You almost sound like you agree with her."

"Darling, you know better than that." Ambrose stood up and took her hands in his pulling her up with him. "It is a beautiful afternoon, and since I finally have you away from your Doctor Schmidt, perhaps we might go for a drive."

"I do wish you would stop saying such things," Bernice said over her shoulder as she left the room, returning a few minutes later with her hat, gloves, and parasol. "Let's go for a walk instead."

Ambrose stepped through the door the butler had just opened for them and extended his arm, which Bernice took along with more of his teasing. "You must admit that you are spending a lot of time with him locked up in that nasty place with all those sick people coming and going. Selfish cad that I am, I miss having you available whenever I wanted your company. However, I am happy that you have found something that interests you, because I know how you missed teaching with Mrs. Reilly once the county opened the new school. Still, you must admit that Doctor Schmidt does monopolize your time these days."

Bernice patted his arm. "I was never jealous of all the time you spend with Mr. St. Vincent." William St. Vincent was not only a business partner, but a close friend.

"No, you have always understood my time spent with St. Vincent." Ambrose gave her an appreciative smile.

They walked in companionable silence until they reached the shopping district and found themselves near Hayward's, a local ice cream parlor and candy shop. "Fancy some ice cream?" Ambrose asked.

"That would be lovely." Bernice let him lead her inside and seat her in one of the white painted chairs at a small table for two.

A few minutes later they were enjoying their ice cream, when they were interrupted by two of Bernice's mother's friends who came into the shop and stopped by their table. Ambrose stood politely while the two women stopped to chat. They exchanged pleasantries and then inquired if Ambrose and Bernice had attended the performance of Madame Pavaleoni at Hampton, the estate of the Ridgely family. Before Ambrose or Bernice could reply, they went into great detail about the performance until finally leaving.

Ambrose looked down at the soupy confection that had been their ice cream. "I should have excused myself and sat and ate my ice cream, and you should have just continued eating. Rude old biddies!"

Bernice sighed. "Why don't you order another?"

"Good idea." He ordered two more dishes and this time they were able to finish eating their treat.

Ambrose set his spoon on the table and wiped his mouth with the table napkin. "I had forgotten about the performance at the Ridgely's. Were you upset with me for not escorting you home?"

"I knew that if Mr. St. Vincent attended, I would be spending most of the evening alone since you and he would be off somewhere huddled together, but I was not happy that Peter was forced to escort me home."

"That was unfair of me. What can I do to make up for it?"

She gave him an understanding smile. "It is all right, Ambrose."

"Have I mentioned the fact that you are a very generous woman? I am a lucky man to have found someone like you for a companion."

"I am the fortunate one to have you as my champion." Bernice rose from the chair he had just pulled out for her. Once they were outside again, she asked, "Where to now?"

He took her arm and held it as they stepped down from the curb. "Seeing the old crows today reminded me that that there is something I must discuss with you."

Bernice looked up into his eyes and read the concern in them. She loved the color of his eyes. It was a soft green, like moss, but whenever he was upset about something, they would cloud over like stormy water. "What?"

"I would rather wait until we are where no one can overhear our conversation." He inclined his head toward people passing them as they walked.

"Very well, but I must tell you that now I am both curious and worried."

They walked home in silence except to exchange greetings with acquaintances they met along the way.

Once they had returned to the Peterson residence,

Bernice removed her hat and gloves and handed them, along with her parasol, to a downstairs maid who had greeted them upon their arrival. She dismissed the young woman, and ushered Ambrose into the parlor. She sat on the heavy gold silk brocaded sofa, and motioned for him to do the same. When he closed the door before doing so, she felt a chill run down her spine despite the summer heat. "Ambrose, whatever is the matter?"

He took her hands in his. "Dearest, it is not quite that bad. I'm sorry if I have frightened you. The other day when my mother was receiving callers, Mrs. Winthrope paid her a visit. The old crone brought up a scandal involving you and Doctor Schmidt. Apparently, Mrs. Delacourte is spreading gossip regarding the two you and an incident that took place at a ball given by the elder Reilly's. Mother dismissed it as nonsense and directed the conversation elsewhere, but she cautioned me that I should make you aware of it."

Bernice shook her head in disbelief. "Why do they waste their time on such viciousness? There was no scandal and the incident of which she speaks took place over a year ago. Peter was merely trying to help me avoid the unwelcome attentions of a certain gentlemen. He had waltzed me out into the hall and we were alone when Amelia discovered us."

"Hmmm….and what exactly were you doing – alone?" Ambrose waggled his eyebrows.

"Nothing for which I need apologize or feel guilty. I find it unfathomable that you of all people would question me thus." Bernice folded her arms in front of her chest.

Ambrose unfolded them and took her hand in his. "Darling, I have no desire to see you hurt. I would never have brought the subject to your attention had not mother asked me to address it."

"And so you have, but I have no idea how to stop the gossips." Bernice heaved a sigh.

"I don't suppose you can, and I imagine your work at

the dispensary is not helping matters."

"Mrs. Delacourte showed up the other day and demanded that I stop working there. She said I was a disgrace to my poor mother, and that you will not want to marry me if I continue. I am sorry if you have a problem with my employment, Ambrose, but I am not giving up something useful that I enjoy just to satisfy a few old crows. They can caw until their voices give out."

He rested his forehead against hers. "I have no problem with what you are doing. As for mother, she applauds your endeavor."

Just as Bernice put her arms around him to give him a hug, the doors to the parlor slid open. "Excuse me, I didn't know you had company," her father said as he gave them a disapproving look.

"How have you been, Ambrose? We have not seen much of you since we returned from New York." Her father motioned for him to return to his seat.

Ambrose remained standing. "Bernice has been busy at the dispensary, and I am afraid I have had some pressing business matters of late."

"So you are here now. Will you stay for dinner?" Her father was trying to be pleasant. Bernice knew he was not overly fond of Ambrose.

"Thank you for the invitation, but I was just about to leave."

"Good afternoon to you then," her father said.

"And a pleasant afternoon to you too, Mr. Peterson."

Bernice started to rise from the sofa, but Ambrose stopped her. "No need to bother, I can see myself out."

"Thank you for a lovely walk, and the enlightening conversation." Bernice gave him a conspiratorial smile.

"You are most welcome."

After Ambrose had left, her father sat next to her on the sofa and stared at the portrait of her mother which hung over the mantle. "Bernice, do not be dictated to by her as to whom you choose for a husband."

Bernice rested her head on his shoulder. "I realize you disapprove of Ambrose, but you only see the first layer. He is much deeper."

"I just want you to be happy." Her father looked away from the picture.

*****

Bernice placed the book she had been reading on the table, glanced at her mother's gilded French Mantel clock, and saw that it was time for bed. As she walked through the hallway to the stairs, she noticed the light coming from beneath her father's study, and softly knocked on the door. Upon entering, she found him studying a sheet of paper lying on the desk in front of him. It was one of many belonging to a large stack. "I came in to say goodnight," she said as she went around the desk and kissed his cheek. "Try not to work too late into the evening, Papa."

He gave her a weary smile. "Just a little while longer."

She was about to turn and leave when he asked her to sit a moment. "There's something I need to discuss with you. I was going to wait until morning, but you leave so early these days that I don't see you for breakfast."

Bernice felt her breath turn to ice in her chest. She could see from the concerned expression on his face that something was troubling her father. What could be so urgent? Had Mrs. Delacourte come to see him spreading her daughter's vicious gossip? Her father cared little for gossip, and would not consider it the disaster that her mother would have if she had been the one receiving the news. No doubt he would dismiss Mrs. Delacourte in a curt manner if she came to call, but he would be concerned for his daughter.

"Sit down, Sweet Pea, and take that look of fear off of your face. My news is not that terrible. I just wanted to tell you that I will be leaving for New York tomorrow."

Her breath warmed and came easier. "Is that all? You seemed so serious. Of course I will miss you, but you always return in a week or two."

"I will be gone much longer this time. I am not sure when I will be returning. Since your mother isn't here and has no need of me for her social obligations, I needn't rush home."

She looked into his eyes, the same shade of blue as her own, and saw an uncertainty as if he wanted to say more. When he didn't, she took the initiative. "It is more than business."

"What makes you say that?" he asked in a relieved tone.

"Papa, I am not naïve. I saw the way you looked at Mrs. Bouroughs - the way you came alive when we spent time with her. You have never been so light hearted in mother's company. In fact, the two of you barely speak anymore unless it relates to some formal event."

He rubbed his eyes with the palms of his hands before answering her. "I would never hurt your mother."

"I am not condemning you, but why keep up the pretense?"

"What would you have me do? Divorce your mother?" The words, though softly spoken, thundered off the dark walnut panels of the quiet room.

After a few silent moments, Bernice asked, "Wouldn't that be preferable to both of you being so miserable?"

He leaned back in his chair, closed his eyes and heaved a weary sigh. "Divorce would destroy your mother. She would no longer be accepted in society. Why should she be punished for something that is not her fault? She did what was expected of her with confidence that her life would follow a given path."

"Did you and mother ever love one another?" Bernice understood what her father was saying, but the thought of two people living their lives without a shred of love or affection was too much to comprehend, and yet she knew that was the case even as she asked the question.

"Your mother and I married because it was what our parents expected of us. I thought we would grow to love one another as we built a life together. When that failed to happen, I buried myself in my work, and she became more and more involved with our social position. Neither of us has been happy with our lives. True happiness is more than just a common background, or similar social standing. There has to be compatibility, understanding, passion, and a genuine love and tenderness. Without these, life becomes a hollow shell where two people exist."

"Until Matthew came to work for you, and you met Mrs. Bouroughs," Bernice interrupted.

Her father shook his head. "Julie and I renewed our relationship because of Matthew. When we were young we fell in love, but she refused my marriage proposal. She said it was because she wanted to pursue her art, that there was no room in her life for a husband. Being the fool that I was, I believed her. I became angry and went home to do my parent's bidding, not realizing that my father had gone to Julie, and threatened to disown me if I married her. A year later, your mother and I were married."

"What happened to Julie?"

"She married John Bouroughs, a man twenty years her senior. His name and wealth helped her get her start in the art world."

"Is Matthew...?"

"Matthew is John Bouroughs' son. It was a happy marriage. I had no contact with Julie until after her son come to work for me. I knew who he was because I had followed her career through the years."

"And then you contacted his mother?" Bernice asked.

"Even then, I kept away. It wasn't until Matthew and I were In New York on a business trip and he insisted I come to dinner and meet his mother that Julie and I resumed our relationship. By that time her husband had died. At first we were just old friends consoling one another, but things changed."

Bernice leaned over the desk and took his hands. "You will get no condemnation from me."

He looked relieved, but also remorseful. "I am not a

very good husband or father."

"You are a loving father, and have remained a good husband, if not a faithful one. Life with mother is not easy." No one knew that better than Bernice.

Squeezing her hands her father said, "Perhaps if your mother were married to someone she loved, and who returned her love, things would be different. See that you don't make the same mistake."

"I doubt that I will ever marry."

"What about Ambrose?"

"That charade is for mother's benefit." Bernice shook her head sadly. "Ambrose is a good friend and nothing more."

"I am happy to hear that. Ambrose is a nice enough fellow, but not the one for you. Do not settle for anything less than someone who loves you, who makes you excited about each day and what it might bring the two of you. Life without that is a dreary existence." He kissed her cheek. "Now off to bed with you."

She rose and was almost to the door when he asked her, "How are things working out with Doctor Schmidt?"

"I enjoy working with him. He is open to using herbal cures, and I am learning so much from him."

Her father smiled. "I like him."

Closing the door behind her, Bernice wondered why he had brought up Peter, but didn't dwell on it. She was more preoccupied with her parents' loveless marriage. Her father had found happiness with another woman who he could never marry, and she had just betrayed her mother. Her heart ached for all of them. Bernice made a firm resolution that she would never marry a man who didn't love her as much as she loved him.

CHAPTER 9

"I am so glad you decided to join us for dinner," Martha said as she poured another glass of lemonade for Bernice.

Taking the glass from her, Bernice said, "It has been nice to have some conversation at the dinner table. Now that Papa is away, I have taken to eating in the library while reading. It seems silly to make the servants go to the trouble of preparing the table for just one person."

"Well then, you will take your dinner with us until your father returns." Martha glanced over at Peter. "You should have thought to invite her sooner."

He shrugged. "I was not aware that Mr. Peterson was out of town. Of course, Bernice should take dinner here at Sara's Glen in his absence."

"I could not possibly do that. It would be an imposition," Bernice protested.

"Rubbish," Rasheen said. "Now that you have begun working with Peter, we have not seen as much of you. "

Peter looked across the table at Bernice and said, "Perhaps Rasheen will get to see you more. I have to go to Baltimore day after tomorrow to give a lecture and to oversee a procedure at the City Dispensary. I would have told you sooner, but I didn't get the letter until this afternoon. I will be gone for about a week." Though he was looking forward to the trip, the idea of being away from her gave him a twinge of reluctance.

"You should take Bernice with you. She could learn a great deal at the City Dispensary, and I am sure your lecture would be of interest to her." A crafty smile adorned Martha's face as she passed a bowl of roasted beets across the table to Peter.

Though he would have enjoyed her company, and his mother's suggestion was not without merit, Peter knew that it would not be proper for Bernice to travel alone with a single gentleman. "Mother, that is not possible."

Connor gave Martha a conspiratorial grin. "Course it is. I have business to attend to for Uncle Patrick, so Rasheen and I can accompany you and act as Bernice's chaperones."

"Oh, that will be wonderful. We can take Clare for a visit with her auntie and uncle and we can spend some time with my family. It will be a nice holiday. And of course, everyone would love to see Bernice." Rasheen jumped up and hugged her husband.

Peter wondered just when Connor had aligned himself with Martha's matchmaking, leaving him to fend for himself. He could not deny that it would benefit Bernice to tour the City Dispensary and see some of the work being done there. Also, the nuns could enhance her medical skills, since they would be more generous than the doctors who frowned on woman actually participating in the healing practice other than to act as their servants. Still, Connor's betrayal annoyed him. He shot a warning look at his former ally in the avoidance of matchmakers, and said, "I suppose it would be all right, but I will not have time for much visiting. This is a working trip."

Connor gave him a smug grin. "Tell that to Aunt Elaine."

Rasheen was already listing all the things she had to do to prepare for the trip, and Martha was assuring her that she did not mind in the least if they took the baby for a visit, since she had her to herself all the time.

"You have not said anything in all the twittering going on around you," Peter said to Bernice. "Would you like to accompany me on this trip?"

She looked thoughtful for a moment before replying, "I think I could learn some things that would make me of more use here, but I feel as if you have been imposed upon."

He gave her an appreciative smile for her perception. "Well, if we put the enthusiasm over the prospect of a family visit aside, I do think it would be beneficial to you. Will you join us?"

"If you have no objections, I would very much like that."

Peter's voice held a note of warning as he looked over at Connor and said, "You can wire Patrick, and let him know we are coming, and that this is a working trip for Bernice and me."

"That may be true, but you will still need a place to sleep, and you can take your dinner with Patrick and Elaine," Martha insisted.

In all the talk about traveling to Baltimore, no one had paid attention to Jack. "Do I have to go along?" he asked.

"But don't you want to come? Granny especially will want to see you," Rasheen said.

"I know, but suppose Thistle has her foal while I am away?" Jack threw a worried glance in Connor's direction.

"She is not due for another month." John reached around and patted the boy on the shoulder.

Connor gave Jack an understanding smile. "Just the same, if you want to stay at home with Martha and John, that will be all right with me, if Rasheen has no objections."

"I will make your apologies. After all, you will be staying with Uncle Patrick and Aunt Elaine come the fall when you start at Loyola. You will have plenty of time to visit with my family then," Rasheen said.

Martha beamed over at Pater. "Then it is all settled and everyone is happy."

"Simply overwhelmed with joy," he said, raising his eyes toward the ceiling.

*****

Peter opened the door, and stepped aside to allow Bernice to enter before taking her arm, and leading her inside where an elderly nun greeted them. Bernice was struck by the elfin features framed by a white wimple and heavy black veil. Warm brown eyes matched the voice that greeted them. "Doctor Schmidt, we have missed you here at the hospital. I trust all is going well in North County."

"Very well, thank you, Sister Mary Joseph. I have missed you also, but I must admit that I do not miss Baltimore. I had forgotten how much I love the country." Peter gave her one of his smiles that Bernice had come to realize was only bestowed on a select few. This woman obviously had been special to him during his time at the hospital. "May I present Miss Peterson? She is working with me at the Dispensary in North County, and since I am in Baltimore to present a paper at the university, I thought it would be a good opportunity for her to tour the City Dispensary and learn from the good sisters."

"You flatter us. Wait here a moment while I go find Sister Imelda. She will want to see you, of course, and no doubt want to conduct the tour herself." She used the small table to push herself up and retrieved a thick wooden cane which hung from the side of the table. Grasping it with a hand whose joints were twisted from rheumatism more than likely, Bernice surmised, she shuffled her bent frame around the desk and through the double doors.

They watched after her in silence for a few seconds before Bernice asked, "Has anything been done for Sister Mary Joseph's rheumatism?"

Peter rubbed the fingertips of his right hand across his forehead as if he had a headache, a sign that he was contemplating something. "I wanted to send her to one of the water cure spas, but she would not hear of it. She rubs some liniment on it that the sisters use, and I have prescribed laudanum to help her sleep if it gets too painful, but to my knowledge, she has not used it. I wish there were something more we could do to alleviate her suffering."

Bernice started to speak and then bite her lip as if uncertain. After all, she was in a hospital with learned doctors. Who was she to question them?

"Come now, you are not going to hold back on me are you?" Peter apparently had noticed her uncertainty. She found the fact that he had been paying such close attention flattering, and encouraging enough for her to share her thoughts.

"I have seen Prickly Ash used, and the results were impressive."

"Then we shall get some for her, and I doubt she will put up any resistance as to taking it. Thank you for the suggestion." He placed his hands on her shoulders, looked into her eyes with an earnest expression and said, "Bernice, I never want you to hesitate to speak your ideas."

There was such sincerity in his voice and the feel of his hands on her shoulders so tender that Bernice felt her heart racing. She wanted to reach up and caress his face, but the doors opened and a tall, slender nun about half the age of Sister Mary Joseph appeared. The face framed by her wimple was one of authority, yet a hint of gentleness could be seen in the cool blue eyes taking stock of Bernice as Peter made the introductions, and then his request for a tour of the ward. Though her manner was more formal than Sister Mary Joseph, it was evident that she, too, was fond of Peter.

Sister Imelda led them through the double doors to a large open room lined with several beds, all filled with patients. A doctor standing at the bedside of one of the patients finished what he was doing, gave a hurried instruction to the nun standing next to him, and walked over to greet Peter before they both disappeared through a side door, leaving Bernice alone with Sister Imelda.

Sister explained that the hospital had once been a girls' boarding school, and some remodeling had been done to make it more suitable for its present use. "We have tried to open as many rooms as possible and make them into wards. There are a few private rooms and two rooms that we have kept for isolation purposes. The room we are in now is the men's ward." Bernice looked about the room and imagined it must have been a double parlor, as there were opened pocket doors in the center. After they passed through the men's ward, they pushed open a heavy oak door that led into a long hallway where there was a large room with a dozen beds that functioned as the women's ward. At the end of the women's ward was a wide staircase which led to the second floor. On the second floor a room that had been the dormitory at the boarding school functioned as the children's ward. There were only two children in the ward at present. Sister stopped to feel the forehead of a small boy who was around six years old. "How are you feeling this morning, Timothy?" She asked the child.

"Me throat hurts and I am hotter than the devil's own fire," he whispered.

"I am going to have Sister Agatha take your temperature, and then we will see what we can do about that throat. Perhaps some ice chips with a little vanilla syrup on them might help." She ruffled his hair.

He gave her an open grin that showed two missing front teeth.

At the end of the children's ward there was a door which led to another small hallway that opened to four more rooms. The doors to all of them were closed. The nun opened one of them and motioned for Bernice to step inside. The room was spotless as was every other inch of the building. Peter had said the nuns embraced the idea of cleanliness and its effect on infection when he instructed them how to see to the rooms. In fact, he said the nuns were easier to convince than the other doctors had been when he tried to introduce them to Lister's Theory of Antiseptics in surgery, which ended up saving countless lives.

The small room was painted white with one window whose blinds were pulled open, allowing the sunlight to stream through. There was a single bed in the corner occupied by a young woman who Bernice guessed to be about seventeen or eighteen years of age. She was mumbling in delirium, her head rolling from side to side. Sister Imelda went to the small table near the bed and poured a glass of water from the pitcher. "Raise her as much as you can."

Bernice did as she was instructed, and the nun tried to get the girl to drink some of the liquid. "Come now, Olive, how will we break that fever if you do not drink?" The girl took a small sip and Sister motioned for Bernice to lay her back down again. Once she was down, the nun pulled the sheet aside and turned the girl slightly revealing a large red stain on the bottom sheet and the girl's gown. "Oh, you poor, poor dear." Sister's voice was as gentle as if she was speaking to a newborn baby. Then she went to a small closet and pulled out new sheets and a fresh gown. Bernice helped her get the girl changed and apply clean packing to help stop the bleeding.

"A few years ago they were using packing that was no more than the leavings of cotton on the textile mill floors. It was not even washed. There is no wonder people said they came to the hospital to die. Doctor Schmidt taught us how to sterilize the packing material by boiling it and then misting it with a carbolic acid solution," Sister Imelda said.

"What is causing her hemorrhage?" Bernice asked.

Sister Imelda gave a weary sigh. "She found herself pregnant, and the father must have refused to marry her, so she sought the only alternative left to her."

"But surely there must have been some other safer solution?" Bernice knew that many young women died from abortions. There was no shortage of unscrupulous doctors, and those claiming to know what they were doing, that would take a young women's money without a care as to her well-being. "What about her family?"

The nun shook her head sadly. "Her family more than likely disowned her, or perhaps she could not bear the shame she would endure. Even if they wanted to help, they would probably not be able, as most of them can barely keep food on the table." Sister took a clean cloth, dipped it in some water, and placed it over the girl's forehead trying to keep it in place as the girl tossed and trembled. "The father is never held accountable, and the poor girl pays with her life just because she had the misfortune to fall in love with a dishonorable blackguard."

The door opened, and an older doctor came in inquiring after the girl. He shook his head. "This is what happens to young women of questionable morals. We reap what we sow, is that not right, Sister? This one will not only pay with her earthly life, but hell fire for all eternity. Tch, Tch, Tch," he clucked his tongue as he shook his head in a superior manner.

The nun's eyes narrowed and Bernice could have sworn she saw shards of ice shoot out of their pupils. "I think God would prefer that we act with compassion rather than condemnation, don't you, Doctor Ogden? After all, it is not up to us to judge since we ourselves will be called to give an accounting some day. Who are we to say someone is doomed to hell?"

The doctor let out a sputtering cough before saying, "Um, well yes, I suppose so, but you ..."

Before he could continue, Bernice broke in, "I have seen Shepherd's Purse used to stop female hemorrhaging.

That might help if we could get it to her in time. I could wire my friend to get some for me from the North County Dispensary, and she could send it on the next train." Peter's encouragement had given her the courage to speak out.

The doctor turned and looked over his spectacles down his long thin nose. "And who are you?"

"This is Miss Peterson. She works with Doctor Schmidt in North Country," Sister answered.

"Young woman, I do not know what kind of medicine Doctor Schmidt is practicing now that he has taken up residence in the country, but this is a nineteenth century hospital, not some medieval castle. We do not practice witchcraft." He waved his hand dismissively before turning his back on the two women and leaving the room.

'Pompous ass," Sister Imelda muttered to the closed door.

Bernice's eyes widened. "He is only quoting what most ministers preach from the pulpit."

"Social sins rarely injure a man, but always destroy a woman. Oh yes, they are full of disapprobation for the girls, but do you ever hear them speak about self control for the young men?" Sister spat out the question.

"Well, no, I have not. Do you see many cases such as this?" Bernice asked.

"Unfortunately, we do. I wish we could provide for these girls so they could have their babies and decide whether to keep them or not, but they would need a place to live and then some kind of employment, but it would be difficult as no one would want to hire them. My order hopes to establish some kind of home in the future, but for now we have no funds. It is difficult to find patrons to help us since most people consider that establishing such a home would be condoning sinful behavior. Yet, it is all right that hundreds of bodies of murdered infants have been found during the past year, scattered in parks and vacant lots."

Bernice was astonished. "I read about the bodies of infants being found in such places and even in privies and ash heaps in the cities of Philadelphia and New York, but didn't think such a thing happened here. I am left to wonder why and how would a woman murder her own child?"

Sister let out a weary sigh. "A wet cloth to the infant's face and sometimes even more violent means is used. Some of these smothered or strangled infants are the unwanted children of married women, a crude method of controlling the number of children in a family. Most are castoffs of raped or seduced unfortunates, who can no longer hide the terrible secret of their shame."

"What about the infant asylums?" Bernice couldn't believe what she was hearing; there had to be some hope.

Sister shrugged. "The state-run asylums are not much better. They have no nurturing and either die of neglect or disease in the first few months of life, if they last that long. The Daughters of Charity have some homes in New York and their rate is slightly better, but they still lose 80% of the babies. There just aren't enough sisters to care for all the unwanted infants." Sister Imelda adjusted the sheet over Olive once more, bent, and kissed her forehead before making the sign of the cross over it, and saying a short prayer. Then she led Bernice out of the room and back downstairs to a small room that functioned as a sitting area.

They had no sooner seated themselves, when Peter appeared. "I have been all over this hospital trying to track the two of you down. I trust your tour was informative," he said to Bernice.

"Sadly, yes, it was," Bernice said.

He lowered his brows in a frown, but before he could say anything, Sister Imelda told him about Doctor Ogden's visit to Olive's room, and Bernice's suggestion to stop the hemorrhaging.

"Ogden is a pompous ass. Go ahead and use the

Shepherd's Purse. I will take responsibility. It won't be the first time he and I have clashed."

Bernice almost laughed when he described Doctor Ogden in the same manner in which Sister had, but the gravity of the situation kept her voice serious. "Even if we wire for it and have it sent on the next train, it will not get here until later tomorrow and that may be too late. I'm not even sure if it will work now."

"I have a friend who operates a pharmacy a few blocks from here. He carries many herbs, since he dabbles in herbal cures. I ordered a lot of the herbs for your workshop from him. We will go and get what you need ourselves, and I will take care of Olive under your supervision. Normally I would have you do it, but since we are in the hospital, we will have to follow the proper protocol. No sense in giving Ogden grounds for more complaint than necessary. While we are there, I will get the Prickly Ash for Sister Mary Joseph, and Sister Imelda will make sure she takes it, though I doubt she will argue this time."

Further encouraged by the nun's agreement with Peter, Bernice suggested, "Perhaps we could try some Meadowsweet for Olive's fever, unless you think she would be better letting it run its course to fight the infection. Or we might try Echinacea for the infection."

"From what Sister has just told me, she has had the fever long enough. We will try anything that might help. With your help, I might be able to save someone this time." He and Sister Imelda exchanged a knowing look between them.

Peter extended his arm to Bernice. "We had better be on our way."

As they were leaving, Sister Imelda said, "I like Miss Peterson, Doctor Schmidt. Perhaps you can bring her to the hospital again soon, and she could share some of her herbal knowledge with the sisters."

"Perhaps. However, do not think of recruiting her to

the order. She is needed in North County." A hint of possession tinged Peter's voice despite the joking manner in which he spoke.

Sister shook her head, giving a serene smile. "Miss Peterson is not meant to be a nun. You have made a wise choice."

Peter thought of asking her what she meant by that last statement, but decided it would be better to leave the question unasked. Instead, he ushered Bernice out of the room and said over his shoulder, "We will return as quickly as possible."

*****

Bernice and Peter arrived at the St. James Hotel late in the afternoon and walked through the lobby to the dining room where the maître d' hotel addressed Peter. "Sir, might I suggest a table in the courtyard if it suits the lady?"

Since it was a rare occasion in Baltimore for a summer day to not have any humidity, they thanked him, and took a seat at one of the tables on the far side of the courtyard next to the brick wall separating it from the busy city cobblestone walkway on the other side. The area was small, but large enough for a dozen tables spaced far enough apart so the diners could have private conversations. Since the sun was on the other side of the hotel, the yard was covered in shade, but it wasn't dark or gloomy because of several flowerpots filled with brightly colored, fragrant blooms.

The waiter came and took their order as soon as they were seated at the end of the courtyard near the gate. "I see our good friend, Doctor Ogden, inside." Peter was looking toward one of the dining room windows. "Will you excuse me for a minute while I go and speak to him?"

"I am certain the last person he would want to speak to is me, and to be honest, I would prefer not to have to see him again either."

Peter rose from his seat shaking his head. "My dear

Miss Peterson, I do believe you have an unfavorable opinion of the good doctor."

A few seconds later, he was inside standing next to Doctor Ogden's table. Bernice stared at the window studying his tall frame. He wasn't dashingly handsome like Connor Reilly, but he was an attractive man in his own right. She imagined he must have had a few women setting their cap for him, and wondered why she had never heard of any attachments, other than the widow Rasheen had mentioned. He was dedicated to his work, but after all, he was still a man. Why did it matter to her? She really needed to stop letting her thoughts wonder in this direction, she chided herself. At that moment, the tea was served, distracting her from dwelling on it further.

Bernice sipped her tea and deliberately took her thoughts in a safer direction - her morning at the City Dispensary. Though her tour had been informative, the image of the young woman they were trying to save haunted her. Peter had given the tincture of Shepherd's Purse to the poor girl in some water and made her drink every drop. They waited an hour and then gave her another dose. The bleeding had already slowed some, but it would take a few hours before the herb took effect completely. He gave Sister Imelda instructions to administer the tincture every hour for the first four hours and then every two after that until morning. By then, they would know if it had worked, but even if the treatment was successful, there was still the matter of her fever and infection. In addition to the herbal tincture and the other herbs Bernice had recommended, Peter had given orders for Sister to continue giving Olive a teaspoonful of sweet spirits of nitre every four hours to produce sweating, and cool the body down. He told Bernice that they would go back and check on Olive one more time before leaving for Patrick and Elaine's, and then they would check again in the morning. "Please let her live," Bernice whispered out loud before she even realized it.

She looked around to see if anyone had heard, but no one was looking at her as if she were unbalanced. The strains of music from a harp being plucked inside floated through the open doorway must have hidden the soft sound of her voice. A sudden breeze caught the ends of the white linen tablecloth flapping it up slightly before it settled into place. The people at the next table received their order, and the scent of terrapin soup wafted across her nose making her mouth water. She had decided against the soup when they had ordered, and was now sorry, but the Maryland crab cakes would make up for any regrets along with the sweet stewed tomatoes and fresh corn. Bernice closed her eyes and tried to relax.

"Psst, Psst, Miss." The voice came from the other side of a black iron gate which sat in the center of the garden wall. The gate was locked since none of the patrons used it when they came through the hotel lobby to the restaurant, and out onto the patio as she and Peter had done. Its sole purpose must have been for show. The man had his fingers tightly wrapped around the intricate scrollwork with his wrinkled face pressed through one large scroll. She couldn't make up her mind as to rather he looked ridiculous or pitiful. Then, seeing the expression on his face, she decided it was definitely the latter. She looked around to see whose attention he was trying to draw. "Psst, Miss, over here."

She gave him a questioning glance and he shook his head. "Yes, you." She rose from her seat and walked the few steps to the gate.

"Are you in some sort of trouble? Shall I get help?" She asked.

"No, no… nothing like that. The man you come in with—was his name Schmidt? Is he a doctor?"

"Yes, he is. Would you like me to get him for you?" Bernice wondered if the man might be ill.

"Don't bother him. I was just wondering if that was him. Is he working at the City Dispensary again?" The man seemed agitated and was looking around as if expecting some unwelcome person.

"Doctor Schmidt is just visiting, but I'm sure he would be happy to see you, if you will let me tell him you are here," Bernice tried to reassure him.

"I got no need to see 'em. Was just wondering where he was doctoring now. Do ya know?" The man suddenly remembered his cap was still on and quickly pulled it off.

Bernice was touched by the gesture. Peter must have treated him or a family member, and he just did not want to bother him. "He has his own medical practice in North County. Now if you will excuse me, I am going to go and get him. I am sure he will want to speak to you, if you will just give me your name."

"The name's Dugan, ma'am, but no need to git 'em," the man insisted.

"Nonsense. You just wait here a moment." Before he could argue, she turned and went to get Peter.

As she walked toward the open doorway, wondering how she was going to interrupt Peter's conversation with Doctor Ogden without irritating the so-called "Pompous Ass," her fears were relieved when Peter stepped through the door smiling at her. When he was close enough to take her arm, he said, "It took me a few minutes longer to persuade Ogden that we use your methods. Actually, I had to lie and tell him it was a treatment used in one of the prestigious French hospitals before he was agreeable. I hope you will forgive me."

Bernice felt comfortable walking with Peter's arm through hers, as if it were something that was a daily occurrence. "I could care less how you manage it, as long as we are able to save that girl, but what would you have done if he had not agreed, since you have already started treatment?"

"He may have disallowed the use of herbs in the future, but he would never know about our current treatment. In case you haven't already guessed, the sisters tend to side with me."

"Yes, they do seem rather fond of you. I suppose that is because you treat them with more regard than most men."

"They deserve my respect, and that of every doctor and patient in that building. Did you come to get me because our meal has been served? You should have just started without me," Peter apologized.

"Oh, I almost forgot. There is a gentleman at the gate asking about you, but he seemed reluctant to disturb you, so I told him to wait and I would get you."

"Are you sure? He must have left." Peter was looking in the direction of the gate.

Bernice sighed. "Well he did seem a bit unsure of himself, and he was very nervous. I thought maybe you had treated him, or perhaps someone in his family. His name was Dugan. Do you remember him?"

Peter stood motionless; his eyes haunted by some unspoken memory.

"What is it?" Bernice felt a chill run through her.

"Probably nothing," Peter said as he steered her to their table and seated her.

Bernice could hear her mother's voice reminding her that a proper young woman never pursues subjects that a gentleman may not wish to discuss. No, instead, she should direct the conversation to general topics such as the weather or perhaps an upcoming society gathering. Yes, but Peter did not fit into the mold of her mother's idea of a gentleman. "Peter, something is wrong. I think you could at least trust me enough to tell me what Mr. Dugan is to you."

"His daughter died under my care, and he holds me responsible." Peter heaved a weary sigh.

"How long ago did it happen?"

"A few months before I came back to North County."

"Is he the reason you did not accept the position at

the City Dispensary?"

"To be honest, I really wanted to come home, and that just pushed me to make a decision. If it had not been for Dugan, I might have accepted the position, but he was making accusations, and even though I was cleared of any blame, it would have been bad publicity. He was hanging around ranting and raving."

Bernice bit her lip. "Is he dangerous?"

Peter shook his head. "Probably not. He makes threats, but I doubt he would carry them out."

"I told him where you are living. Suppose he follows through on those threats?" Bernice felt her blood run cold even with the gentle warm breeze caressing her skin.

Peter reached across the table and patted her hand as she reached for her teacup. "Dugan is harmless. He probably just saw us and wanted to know what I was doing. I think he wanted to hear that I was ruined. Perhaps he might think my current practice is the equivalent of that."

"Are you sorry you had to leave?

"No. I have the best of all worlds. I get to keep up on things here, present my research, and I am home with my family. There are many doctors in the city, but I am practicing where there is a real need. Besides, I have the very best assistant a doctor could ask for."

Bernice felt a flush of pleasure at his compliment. "What was wrong with Mr. Dugan's daughter?"

"She had a failed abortion, and a friend brought her to us to try and save her, but there was nothing we could do. Dugan tried to say I was the one who had performed it, and that I had brought her to the hospital to save myself."

"But that would only draw attention to you." Bernice drew her brows together.

"The man is out of his mind with grief. There is no reasoning with him. Maybe in time he will regain his senses."

Just then their meal was served, and after the waiter left them, Peter said, "Let's just enjoy our meal. If we finish at the Dispensary early enough, we could take a carriage ride to Mount Vernon and stroll a bit before dinner. Would you like that?" He gave her one of his warm smiles, not the professional one he normally used.

Bernice made every effort to keep her expression neutral when she was filled with excitement. She was happy to spend time with him anywhere. "A little exercise would be nice after all this food."

CHAPTER 10

Peter stood just to the side of the doorway so that he could watch Bernice without her noticing his presence. It was probably rude to do such a thing, but he was about to enter the room when he saw her standing over the bouquet he had purchased for her from a vendor's cart in the park. It was one of the nicest afternoons he had spent in a long time. He enjoyed her company so much, that the hour he allotted for their outing drifted into two, and if it had not been for the fact that he wanted to see if they were successful in stemming Olive's hemorrhage, he would have gladly spent the entire afternoon in the park with Bernice.

The time away from the hospital allowed time for more personal conversation. He got the sense that she was as lonely as he, though she had never said as much. It was apparent in the way she spoke of her friends and family; as if she were the outsider. Yet, there was no trace of bitterness in her voice or expression. Bernice did not have an acrimonious cell in her body.

When they arrived at Patrick and Elaine's, she asked him if he would mind if she put the bouquet in a vase in the parlor since it was too lovely not to share with everyone. Now she was rearranging the roses, baby's breath, and carnations so that they fit the vase perfectly.

To his surprise, she took one of the carnations, brushed it against her cheek and then pressed it into a book she was holding. Then she sat at the ornately carved rosewood desk near the window, opened the book, and began writing. He stepped out from the side of the doorway, and was about to walk into the room, when she looked around as if suddenly sensing someone was watching. "I was just making notes on Olive's treatment for future reference."

Peter grinned. "Ah, the mark of a true scientist."

"I just hope the treatment works," Bernice said.

"Well, it has already slowed the bleeding by half. The problem will be how much blood she has already lost. We will know for sure tomorrow. You probably saved that girl's life. I am grateful you came along on this trip." As soon as he spoke the words, Peter realized they were true on more than just the medical level.

Bernice put the pen back into the ink well, reached up, and rubbed the back of her neck. "I have learned a great deal."

Peter strode across the room and studied her closely. "Did today's activities tire you?"

"No, not all. I seem to have pulled something when I was helping Sister Imelda change Olive's bed linens." Bernice started to rub her neck again.

"Here, let me." Peter began messaging her shoulders and neck. "Does that feel better?"

She shrugged her shoulders up into his hands. "Mmmmm, much better."

It felt good to let his hands roam over her neck and shoulders, but he realized Elaine and Rasheen would not approve of such familiarity. He reluctantly removed his hands. "Where is everyone?"

Bernice gave a sigh of protest. "Elaine and Rasheen are upstairs putting the baby down for the night. Patrick and Connor are in the library discussing business."

Since there was no chance of them being interrupted for awhile, Peter resumed his gentle message, his fingers going into her hair, and then taking his hands down into her shoulders and dangerously close to the opening of her neckline. "I had almost forgotten what it was like to take some time off and enjoy the company of a beautiful woman. I owe you a debt of gratitude."

Bernice turned her head and gave him an appreciative smile. "It is I who should thank you; not only for this afternoon, but for the opportunity you have given me to learn." Wistfulness stole across her normally composed features as her voice echoed his own longings. "I like spending time with you no matter the circumstances, and it was thoughtful of you to buy me the flowers, but you need not flatter me with false compliments."

"Why would you doubt my sincerity?" He continued to gently rub her neck allowing his fingers to stray to the soft skin of her cheeks.

"Because I have a mirror." She gave a small self-depreciating laugh.

"Then we must get you a new mirror, for the one you have is damaged."

"No one has ever referred to me as a beauty before. Thank you for the compliment."

A strange, faintly hopeful feeling planted itself in his chest when he noticed the smile on her lips. "Elaine informed me that each of the flowers has a meaning, but Mrs. Garrett came to call before she could translate for me."

Bernice laughed. "When I was in boarding school, the girls read the book on the language of flowers. I am afraid more attention went into that reading than our studies."

"So you are familiar with floral nomenclature?" He inclined his head. "Perhaps you could educate me so that I could impress Elaine."

Her gentle laugh rippled through the air like the sound of birds singing in a spring garden. "I would not take it too seriously, but as I recall, a pink rose means a secret love, a carnation indicates fascination, and baby's breath signifies happiness.

"You are definitely a fascinating woman, Bernice Peterson." He leaned over and put his cheek next to hers, his lips a whisper away. "What about a red rose?"

Her breath caught. "Passion."

He could smell the lavender in her hair. "When I am with you, I feel passion, but also a peace and happiness that I had forgotten existed. Have you used an herbal potion to make me lose my good sense, because I have the impulse to throw caution to the wind right now?"

"Cough, cough, cough." Startled, Peter looked up to see Rasheen's Uncle Frank standing in the doorway. Father Frank Hughes was a good friend of the Reilly family since he had once been Connor and Peter's teacher when they attended Loyola Boy's School. "Where is everyone?" Frank asked as if he had not witnessed an intimate moment.

Peter straightened and repeated Bernice's earlier explanation. "Rasheen and Elaine are upstairs with Clare; Patrick and Connor are in the library. You will have to do with Bernice and me for a bit. Would you like a drink?" He walked over to the side table and poured a small glass of whiskey from a crystal decanter without waiting for an answer.

Frank reached out and took the drink. "That is grand. Thank you."

Bernice sat in her chair completely composed and said, "It is good to see you again, Father Hughes.

The priest took a swallow of his drink. "Elaine tells me you are working with Peter in his new practice. Do you like it as much as teaching?"

"Do not tell Rasheen, as she was kind enough to let me teach with her, but I like it even more so, because I can put my knowledge of herbal cures to use."

Peter gave Bernice an admiring glance. "She is very skilled, and is teaching me a few things. It is quite probable that one of her herbal cures saved a young woman's life today." He told the priest about Olive and also asked if he would look in on her the following day. Most clergy would have condemned the poor girl, but Frank would offer forgiveness and hope.

Bernice waved her hand in protest. "I am just glad Sister Imelda saw the merit in my suggestion. She is the one responsible for Olive's improvement."

"Given Sister's history, that is no surprise." Frank sat his empty glass on the side table.

"What do you mean?"

"It is not my story to tell. You will have to ask her. "

Bernice looked to Peter for an explanation, but he raised a shoulder in a silent gesture to denote his lack of knowledge regarding the matter.

Frank switched the subject to Granny Hughes. "My mother was disappointed that young Jack did not accompany you on your visit."

"It is not a visit," Peter insisted. "I have things to attend to at the City Dispensary and wanted Bernice to come along so she could observe the nuns at work. As for Jack, it was a difficult decision for him, but he didn't want to miss the birth of Midnight's first offspring. We should be home way before that happens, but you know how Jack loves that horse, and he is almost as attached to the mare that Connor bred with Midnight."

"Well, he will be in the city all winter for school, so Granny and the rest of the family will have ample time to see him then," said Frank.

Peter nodded. "I believe they made arrangements for him to live with Patrick and Elaine, but given how much visiting goes on between the two families, you are right about Granny seeing him often."

"By the way, Bernice saw Dugan today while we were at lunch."

Frank gave them both a worried look. "Did he cause any trouble?"

'No – just wanted to know where I was practicing

medicine. Poor creature. I wish we could do something for him, or that he would at least let us try."

Bernice folded her hands, clenched her fingers and then released them. "I regret that I told him where Peter was practicing medicine."

"Stop worrying. Anyone would have done the same as you under the circumstances," Peter reassured her.

"You are probably right. Now if you will excuse me, gentlemen, I need to go freshen up before dinner."

After she left, the two men sat in silence. Frank stared thoughtfully at his steepled fingers with a judicial expression on his face before finally saying, "I am happy to hear that things are working out well with Bernice."

Peter poured them both another drink, handed Frank his refilled glass and took a seat. "She is a quick student and an excellent teacher."

"Your mother and Rasheen are very fond of her, along with the rest of the family. The first time I met Bernice was here at Patrick and Elaine's New Year's Ball. At the time, I was more concerned for Rasheen. She was still struggling with her emotions over Daniel's death, and closing her heart to the possibility of happiness with Connor."

"Well they are happy enough now." Peter knew where this was going. Frank had been involved in orchestrating Rasheen and Connor's marriage, and apparently was of the same mind as his mother and Rasheen where Bernice was concerned. Maybe if he tried to focus the conversation on Connor and Rasheen, Frank would leave it be. "Not bloody likely," he muttered under his breath.

If Frank heard him, he ignored it. "Rasheen had to be willing to open herself to a new life. Sometimes a second love is greater than the first. Now she has everything she has ever wanted."

"So does Connor." Peter knew that as much as Connor loved his aunt and uncle, there had always been something missing in his life after his father died. Rasheen filled that emptiness for Connor.

"Yes, they are well suited, and lucky to have found one another. Speaking of finding someone, you had better be careful. Someone is going to realize what a gem Bernice is someday and steal her away from you."

Peter knew Frank was not going to let it be. All right then, he would keep the conversation on a professional level. "I will have to find a replacement when that happens."

"You are only fooling yourself, if you think you could find someone to take her place. Women like Bernice are rare." Frank was not speaking of medicine.

Peter agreed with him, but he could not, or would not, admit the need for someone in his life. "Perhaps you are right." Mercifully, Rasheen and Elaine came into the room and the conversation switched to baby Clare.

*****

Upon reaching the City Dispensary the next morning, Bernice and Peter found Olive sleeping peacefully with Sister Imelda seated in a chair next to the bed fingering her rosary beads. Sister rose from the chair silently, and motioned for them to step outside the room. "Her bleeding has slowed to a trickle and the fever broke around dawn, but she was still restless. She kept crying and saying she wanted to die, that she deserved to die for what she did. There was nothing I could say to calm her, but then Father Hughes came to see her. After his visit she calmed. Whatever he said restored her hope, and gave her the will to live."

Peter nodded. "If anyone could reach her, it would be Father Hughes. Give her one more dose of Bernice's tincture, and stop the Meadowsweet. See if you can get her to eat some light broth and some toast."

Before Peter could continue, Doctor Ogden came barreling down the hall. "Doctor Schmidt, what a break that you are here. There has been an accident at one of

119

the warehouses, and we have several men who need treatment and some will require surgery. Can you help?"

"Excuse me, ladies. Bernice, I will leave you in Sister Imelda's capable hands." Bernice heard him asking Doctor Ogden what had happened as they rushed down the hall, but was unable to hear the reply, as they were already turning the corner.

"Miss Peterson, would you mind if we went to the convent for a bit so I could have some coffee? It was a long night and I missed breakfast this morning."

Bernice noticed the weariness in the nun's eyes. "Not at all, but I would be happy to sit with Olive, and let you get some rest if you like."

"That is very thoughtful of you, but I will send one of the other Sisters to sit with her for a spell to see that she eats something as per Doctor Schmidt's instructions." Sister Imelda led Bernice down the long hallway that lead to the small courtyard in the back that connected the convent to the hospital. They went in the back door through the kitchen where a cheerful nun was washing dishes. Sister Imelda introduced her as Sister Mary Agnes. "Sister Mary Agnes is in charge of the kitchen and is a wonderful cook."

Sister Imelda went to a cupboard, pulled out two cups and saucers, and then poured coffee from the pot on the stove. She reached into the icebox, and got out a pitcher filled with milk. "Do you take cream and sugar in your coffee?"

"Just cream." Bernice said.

"Now you are not going to be sitting in my kitchen while I clean up. Go into the parlor and I will bring you a tray." Wagging her finger at Sister Imelda, Sister Mary Agnes said, "And you have not had any breakfast. What would you like?"

Sister Imelda smiled at the older nun. "Are there any more of those blueberry muffins you made yesterday?"

"There's enough for each of you to have one."

"Only coffee for me. I had a big breakfast just an hour ago," Bernice protested as Sister Mary Agnes put the muffins on the tray anyway and led the way to the parlor. It was a large room crammed with an abundance of furniture, with a piano in one corner. The heavy green drapes were pulled aside allowing light that was filled with dancing dust motes to stream through the two front windows. It would not have been any different than other parlors Bernice had been in other than the fact that there was a crucifix on the wall. There had been a crucifix in the kitchen too, and a small table with a statue of the Virgin Mary stood in the hall leading to the parlor, not something one found in the average home. At least not in the homes Bernice had visited, but then she was not Catholic and not familiar with their customs. Rasheen and Connor had a crucifix in their bedroom over their bed, but nowhere else in the house. The only reason she had seen that was because she had been with Rasheen when she was nursing the baby. Since this was a convent, she supposed they would have more religious artifacts.

Sister Imelda adjusted a napkin on her lap, and handed one to Bernice. "If you are not hungry, do not worry about the muffin." She took a muffin and began to nibble at it.

"I hope Sister Mary Agnes will not be upset with me." Bernice took a long sip of her coffee.

"Do not worry with it, Miss Peterson. Mary Agnes will understand."

"Please call me Bernice." Bernice wanted to be on friendlier terms with this woman, especially since she was about to propose something that would require them to be in a much closer relationship.

"All right, Bernice." Sister smiled and Bernice noticed warmth in her expression. "I noticed that Doctor Schmidt has dropped the formalities, and also calls you by your given name. It is good to see him more relaxed. I told him he made a good choice; that you are good for him."

"I think we have been good for each other. He has been open to my herbal cures, and I have learned so much from him."

Sister shook her head. "I was not referring to your work, though I am certain you complement one another there too. I meant that he seems to be happier than when he was here at the Dispensary. He rarely smiled, and there was no joy in him. I think his spirit suffered a deep wound. You must be healing that wound. I have never seen Doctor Schmidt so content. Be patient with him, Bernice, it will not be easy to earn his trust, but once you do, you will have all that goes with it."

"I have always found him to be strong and self-assured. It is difficult for me to imagine him as you describe, but if that were the case, I doubt his recovery had anything to do with me."

"Do not have such a low opinion of yourself. I have only known you for two days, and I find you to be an extraordinary young woman." Sister folded her hands in her lap and gave Bernice a warm smile.

Encouraged, Bernice decided this was the time to offer her proposal. "Sister, I have a proposition for you."

The nun raised a questioning brow.

"There is no sense in dragging this out, so I will make it as brief as possible. My mother's aunt has died recently, and left me a rather large mansion and a considerable amount of money and jewels. I have no intention of using the mansion, and I thought perhaps you could use it to start a home for girls like Olive. I intend to sell the jewels and could provide the funds to run the home. My thoughts were that we could take the girls in, and allow them to decide if they would like to keep their babies or give them up for adoption. We could also provide training so they could get decent employment. The home would provide care for their child while they worked, and also shelter for them until they could make other arrangements.

I thought perhaps the sisters could provide care for the babies. The girls would pay a small amount toward their room and board after they were employed."

Sister was quiet for a few moments as she processed the information. Finally she nodded and said, "I like your idea, but how would we find employment for the girls? No one will want them."

"I have a friend, Ambrose Kingsley, who is a well-known member of society, and a good businessman. He would see to their training and has the ability to open closed doors. What I need from you is for your Sisters to run the home."

"I can provide the nuns, but what about you? Why are you giving up such a fine home? You may marry and wish to live there someday."

Bernice shook her head. "My mother's aunt never had any children. I think she would have liked the idea. Besides, I do not see marriage in my future."

"Do you not wish to marry?"

"Very much, but I want to love and be loved. I will not marry out of duty."

"No – you would not."

"Then you will help me? I saw the way you took care of Olive; the tenderness you gave her. You and your sisters are the only ones I would entrust this project to."

"The plan is a good one, the sisters would be willing, but how will we find the girls before it is too late?"

"Leave that to me. I have a friend who is a midwife, and she gets many requests to end pregnancies though she has never done it. I will ask her to send these girls to us."

"Quiet, competent, and persistent – Bernice, you would make a good nun," Sister mused.

"I suppose so, if I were Catholic. What made you become a nun, Sister, if you don't mind answering." Bernice was curious about the woman sitting across from her. Father Hughes said Sister Imelda had a story.

"Girls like Olive have a special place in my heart. I

once knew someone who ended up like that." Sister's expression became thoughtful and quiet for a few minutes. "I was the only daughter of a prominent, New York Protestant family, and my mother had decided I would marry well above her peers. There was a Duke visiting, and everyone knew he was here to seek a bride with a fortune. He went to my parents and asked for my hand in marriage after only being in my company a few times. My parents did not know it, but I had secretly converted to Catholicism because of my ladies' maid who was close to me in age and temperament. In spite of our different stations in life, we became close friends which is forbidden. I need not explain that to you."

"Maggie found herself in the same situation as Olive. When my mother found out, she discarded the poor girl like she was no more than a pile of rags. She made sure I did not find out until much later. She arranged a trip to Europe for the two of us to visit the Duke's family in preparation for the pending engagement. She told me Maggie would have to stay at home due to her condition, but as soon as we were gone, Maggie was thrown out on the street. When we finally returned and I learned the truth, I searched for Maggie, but it was too late."

"I knew I could never marry the Duke, as I was being called to my vocation to the religious life. When I went to the Mother Superior of our order, she cautioned me that the convent was not a refuge from the world, and under the circumstances, they could not allow me to enter the order. She arranged for me to stay with a family here in Maryland where my family would not find me. While with them, I nursed the elderly grandmother, and decided that even if I could not become a nun, I would devote myself to caring for the sick. In the meantime, desire to become a nun never waned. Upon the recommendations of the family I was staying with, the Mother Superior allowed me to enter the convent. So here I am."

Bernice could see herself leaving her mother behind,

but to never see her father again was unimaginable. "Have you ever regretted leaving your former life?"

"Never." There was serenity in sister's voice and on her countenance.

Bernice found herself envious. "I wish I had some kind of purpose for my life."

Sister's voice was gentle as she said, "Hear with your heart, and you will find what you seek. The heart knows its own truth."

.

CHAPTER 11

When they disembarked at the North County Train Station, a carriage was waiting for them, along with a small wagon driven by John. As the men loaded the luggage onto the wagon, Connor looked around and said, "Where's the lad? I thought he might be able to tear himself away from the stable long enough to come greet us."

A concerned crease crossed John's brow. "He was all ready to come with me, and then he had a stomach upset that sent him to the water closet."

"Has he been ill while we were away?" Connor asked.

"He was fine up until the minute we were ready to leave. It came upon him all of a sudden."

As Peter helped Bernice, and then Rasheen and the baby into the carriage, he said, "I'll have a look at him when I get there."

"Are you sure he hasn't been feeling bad?" Connor asked again.

"Will you stop acting like an old mother hen? I said I would see to him." Peter slapped Connor on the back as they got into the carriage. "We will be home in a bit, and then you can put your mind at ease."

When they arrived at Sara's Glen, Jack was in his room. Peter went upstairs while the others settled themselves, and gave Martha all the news from Patrick and Elaine. A short time later, Peter came downstairs with Jack. "Jack is coming home with me."

"Nonsense, I can take care of him." Martha jumped up from her chair and put the back of her hand to Jack's forehead. "Why, he is burning up," she said in surprise.

"Jack needs to be quarantined until I know for sure what we are dealing with." Peter gave Jack a reassuring pat on the shoulder. "Don't fret, son. I just want to make sure everything is all right. Go on up to your room and pack whatever you would like to bring. It will be fun, just us men."

Once Jack was out of hearing range, Martha fell into her chair. "You must think it is something serious or you would have left him with me. What do you suspect?"

"He has some of the symptoms of typhoid fever, but I won't know for sure for a few days."

"But that cannot be," Rasheen interjected. "Martha and John are fine."

Peter gave his parents a questioning look, but both assured him they felt fine. "I will keep check on the two of you just the same. In the meanwhile, make sure you and Connor keep away from Jack's room, and no one is to come to my house until I find out for sure what this is. We do not want to expose the baby to it."

"But we can't just abandon the lad." Connor glanced anxiously at the stairs Jack had just trod.

Peter placed a reassuring hand on his shoulder. "You know I will take good care of him, and I'll make sure he knows you would be with him if you could. Please, Connor, don't make this worse."

Connor ran his hands through his hair tugging at it. "Jaysus, this isn't fair. The lad has had such a hard life; just when he is comfortable and secure this has to happen."

Rasheen handed the baby to Martha, and got up to put her arms around her husband. She didn't bother to scold him for his blasphemy. "Darling, we have to trust Peter."

Connor nodded and let out a long breath. "You're

right. I better see if Willie has not unharnessed the horses yet, and make sure the carriage is ready for another trip." He kissed Rasheen, and hugged her hard before leaving.

Looking at his parents Peter said, "If the two of you feel the least bit sick, you are to let me know immediately. For now, we have to make sure his room is thoroughly disinfected."

"And just who is going to take care of Jack while you tend to your duties as the county doctor?" Martha asked.

Bernice had seen the concern in Peter's eyes as he looked over his parents. Even if it weren't for the baby, if they were to get typhoid, it would be dangerous for them at their age and caring for Jack would wear Martha down. Raising her chin, she said, "I will."

"You cannot stay with Peter without a chaperone. Your reputation would be ruined." Martha gave Peter a pointed look.

"Mother's right," he agreed.

"Bother my damned pristine reputation!" Bernice said in a loud, exasperated voice. Seeing the shock on the faces around the table, she softened her voice. "Jack is most likely frightened. He needs someone he trusts to be with him all the time. You won't be able to do that, Peter. What if there is an emergency and you are needed? Please, let me do this."

She could see she had won her case when he nodded, and raised his hand to quiet Martha's continued protests. "I'll see to his room here first." Bernice began to roll up her sleeves and plucked an apron from a hook near the sink.

"I can at least do that," Martha argued.

Peter shook his head. "I do not want you exposed anymore than you have already been. And besides, the nuns taught Bernice the proper way to clean a sick room.

"Hmmmp! You would think I never cared for a sick person."

Bernice gave her a sympathetic pat on the shoulder.

"We are concerned for you and the rest of the family. Besides, you know Rasheen needs your help."

Martha took some solace in that reassurance. "I suppose you are right."

*****

Peter put Jack in the bedroom closest to his own and gave him something to aide his sleep before going downstairs to wait for Bernice. She had surprised him tonight with her show of temper when she insisted that she would nurse Jack. It was like the afternoon when he had returned to find her ripping herbs apart. It would seem Miss Peterson was not a meek little mouse after all, and he was happy for that fact. If his suspicions were correct, the coming days and weeks were going to be arduous for her to say the least. There would be sick pans to empty, and if Jack couldn't make it to the water closet, there would be sheets to change. She had shown herself to be made of sterner mettle than he had imagined thus far, and he had confidence she would handle this crisis with her usual competence.

He was pulled from his contemplation by the sound of a carriage pulling up in front of the house. When he went to the door, he found Bernice standing on the front porch with her bag. She had dismissed Willie, and the carriage was already rolling down the road toward Sara's Glen. Peter took the bag from her and stepped aside for Bernice to precede him.

"I will take your bag up to your room and get you settled in," he said. "Then we will discuss Jack's care."

Bernice followed him up the stairs. "Where is he?"

"I put him to bed and gave him something to help him sleep. He's in the room next to mine and you'll be in the room across from his so he'll have one of us near when he calls for help." He set her bag on the chair near the window and motioned for her to follow him downstairs again where he led her into the parlor. He bade her have a seat on the settee before taking his own seat in one of the armchairs. Rasheen had helped him pick out the set, and though it was stylish being carved of rosewood, covered with a heavy brocade of ivory and gray print, he found the pieces most uncomfortable. Since he never spent any time in the room, it had never mattered to him. The one thing in the room that caught one's attention immediately was the ebony cabinet inlaid with ivory. He had selected that himself with the enthusiastic approval of both Rasheen and Elaine.

Bernice looked around the room. "You have done an admirable job of decorating for a bachelor."

"I can only take credit for the cabinet. Rasheen and Elaine did the rest." He couldn't explain why, but her praise relieved the worry he was having over Jack if only for a few seconds.

She folded her hands in her lap, and took on a more serious expression. "Do you really think Jack has typhoid?"

"I'm not sure." He ran the fingers of his right hand over his forehead thoughtfully. "He has the fever and is vomiting, but the timing isn't right. And children usually get diarrhea with typhoid. We are going to have to keep watch over him, and hope for the best. Are you sure you will be able to care for him? It is not going to be easy."

She gave a curt nod. "I will be fine."

"I hope so, because if it ends up being typhoid, he won't be the only one. I will be busy dealing with an epidemic, not to mention trying to find the source of the contamination. A typhoid epidemic can wipe out most of the town's children and elderly. In the meantime, I want you to make sure the windows in his room stay open, even if it rains. Do not worry about the water coming in as the fresh air will be more important. Make sure you wash your hands every time you come into contact with him." Peter was concerned that she would contract it from Jack. He tried to reassure himself that his diagnosis could be wrong. It had to be wrong. Otherwise, his parents had been exposed to something very dangerous, and Bernice was going to be in harm's way.

As if reading his thoughts, she reached over and patted his arm. "Your parents will be all right, and I will be careful; but it is better for me to be caring for him than your mother. If I were to get sick, I am in a better position to ward off illness than Martha because of my age."

She was right, but thoughts of Jenny's illness and how quickly he had lost her floated through his mind. Memories left him with a sense of vulnerability when he had to keep a clear head. Trying to rid himself of it, he gave Bernice a brusque reply. "That is the only reason I agreed to let you take on this task."

Then seeing the hurt in her soft blue eyes, he rose from his chair and offered her his hand. Softening his voice, he said, "Now you had better get some rest." She took it and kept her hand in his even after she was standing so he saw no need to release it and held it as they climbed the stairs. When they had reached the top landing, he reluctantly dropped it, and bid her good night.

*****

Bernice slipped out of her clothes and into a soft cotton nightgown. The gown was one of her favorites because it was both pretty and comfortable with daisies embroidered across the empire waist and cuffs. She carefully hung her dress and the two skirts, and blouses she had packed in the wardrobe before placing her folded undergarments and stockings in the drawer. Then she laid out her hairbrush and comb on the small dresser before removing the pins holding up her hair until it fell free. She stared at her reflection thinking about how Peter had brought up doubts about her ability to care for Jack. Even after several weeks of working in his office and assisting with patients, he questioned her capability. She picked up the brush and angrily pulled it through her locks. What did she have to do to prove herself worthy of his trust? She was in the middle of another vigorous stroke when the sound of a thud in the hallway caught her attention. Quickly dropping the bush on the table, she ran from the room without bothering to don a robe. There on the hallway floor just outside the water closet door was poor Jack retching what little remained in his stomach. She knelt beside him and raised his head. He tried to get up as he cried, "Sorry, sorry, sorry….."

"Shhh, shhh, it was not your fault." Bernice put her arm around him and was about to lift him when she noticed Peter standing above them buttoning his trousers. He was shirtless, revealing a well-muscled chest with a light golden fleece. For a few seconds she was distracted by the strange warmth that ran through her all the way to her toes, until Peter took charge.

"Here, let me." He picked Jack up and carried him back to his room gently sitting him up on the bed.

Bernice followed and pulled a new nightshirt from one of the drawers in the small oak dresser. She crossed the room, put the garment on the bed and was about to remove the soiled one when Jack turned bright red. "No, no," he protested.

Realizing her mistake, she quickly backed away. "I…will attend to the hallway then."

Peter put a reassuring arm around Jack's shoulder. "We men will take care of getting the lad changed and seeing to things in here. There are rags in a box in the pantry off the kitchen and a bucket and mop. After you are finished, see that you wash your hands and that there is nothing on your gown. Leave the rags in a bucket of water on the porch. I will deal with them in the morning before Ivy gets here." Ivy was a local girl he had hired to do his housekeeping and fix his breakfast and lunch after convincing Martha that it would be impossible for him to treat patients if half his time was spent running between the stone house and Sara's Glen for all his meals. Rasheen had been the one to help them finally reach a compromise by suggesting that one of her former students, Ivy, be a part time housekeeper for Peter. Martha agreed on the condition that he have his dinner with the family at Sara's Glen. So far the arrangement was working out well for everyone.

*****

After he had gotten Jack changed and comfortable, Peter made sure the boy drank some water. Then he took the soiled nightshirt downstairs and placed it in the bucket with the rags. They would have to be boiled in soap and water in the morning. He decided to take care of that task himself as he didn't want Ivy exposed to any contaminants, and Bernice would be busy enough with Jack. He hurried back up the stairs to check on Bernice and make sure she had washed as he instructed. To his surprise, she had left the door to the water closet room open and was standing at the sink with her long silky tresses flowing to one side while she pressed a wet cloth to her neck. Outlined against the soft light from the oil lamp she took his breath away. When she reached over to hang the cloth on a nearby rack causing the fabric in her gown to pull across her breasts in a snug outline, he was keenly aware of thoughts that were taking him down a dangerous path until she looked over at him and broke the silence.

"Is Jack sleeping?" she asked.

Peter gulped for a breath. "Um.... Yes, he is comfortable for the time being. Did you make sure you washed thoroughly?"

She held out her hands for inspection. "Doctor Schmidt, if I have learned one thing from these past weeks working with you, it is the proper method of washing my hands."

Though she had addressed him in a formal manner, he could tell by the way the corners of her mouth were struggling not to turn up that she wasn't annoyed with him. He wondered how long that smile would remain if he gave into his desires. She was the picture of innocence with her modest gown and yet every bit a temptress. He searched the gown to make sure there were no traces of Jack's misfortune on it to take his mind in another direction, and was amazed to find the gown looked as if she had just gotten out of bed rather than cleaned up from a sick person. Of course, she wore an apron which was now in the bucket with the soiled clothes and rags. Still, he thought the woman was amazing. "You seem to be no worse for your nursing duties. Now off to bed with you." He started to reach out to give her a gentle push in the direction of her room, but quickly dropped his hand. There was no telling what would happen if he let himself touch her. Stepping aside for her to leave the room, he leaned one shoulder against the door frame and watched as she walked down the hallway, her gown swishing around her slender hips. "God help me," he whispered.

*****

Peter threw the book across the desk in frustration because it gave him no answers. A week had passed and Jack was not responding to the normal treatment of salt water, sugar water, and plain water. The fever would go down during the day, and then spike at night making him delirious. Bernice asked him to move a small bed into the room on the second night so that she could be with Jack to keep a cool cloth on his face. During the day she managed to get some broth and the water mixtures into the lad, but nothing solid. Jack hadn't developed diarrhea or the rose spots that normally accompanied typhoid, which made it difficult to diagnose and treat him.

A noise outside his open door caused him to look up and see Bernice passing on her way to the kitchen to get fresh water. He got up and followed her. "Is he asleep?" He asked.

She filled the pitcher before turning and answering. "For now."

Peter studied her carefully to look for signs of fatigue and found light circles beneath her eyes from lack of sleep.

He took the pitcher from her. "Let me sit with him for a bit so you can get some sleep."

She shook her head. "No, he is used to me."

"It will not do him any good if you collapse and are not there at all," Peter argued, but knew it was futile.

Avoiding the discussion, she answered, "Would you mind if we tried some herbal remedies?"

He gave up the argument. "I see no reason why not. At this stage, anything that might break the fever would be welcome."

"Would you stay with him while I get what I need?"

"It is almost dark outside. Give me a list. I'll get whatever you require." He did not like the thought of her going out and fumbling around in the dark with just a lamp, or the idea of her being alone in the office after dark. Thankfully, she didn't give him an argument, but instead went with him to his study, and waited while he produced paper and pen. Dipping the pen in the ink well, he held it over the paper waiting for her instructions.

She tapped her finger to her lips for a few seconds as she considered what she might need. Then she dictated, "Peppermint to help ease his anxiety, and some boneset and yarrow to mix with it. Ginger root will help settle his stomach and spotted Joe Pye weed will induce sweating."

He raised a questioning eyebrow at the mention of the Joe Pye. "He is already sweating."

She nodded. "That is true, but the woman who taught me about herbs at the school I attended used it on one of the girls who had a bad fever, and it resulted in a cure."

"All right, I supposed it cannot hurt. Anything else?"

She shook her head. "No, that should be enough. You will find them labeled and arranged alphabetically on the second shelf in the back of the room."

Peter set the pen in the silver tray next to the inkwell and went to get her herbs. The task took less than ten minutes. Everything was meticulously ordered just as she had said. He found himself once more amazed at her capabilities. He had suspected there was more to her than an empty- headed society belle, but the way she assisted him with patients, her spotless well-ordered herbal work space, and the manner in which she cared for Jack, and kept things pristine without any direction from him was equal to the nuns at the City Dispensary. In fact, if Sister Imelda were to see her in action now, she would probably try to recruit her for the order. He shuddered at that thought of his Bernice as a nun. His Bernice, now where did that come from? Mentally shaking himself, he gathered up the requested herbs, and returned to the stone house.

She was in Jack's room wiping his face and arms with the cool damp cloth. "His fever is rising again."

Peter set the herbs on the night stand, and put his hand to Jack's forehead. "Let's get some of your herbs in him and see if they help. I'll stay with him while you prepare them."

She picked up the herbs and went down to the kitchen to prepare some herbal tea. When she returned, they placed the cup of liquid to Jack's lips, and coached him to drink as much as he could. When Bernice pulled sheets aside so Jack would be cooler, she noticed a red mark just below the neckline and pointed it out to Peter.

Peter let out an exasperated breath. "He has all the symptoms of typhus except diarrhea. All we can do now is add your herbs to the treatment and wait."

CHAPTER 12

The next morning there was a loud commotion at the back door, and then the sounds of Ivy pleading with someone that they could not come inside. Peter ran down the stairs buttoning his shirt on the way. When he reached the kitchen, he found Connor trying to push his way past Ivy as she pushed against the door in a futile attempt to keep him from barging in.

"What in the hell are you doing here? I told you to stay at Sara's Glen." Peter knew the answer to the question. Connor would never abandon Jack, even to the best of care.

"I need to see Jack," Connor pleaded.

"Jack is quarantined. No one is permitted in his room except Bernice and me. Would you risk harm to Rasheen or Clare?"

"I'll stay here with you. Rasheen and I talked about it, and she sent me to reassure Jack that we have not abandoned him." Connor ran his fingers through his hair a sign of agitation Peter recognized from the years they had spent together as boys. "Peter, it has been over a week now, the boy could... I cannot abandon him when he needs me most."

Peter stepped outside and took Connor by the arm leading him away from the door. "I am doing everything I can, and we have added some of Bernice's herbal treatments. As soon as he improves, I will send word for you to come and see him. Until then, you cannot expose yourself and possibly spread the disease."

"Is it typhoid?"

"He has all the symptoms, except one. Even if it is not typhoid, I cannot risk an epidemic of something unknown. Go home. I promise to let him know you were here, and doing everything in your power to get past me to see him."

"I want to know if there is any change – any change, at all. I need to be here with him if he takes a turn for the worse."

"You have my word. Now go home and take care of your family and my mother. I'm sure she is about as anxious as you are, and I don't want to have to deal with her." Peter said a silent prayer of thanks that he hadn't had to face both Connor and Martha.

*****

During the next several days there was more vomiting during the day, high fever at night, but mercifully, the diarrhea was kept at bay for some reason. Peter was inclined to give the credit to Bernice's herbal remedies. They kept up the treatment of salt water, sugar water, and herbal teas and tinctures. Connor showed up at the front door every day, and every day they gave him the same report on Jack's lack of progress as they turned him away.

By the second week, Connor's temper broke. "Damn it, I want to see Jack. At least he can have the comfort of knowing I was here if he leaves us. Jaysus, Peter, have some compassion and stop being a doctor for once."

Peter gave him a big grin. "Go get me some fresh tomatoes from the garden if you want to do something useful."

"Jaysus, Mary and Joseph! The lad is gravely ill and you are asking me for tomatoes?"

"I thought Rasheen cured you of using blasphemy." Peter said as he ushered him through the back door.

"My wife is not here. Stop changing the subject,"

Connor argued before realizing he was inside and noticed Peter's grin. "You let me in," he said softly. "Does this mean…?"

"The fever broke last night, and he is asking for food this morning. The tomatoes will help reduce the inflammation of mucous membranes in his nose and throat."

"But how are you going to get him to eat tomatoes after being so sick?"

"Get my mother to stew them with lots of sugar. It will be Bernice's task to get him to eat them. She has proven better at coaching him into taking his medicines than me." Peter motioned for Connor to take a seat at the kitchen table, and then poured them both a cup of coffee from the pot on the stove. "Jack is sleeping right now, but as soon as he wakes, you can have a short visit."

When Bernice joined them a few minutes later and started toward the stove to get herself some coffee, Peter rose from his seat and gave her a warm smile. "Sit and rest a bit. Let me fix your coffee."

He could tell by the way she moved her head that her neck and shoulders were stiff from sitting for long periods of time in the straight-backed chair in Jack's room. Silently, he cursed himself for not thinking to have a more comfortable chair put in the room. Once he had set her coffee in front of her, he moved to the back of her chair and gently massaged her shoulders. "Better?"

"Umm, much better, thank you. Have you given Connor the good news?"

Both men nodded.

After they had finished their coffee, Bernice took the cups, rinsed them out, and dried them before excusing herself to see to Jack. "As soon as he wakes, I promise to come and get you."

When she had left the room, Connor gave Peter a sheepish grin. "It appears that my wife and Martha's little scheme just might be working, but I would rather break a difficult horse than tell them. Your secret is safe with me."

Peter glared at him. "There is no secret. You have lived with Rasheen too long. You are getting romantic."

"Tell me you do not have tender feelings for Bernice."

"You know I will never let myself have those feelings again. Look how you have suffered these last few days over the fact that you might lose Jack. What if it had been Rasheen? No, I'll not put myself through that torment."

Connor reached across the table and grabbed Peter's forearm. "To love is to risk loss. It is the price we pay because it is worth it. Don't end up a lonely old man because you were a coward."

*****

Once Jack's fever broke, he made a speedy recovery and his appetite was back to normal. Martha sent cakes and cookies to go with the meals Ivy prepared. But unless someone was there to entertain him, he would pace the front porch restless to be outside. Connor brought a cast iron set of toy soldiers that Jack would spend time arranging in battle, and the two of them played marbles on the parlor floor.

"Where's Connor this morning?" Jack asked when Connor failed to appear at the normal time.

Peter winked at Bernice before saying, "He'll be by later. He has work that has been neglected, and he wants to be free to spend the entire day with you when you go home tomorrow."

Jack gave a loud whoop. "Can I see Midnight and stay with the mare when she delivers his foal?"

"Yes and yes, but I want you to stay close to the house for a few days so Mother and Rasheen can make sure you are completely recovered. I don't want you going off on adventures with your friends until we know you have your strength back." Peter put his arm on Jack's shoulder and looked him in the eye as he would a grownup. "Do I have your word on that?"

"Yes sir."

Peter raised his brow at Jack and nodded toward Bernice. "Jack?"

"Miss Peters, thank you for taking such good care of me."

Bernice gave him a gentle hug. "I was happy to do it."

*****

Peter looked up from the medical journal he was reading at the sound of footsteps in the hallway. A few seconds later Bernice appeared at the open doorway. "I was going to make some tea, and maybe have one of the apple tarts Martha sent this morning. Would you like me to bring you something?"

He rubbed his weary eyes with the back of his palms. "Perhaps I'll join you in a few minutes, but I want to finish this first. Is Connor still with Jack?"

She stepped inside his study and perched on the edge of one of the leather-upholstered chairs. "He wanted to stay with Jack until he goes off to sleep even though he will be going home tomorrow. The man must be exhausted, but he is beyond happy now that his family will be reunited."

Peter wasn't surprised that Connor had shown up on the doorstep right before Jack's bedtime. Family was important to Connor, and as his adopted son, Jack was every bit as much family as any blood ties. That was the way it was with him and Connor too. They were brothers in every way but blood. "Connor's mother died before he had a chance to know her, and his father died when he was very young. That's why he came here from Ireland to live with his aunt and uncle. Patrick and Elaine have taught him the value of strong family ties."

Bernice nodded and then lifted herself from her perch to leave the room. "Should I set out a cup and saucer for you?"

"I think I might take a break and join you. When Connor finishes with Jack, I'm sure he will want to talk with me for a few minutes before rushing home."

A few minutes later when they were in the kitchen having their tea, Connor joined them. "Jack is in fine spirits. Thanks to both of you for the care you gave him. Do you think it was Typhoid?" He directed the last to Peter.

Peter took a quick swallow of his tea before answering. "All the signs were there, but he recovered too fast. I have been trying to find some answers in my medical journals, but thus far it has been a futile search."

"Do you think the herbs sped up his recovery?" Bernice had her elbows on the table in a very unladylike pose with her chin resting on her folded hands.

For some reason he found the pose charming and irresistible. He wanted to kiss the top of her head and then her lips and.... Irritated with his thoughts, he replied in a curt tone, "I doubt that herbs could have done what science failed to do in this case. It was just luck that he got well as quickly as he did. Let's just be thankful for that."

Connor shot him a look that said, "You're a jackass," and he knew there would be a discussion about it when the two of them were alone.

"Oh, I suppose you are right," she said, "I didn't mean that ...I was just...I'm sorry." She looked crushed. Connor was right. He had acted like a jackass.

"When can I come and get Jack tomorrow?" Connor asked as he rose to leave.

"No need for you to come for him. I'll bring him home first thing in the morning." Peter walked to the door and watched as Connor mounted his horse and rode away. When he came back to the table, Bernice was at the sink with her back to him. He wanted to take her in his arms and tell her he was sorry, that the fault was all his, but instead he said, "I have to get back to work. I'll be in my study if you need me."

She remained silent with her back to him, and simply

gave him a nod.

A short time later he came upstairs to check on Jack before retiring, and found her bent over the boy giving him a kiss on the forehead. The maternal gesture sent an overwhelming wave of tenderness through him. He made a hasty retreat to the safety of his room in an effort to escape the unwelcome emotion. What in the hell was the matter with him?

He dropped into the bed, not bothering to remove his clothes. Once more he reminded himself that there were more serious matters to ponder than the carnal desire that was sneaking into his thoughts. He was a bloody doctor. Yet, he couldn't seem to muster the medical professionalism he possessed when thoughts of her tormented him. Perhaps this was true, but he sure as hell could control his behavior, even if it took every ounce of willpower he possessed.

He had acted like a jackass. Though she tried to hide it behind that calm façade, he could tell when something troubled her. It showed in her eyes for just a few seconds before she masked it. No one else would notice, but he had come to recognize that look because he had seen it once before on the night Mrs. Delacourte snubbed her at the Ridgley's. Jumping up from the bed, he went to her room and softly tapped on the door. To his surprise, it wasn't closed all the way. He poked his head inside and saw her empty bed. A moment of panic hit him as he thought she might have decided to leave in the dark.

She couldn't have gone, he assured himself as he raced down the stairs. She didn't have a carriage, and even if she did, she wouldn't know how to harness the horses. He checked the library to see if she had come downstairs for something to read, but it was dark. Then a light coming from the kitchen caught his attention, but she wasn't there. The oil lamp on the table was turned down low, and the back door was open. Through the screen door he saw her silhouette and let out an audible breath of relief.

He crept to the screen door, softly opened it, and closed it. She didn't move, but sat with her back against the porch rail, her eyes closed. Droplets from the misty rain fell on her cheeks. From the desolate expression on her face, he wondered if they might be mingled with tears; tears that were the result of his callousness. He couldn't bear to be the cause of such misery. "I was wrong," he whispered.

Her eyes flew open as she jumped up. "Is Jack having a relapse?"

Before she could get past him, he grabbed her arm and pulled her toward him. "No, no, he is sleeping soundly. I meant I was wrong when I said the herbs didn't work. I'm sure that they were a great help."

"I don't understand." She looked up at him with those innocent blue eyes, and it was all he could do not to take her in his arms, but he couldn't get trapped in an emotional tangle. It would be bad for both of them, he reminded himself.

"I was wrong about the herbs. I was just frustrated that I can't make a diagnosis."

She gave him a weary smile. "Then they did help?"

"More than that; they sped up his healing. I've made notes of the symptoms he had, what you used, and how long it took before taking effect. We will have them for future reference, but thankfully for now, it doesn't look like we have any other cases." He stroked her arms through the long sleeves of the gown and realized the fabric was damp, not soaked through, but still wet enough to give her a chill. "You need to get upstairs and change into something dry. I will be up with some warm milk and honey in a few minutes." Before she could protest, he led her through the screen door and gave her a gentle shove toward the hallway. "Doctor's orders."

He waited a few minutes before going upstairs and tapping on her door. She granted him permission to enter.

Once inside, he motioned for her to get into the bed. To his surprise, she did so without arguing. As he set the milk on the table next to her bed, he noticed the dark circles under her eyes from the last few weeks without a decent night's sleep. Well, at least she would get some rest tonight; because he had insisted she would sleep in her own room. Jack was sleeping through the night, and even if he should require someone, Peter would be the one to go. Her hair hung in two long braids over her shoulders reminding him of a little girl as she lay against the propped up pillows. All his previous thoughts disappeared when he thought of how vulnerable she looked, and how she made him feel the same. It was an uncomfortable feeling that he had buried long ago. When she finished the milk and handed him the cup, he said, "I haven't taken the time to thank you for all you did for Jack. You were magnificent. The sisters from the City Dispensary could not have done any more for him than you did."

Her face lit with pleasure from the compliment, but she replied humbly, "When we respond to the needs of others, we nourish ourselves."

"Now you are speaking like Sister Imelda. You have helped Jack and me both. I don't know what I would have done without your help in this crisis. I've also come to depend on you at the office. You make a great nurse. I'm glad Sister hasn't seen you in action, or she would try to recruit you to join the convent."

Bernice laughed. "I'm not even Catholic."

"She would convert you."

"I think I would rather stay where I am. I've learned so much from working with you the last few months. Thank you for giving me the opportunity."

"Perhaps we teach each other." He tucked the sheets in around her. "Sleep well. You have earned a decent night's rest."

*****

Standing in the doorway, Bernice took a breath of

the humid morning air, and waved goodbye to Peter and
Jack as they left for Sara's Glen. Later in the day, when the
heat intensified, moving around would be miserable.
When she came inside, Ivy had already cleared the
breakfast dishes and was busy washing them.

"I'll get to the boy's room as soon I'm done with the
dishes, Miss Peterson," Ivy said over her shoulder.

"We'll work on it together. I'll go up and strip the bed
while you finish up here," Bernice said as she left the
room. "It will probably be best to get things done as early
as possible, since it looks to be an uncomfortable day
ahead."

By the time Bernice had reached Jack's room, her
energy was already ebbing. Even though she had not kept
watch with Jack last night, she found it difficult to sleep.
Force of habit kept her awake listening for any sound that
might come from his room. She took a breath, and forced
her weary body into action as she removed the bed linens
and then took them downstairs where she placed them in a
basket in the basement next to the wringer washer.
Though she had never used the device before, she had
seen the laundress at her boarding school operate it by
turning the hand crank which moved the two rollers in the
iron frame and wrung out the clothes over a bucket. It
was hard work, but better than beating the clothes on a
rock as they had done years ago. Thank heavens for
modern inventions, she thought, yet grateful that she did
not have to use this one.

Ivy would see to the dirty linens on laundry day. For
now, Bernice would do what she could to get Jack's room
in order. On her way to the stairs, she noticed the door to
Peter's study open and decided to step inside and sit for a
few seconds. Lack of sleep, along with the heat and
humidity, must be the reason for her weariness, she
thought. If she just rested a bit, she would get her second
wind. The drapes were pulled closed to block out the
morning sun and heat. The coolness of the room made

her feel a bit better, but the air was still heavy. She left the door open and dropped into one of the dark brown leather upholstered chairs in the corner of the room looking around her. This was his room, in his home, where he read the books on the surrounding shelves, where he wrote his papers, and corresponded with his colleagues. How many late nights had he sat at the mahogany desk pondering over a diagnosis?

She could see two of the books in a nearby glass bookcase; one was in Latin and one was Greek Mythology. Most of the other books were medical tomes, with some novels among them, but she wondered if he would take the time to read for pleasure. Perhaps the Greek Mythology was something left from his college days. Then she spotted the jar of marbles that Connor and Jack had used sitting on the edge of the desk. They must have been from his childhood. He was so serious most of the time; it was difficult to imagine him as a child.

From what Rasheen told her, Connor and he got into a great deal of mischief when they were adolescents and were often in trouble with Martha. He must have been mischievous, but it was hard to imagine him like that now, though she had seen a glimpse of that side of him when he was with Connor. The two men had a bond even stronger than the friendships she shared with Rasheen or Ambrose.

Yet, even with that, there was a sadness about him. She recognized it, because she knew it all too well. He was so kind and compassionate in his treatment of others. She remembered the tender way he had taken care of her last night. If only she could do something to care for him, to make him smile more, give him some joy. Dropping her head in her hands, she realized she was in love with him. Not the romantic love she had felt before, but a deep love for the man and all that he was – his work, his character, his kindness. This was all wrong. Attraction was one thing, but how could she survive this? This was insane.

She had to get control of her emotions. She pulled herself up from the chair, using the arms for support and was about to leave the room when he appeared in the doorway. He didn't speak, but leaned one shoulder against the frame and gave her a questioning look.

Her heart skipped. "I am sorry. I did not mean to ... to...it was just that after I brought the bed clothes downstairs I needed to sit a minute, and your study was here. I should have gone to the parlor. She jumped up from the chair. "I'll go help Ivy finish now, unless you have something you need from me."

He moved in front of her blocking her exit. Putting her chin in his hand he tilted her face upward; concern filled his eyes. "You need some rest."

She wanted to argue with him, but she knew he was right, and the thought of sleeping in her own bed was more than tempting. "As soon as Ivy and I get the room finished, I think I'll do just that."

"I'll help Ivy with the room after I've taken you home, and seen that you are settled." He took her by the arm and led her into the kitchen where he left instructions with Ivy to keep an eye on her, and not let her do another thing while he got the buggy ready to take her home.

*****

Bernice was about to change into a house wrapper when the maid came into her room bearing a silver tray with a calling card on it. "I'm too exhausted to see anyone, please offer my apologies," she said as she absentmindedly read Ambrose's name on the card. "Never mind. Show Mr. Kingsley into the sitting room, and tell him I will be down in a minute."

Ambrose was looking out the window, hands clasped behind his back, watching something intently. Upon hearing her enter the room, he turned around and said, "You look like hell. What's he been doing to you?"

She plopped into the nearest chair and gave him a tired smile. "Thank you. It's good to see you too."

He came over and knelt next to her, his eyes filled with worry. "I'm serious, darling, your appearance worries me. Are you ill?"

She ran her hand through his hair and ruffled it like one would a small boy. "I'm just very tired. Jack was ill, and I stayed at Peter's to nurse him. Peter was concerned it might be typhoid, and we didn't want to risk spreading the disease."

Ambrose brows rose in disbelief. "You mean you spent the night there?"

"I can assure you nothing illicit took place, unless you consider cleaning up from a sick person, and emptying bedpans as such. Peter couldn't very well attend to Jack, as well as his patients, and we couldn't leave Jack at Sara's Glen with the baby there, not to mention Martha and John."

Ambrose stood up quickly, and stepped back in mock horror. "Oh, my heavens, you aren't contagious, are you?"

"Will you stop being silly? We were really worried about Jack. It was serious, Ambrose." She had to struggle to keep her voice steady. For some reason, she was on the verge of tears. It must be the lack of sleep, she assured herself.

Ambrose sat in the matching rose brocaded chair next to Bernice's. "My poor, dear girl, the whole experience sounds ghastly. Is there anything I can do for you? Perhaps take you out for a nice luncheon?"

She shook her head. "I am too tired. Would you like to have a bite to eat with me here? I can have Mrs. Dunkirk fix us something. Besides, there is a matter I wish to discuss with you."

Tapping his fingers on the chair's walnut trim, he said, "I knew there was more. Tell me what is happening with you and the good Doctor. Am I to lose my fiancé?"

Bernice was too weary to argue or laugh with him. "Will you stop it? The matter I wish to discuss involves my aunt's house."

Disappointment washed across his face. "Can we eat first? I didn't have breakfast this morning, and I'm starved."

A short while later, they had finished their lunch, and were in the small garden seated in a swing beneath the shade of a maple tree, each of them sipping lemonade. Ambrose leaned his head on her shoulder, and gave her an impish grin. "How are things going with the doctor?"

"They are going very well. I am learning a great deal and find that I like the work."

He raised his head. "That's not what I meant."

Bernice glared at him and said nothing.

Not the least intimidated, he persisted, "Well?"

"I do not wish to discuss a non-existent personal relationship with you. If you insist on questioning me in this manner, I am going to dismiss you and go to bed."

"You look like you could use the rest. Perhaps it would be best if I leave."

"If you promise to stop badgering me, you can stay. Besides, there is the matter of my aunt's house I want to discuss with you."

He twirled a loose strand of her hair around his finger. "Unless you plan on marrying me and living there, I don't see what there is to talk about."

"Ours would be a marriage of convenience only. You know very well that I will not live like that. You wouldn't want that either, no matter how close we are as friends."

"Tell me your plans." He let the strand of hair fall from his finger, and gave her his full attention.

She told him of her discussion with Sister Imelda, and how the nuns would use the mansion as a home for unwed mothers. He sat his glass on a nearby table and listened with one arm resting across his lap and the hand of the other fisted in front of his mouth with the thumb holding his chin. His eyes never left hers the entire time she spoke. It had been like this ever since they were children whenever she discussed something important with him.

When she stopped for a moment to take a sip of her drink and then set it next to his on the table, he said, "I had a friend in school whose sister found herself in the same situation as the girl you attended. Fortunately, he found out before she did something drastic. They sent her away to have the baby to avoid a scandal. She came home after the baby was born; leaving it in the care of the family she had stayed with. After a few months, her parents sent for the child. They told everyone it was the child of a cousin who had lost her husband and was too ill to care for the baby."

"These girls don't have that kind of support."

"No, I would suppose not. Well, darling, if you won't live in the place with me, at least I know I'm making a sacrifice for a worthy endeavor." Ambrose put his arm around her shoulders and gave a gentle squeeze.

"I'm glad you feel that way, because there is more to my plan." She gave him an imploring smile.

He gave her a skeptical glance. "Am I to assume that the next part involves me?"

It had always been like this between them, as if they were brother and sister, each knowing what the other was up to. "It does. The girls will need jobs after they have their babies, whether they keep them or not. With your contacts you could secure good positions for them. They will be well trained so you will be able to recommend them with no reservations. Should they obtain a position that requires them to live in their employer's home; their child would be cared for by the other girls in the home and the sisters."

"You have given this a lot of thought. I will not only help you find employment for them, but I would also like to contribute funds for the home's operation," he said enthusiastically.

"Thank you, Ambrose. I knew I could count on your kind heart."

He got up and reached down for her hands to pull

her out of the swing. "Now, my dear, I am going to leave you so you can get some rest.

*****

Bernice took a leisurely bath after Ambrose left, and then instructed the maid not to wake her for dinner if she were sleeping as she intended to sleep through until the next morning. Just as she was about to get into bed, she spied the letter from her sister she had placed on her dresser earlier in the day. She propped up her pillows against the bed's headboard, tore open the letter and began reading.

Dearest Bernice,

How I wish you had accompanied mother on this trip. Perhaps you would be able to make some sense of her behavior, for I surely cannot. It would seem our mother has become very friendly with a widowed Duke. She is acting as his hostess, and has completely abandoned the Drakes, leaving me in their care. Though her actions would be scandalous back home, apparently no one dares criticize them because of his title. You should see her. She acts like a different woman when she is around him. It is amazing to hear mother giggle at the dinner table when he has told some funny story. I have never seen her smile as she does in his presence. The only smile I have ever seen on her countenance is a formal one. I doubt that you would approve of her conduct if you were here, though to my knowledge theirs is simply a friendship and nothing more.

Bernice skipped over the remainder of the letter and tossed it on the nightstand with a sigh. Her sister must be imagining things. Their mother would never do anything that even hinted at a social impropriety. She would write to her in the morning before going to the dispensary. For now, she just wanted to get some sleep. She got out of bed, and pulled the drapes closed herself rather than disturb the maid again. Once she was back in the bed, she pulled the sheet over her loosely and dozed off for a few hours before waking from a restless sleep.

There was no light peeking through the crack in the drapes so it must be night, she reasoned as she tried to go back to sleep, but it was no use. Too many thoughts were swirling around in her brain. She propped the pillows against the ornate carved rosewood headboard, and stared into the darkness of her room, giving into the thoughts winding through her restless mind.

Up until today, she had been able to conceal her feelings toward Peter, but the tender way he had tucked her into bed, his concern for her well being, and the glimpse into his childhood, brought her closer to the realization that she loved him deeper than she thought it ever possible to love another person. Now there was more than the romantic longing; there was emptiness in her, a longing for something she feared she would never know.

Perhaps it would be better for both of them if they stopped their present arrangement. After all, he had said that her herbs were of no help. Maybe he had come back to say he was wrong only to spare her feelings. She had been a fool to think she was of any use to Peter in his work. She had been an even bigger fool to think he might come to care for her in the way that she cared for him. More than likely he had just allowed her to work in his office to appease Martha and Rasheen. But he had championed her suggestions in Baltimore, and praised her for the success. Maybe he had just been tired last night, and hadn't meant to be so curt when she had asked about the herbal cure for Jack.

She wondered if he had any attraction to her at all. He had acted more like a suitor the day they had been at the park. Reaching up, she touched her cheek with her fingers, remembering how his breath had felt on her skin. Was he about to kiss her before Father Frank came in the room at Patrick and Elaine's? Maybe this was all a fantasy in her mind.

Perhaps she should stop thinking she was entitled to

more than the life her mother wanted for her, and just marry Ambrose. They may not love one another in the physical sense, but there was affection between them, and he had been her best friend until Rasheen came into her life. Ambrose would not want to change her. Perhaps her father was wrong; maybe there could be marriage without the kind of love he suggested. Maybe friendship could be the foundation of a marriage. They got on a lot better than her parents. At least they both understood one another and were honest with their feelings. She knew Ambrose's true self, and he knew her. Ambrose would never give up his lover, nor would he expect her to be faithful. Yet she knew she could never have an adulterous affair like her father. If she married, it would be a marriage built on trust, love, and passion. Who was she kidding? Her mother and society would rule her.

What was she going to do with the rest of her life if she couldn't at least work with Peter and be near him? The question whirled around and round in her head, along with considerations of marriage to Ambrose, her mother, and society. She finally drifted off to sleep and had nightmares of a marriage where she was being sacrificed on a golden altar with society's matrons chanting proprieties at her and Mrs. Delacourte raising a gilded sword encrusted with jewels over her. The sword was poised to cut her in two when she let out a scream that shook her body and woke her. The upstairs maid came running into the room. "Are you all right ma'am?" The frightened woman asked.

Bernice shook her head and shrugged her shoulders. "I seem to have been having a nightmare. I'm sorry for all the bother."

"Not at all, ma'am. Would you like me to bring you up a breakfast tray or would you prefer to sleep longer?"

Bernice looked over to the drapes and saw a shaft of light cutting across the carpet. "I'll have the breakfast tray and then dress and be off to the doctor's office. What time is it?"

"A little past ten."

"Oh my, I slept later than I planned. I'll get myself dressed while you get the breakfast tray." Bernice was already out of bed and rummaging through her closet looking for something cool to wear. She could tell it was going to be another hot, humid day by the stickiness in the room. By noon it would be worse.

CHAPTER 13

Peter leaned against the edge of his large desk while Mr. Sauter sat in the chair opposite him rubbing his fingers. The older gentleman had the beginnings of rheumatism, and it was becoming more difficult for him to use his hands. "Am I going to have to stop working, Doc?"

Handing him a bottle of medicine, Peter said, "Take this in the morning with your breakfast. It will alleviate the pain enough so that you can continue to make furniture. Nothing that comes out of a factory can compare to your craftsmanship."

He was about to see Mr. Sauter out, when Bernice came through the door. "I am sorry to be so late," she apologized.

He noticed that she still had the dark shadows beneath her eyes. If anything, they were worse than before, appearing as bruises against her translucent skin. "You should have taken another day to rest." He didn't give her a chance to respond, but continued, "But since you are here, could you provide Mr. Sauter with some herbs to help with his rheumatism?"

She disappeared into the lab for a few minutes before returning with a packet of dried herbs and a bottle of liquid. Handing them to the older man, she said, "The dried herbs are birch and meadowsweet. Use them to make a daily tea. The liquid is the same, but you will rub that on the troublesome area. It should give you some relief in a short time. If you use it faithfully, it will keep the pain at bay."

Mr. Sauter looked doubtful, but Peter assured him the combination of his medicine and Bernice's herbs would be the most beneficial treatment. As he walked the older gentleman out to his horse, he extracted a promise from him to take the herbs just as Bernice had instructed.

When he came back inside, Bernice was busy working with her herbs. He leaned against the doorframe watching her as she made notes in a small book. She finished writing, and looked up giving him a tired smile.

He wanted to tell her to go home and not come back until the circles beneath her eyes were gone, but there was something else in her expression besides the weariness. Normally, he would have forced it out of her, but there was a fragility about her that made him hold his tongue. This time he would have to wait until she was ready to share her thoughts. He left her to her work without saying anything and went into his office. There were no patients scheduled until later in the day, so he began to make some notes of his own about Jack's recent illness. He wasn't sure how long he had been writing until his stomach rumbled; reminding him it was past lunchtime. His pocket watch read half past one. He rose from the desk to tell Bernice it was time to break for lunch, when the front door burst open.

"Doc, you have to come quick. There's been a train wreck over at Tinner's Run." The young man could barely get the words out he was breathing so hard. "It's bad – really bad."

"When you leave here, stop by Sara's Glen and tell Mr. Reilly what has happened and ask him to bring his men. After that, go into town and get as many men as you can to help. Tell them to bring their shovels, axes, saws – anything we might need to free passengers," Peter instructed while he and Bernice went around the office gathering things they would need. The man nodded, and quickly left to get more help.

They were headed out to the barn to have the hired hand ready Bernice's buggy, when Rasheen pulled up in her buggy. "We just heard the news. Connor has already started for the wreck. I thought perhaps Bernice could ride with me, if you wanted to take a horse and get there faster."

Peter began shoving things into a saddlebag. "Remind me to tell Connor what a brilliant woman he married. If the two of you take the Pike Road along the Little Gunpowder Falls, that will get you there faster," he said as he swung his leg over the horse the young man who worked for him had just saddled. Without the bother of the buggy, he would be able to ride through the woods and creek, getting there in half the time. He tore out of the barn and galloped down the road, leaving the two women to check one more time to see if they had forgotten anything.

Half an hour later, Peter arrived at the scene of the accident and surveyed the wreckage. The engine was in a ditch engulfed in flames as were the first two cars. It was a gruesome sight. Brilliant carmine colored the sky as the flames mounted high in the heavens, undulating like giant demons performing an evil ritual. For a split second, he stood frozen, his eyes fixed on the horror, thinking of the poor souls who had gone to their death trapped inside the charred mangled tomb. It was probably just as well for the engineer and the fireman, because even if they survived by some miracle, their lungs would have been scalded.

A short time later, Connor's men arrived with wagons, horses, and tools to help free the trapped passengers. Connor directed them to check the two derailed cars that were on their sides to make sure everyone was out of them. While they performed their rescue mission, Peter started his own task of providing medical assistance to the seriously injured.

When Bernice and Rasheen arrived, Peter steered them toward the open field at the edge of the woods where the dazed and injured sat, and instructed them to spread some of the blankets out so the men could lay the more severely injured on them instead of the weed-covered ground where infection would get into the wounds. Once that task was accomplished, the two women went about comforting the women and children, some of whom were screaming in a frenzy of fear and grief.

The afternoon sun blazed down on them sending waves of heat, which not only made it miserable for everyone, but intensified the smell of the burned cars and human sweat mixed with body odors. The stench filled the humidity-laden air making the simple act of breathing a labor. Peter identified the critically injured, and did what he could to treat them, and then moved onto the minor injuries. He wasn't sure just when Bernice had joined him, but she was by his side, doing what was needed before he asked. An hour later, the hospital train arrived with doctors and medical students from Baltimore. After that, things went faster, as the team tended major lacerations, more than a few cases of crushed ribs, and broken arms and legs from where passengers had been thrown around the cars from the impact. Miraculously, there were no severed limbs or mangled bodies, and no one had been blinded.

It was early evening by the time the hospital train had left for Baltimore with the injured and another train arrived to take the remaining passengers back to the city. Connor put his arm around his wife and kissed her cheek. "Go on home, I promise to be along as soon as I check on a few things. Our baby girl must be wondering where her parents are, even though Martha is spoiling her rotten."

Peter looked over at Bernice. "You go on ahead with Rasheen, and then I want you to go home and get some rest."

While Connor was walking Rasheen to her vehicle and making sure everything was secure, Peter put his hands on Bernice's shoulders and touched her forehead with his own. "You are amazing."

She gave him a weary smile. "No one has ever given me such extraordinary praise. I may become impossible to work with now."

"I doubt that," Peter said as he took her arm and assisted her to the wagon, and then helped her up. "Remember what I said, "Go home and get some rest.""

"Yes, Doctor."

He stood next to Connor and watched as the wagon bumped along the meadow until it reached the dirt road next to the woods. It would be a bumpy ride as the road was filled was ruts. When the wagon was finally out of view, Connor went to speak to some of the men who had been working at the wreck all day.

Peter gathered his things and made some notes in the journal he kept in his medical bag. He found that going over such written material later gave him new insights into injuries and cures. His thoughts kept returning to Bernice and how tired she looked. Now he wondered if it had been a good idea to let her go home alone. He finally gave up trying to concentrate on his notes, and shut the book just as Connor approached.

"Any idea as to what caused the accident?" Peter asked.

Connor removed a handkerchief from his pocket and wiped the sweat from his brow. "Looks like the flange on the engine wheel may have broken, but they will know more when they investigate. One thing is for sure – the engineer was trying to make up time, and may have pushed for more speed."

Peter shook his head in disbelief. "I heard one of the farmers who live nearby saying he heard an explosion and came as quickly as he could. Before he got close enough to see the wreckage, he heard the sounds of crashing woodwork and hissing steam. Apparently, the initial derailment didn't kill the victims. Most were caught in the burning derailed cars that were on their sides. Even though protruding arms and legs and other parts of bodies could be glimpsed through the flame and smoke, it was impossible for him and his sons to get close enough to attempt a rescue, because of the intense heat. They will have to live with those images haunting their memories the rest of their lives."

Connor nodded. "It is going to take a long time for any of us to erase today's memories from our minds."

"Go home and hug my godchild. That will be a start for you." Peter picked up his medical bag and loaded it in the buggy.

Connor mounted his horse and gave a mock salute. "See you for supper."

"I am too tired."

"You know if you fail to show up at the dinner table, Martha will either bring it to you or send your father or me. Come, get something to eat, and make a hasty retreat. Spending time with the family will ease some of your memories of today as well."

Peter knew he was right. He didn't want Connor to have to come out after such a hard day. He decided to stop by Sara's Glen on his way home, but he was going to eat dinner and leave. There would be no visiting tonight.

*****

Peter pulled up behind Bernice's buggy in front of the building he used to house his phaeton, buggy, and maintenance equipment. Why was she still here when he told her to go straight home over an hour ago? He jumped down from vehicle and was about to go get her, when Joshua came out of the building. "Why is Miss Peterson's buggy still here?" Peter asked the young man.

"I was waiting for her to return," the bewildered young man replied. "Should I ready it now?"

"Just feed and water my horse before you bed him down for the night. I'll take care of Miss Peterson's buggy if she is here." The thought occurred to him that perhaps she might have asked Rasheen to drive her home. She had looked exhausted when they left the accident scene. "Did you see if Mrs. Reilly dropped her off?"

"No sir. I was out in the back field cutting most of the afternoon, and then came inside the stable to tend the horses. Just now I was repairing a harness. I figured she'd be coming back with you."

"I sent her home earlier. Don't fret on it, Joshua. I'm sure she just got another ride home. As soon as you finish with my horse, go on home." Rasheen had mentioned how tired Bernice was, and how she barely made it up the steps. He just assumed she meant the steps to the stone house, but she could have meant the steps to the Peterson mansion. He had not even considered clarifying whose steps she referenced. Come to think of it, why would she be going into the stone house when he had told her to go home?

He left Joshua, and walked across to the house going in the back way through the kitchen door. He was about to head upstairs, when he saw Bernice sitting on the floor with her head resting on the seat of a chair. He knelt and cradled her limp body in his arms while he checked her pulse, and found it weak. "Bernice, talk to me. Come on Angel, wake up." Her breathing was so shallow that he had to put his head against her chest to hear it. Terror cut into him like a surgeon's knife. Get it together, he reprimanded himself. She needed his medical skills, not his panic. He checked her skin for signs of heat exhaustion. God in Heaven, if she had had heat exhaustion, and lain here all that time, she would surely die. At the very least, her mind would be addled. He unbuttoned her dress and then got a drink of cold water before dropping to the floor next to her. "Wake up, Sweetheart. "

She stirred, noticed her open top and began to pull it closed. Peter moved her hands and placed the water in them, steadying the glass with his hands wrapped around hers. "You need your clothing loosened. Now drink this slowly. I have no idea how long you were laying here. It has to have been at least two hours or more, unless you did something else before coming inside, did you?" He had made good on his statement to Connor that he was eating dinner and coming home, so he calculated that he had been there less than an hour and it hadn't taken Connor and him that long to get home from the accident since they were on horseback and took the shortest route.

She took a few sips of water and looked around wide-eyed. "I…came in…to get a drink of water. It was so hot. I just wanted something cold to drink before driving home. Then I went to the surgery and put the things we didn't use away. I was still thirsty, so I came in to get another drink. I must have fainted, but I have never done that in my life." She sat up away from his arms and drank some more before struggling to stand.

"Whoa, Princess, what do you think you are doing?" He pulled her back to him holding her securely in his lap.

"I have to get home before it gets dark," she said, yet made no effort to move.

Stroking her hair with his free hand, he said, "You are not going anywhere. I'm going to fix you a cool bath and you are going to soak in it until you bring your body temperature down. Then you are going to bed, and have a long rest."

"Peter, I cannot stay here," she whispered against his chest, "We would both be ruined."

"Everything will be fine. No one knows you are here." Before she could protest further, he swept her up in his arms, and carried her up the stairs. He took her to his own bedroom and gently placed her in the bed. "You lay here while I get your bath ready and then I will come and help you undress."

"I cannot…. It would not…"

He gave her his best professional smile. "I am acting as your doctor, not some rogue hell bent on seducing you. Be a good girl and stop arguing."

She gave him a skeptical look, but stayed put as he left the room. When he returned, she was stepping out of her petticoat. All that remained to be removed were her chemise and drawers. For a brief moment, he struggled to inhale. Keep your wits, Doctor Schmidt. He pasted a nonchalant expression on his face and held up a sheet for her to wrap herself in once she was completely stripped. "Take the pins out of your hair and put them on the dresser. I want your entire body – head to toe – in the cool water."

She wrapped herself in the sheet, and did as he asked and then let him lead her to her bath. When he stood in the doorway, leaning one shoulder on the frame, she protested. "Peter, it is not necessary for you to stay."

Straightening, he said, "All right, but you are to leave the door open, and call me if you feel the least bit faint." He had no intention of going any further than right outside the room, just out of her sight, and sit on the floor with his back to the wall until she was out of the tub. Half-hour later she appeared in the hallway, sheet wrapped around her, hair wrapped in a towel. She was a temptress and completely unaware of it, which made her all the more dangerous. God help him!

She started to go in the direction of one of the other bedrooms, but he held up his arm to block her. "You are sleeping in my room tonight."

"But where will you sleep?"

"I'll sleep in one of the other rooms."

"That is ridiculous. I have caused you enough trouble. I will not be responsible for…" Before she finished the sentence, she swayed and fell against him. "I must still be a little unsteady on my feet."

He kept his arm around her and led her to his room. "My room has the most windows to catch a breeze should there be one this evening. I want you to be as cool as possible. She looked around the room. "Do you have a night shirt that I might sleep in, or I suppose I could sleep in my under garments."

"You are not wearing anything tonight. I want you to be as cool as possible. You had me worried when I found you. I feared you might have suffered a heat stroke. Though that was not the case, we are not tempting fate. Get in the bed. If you are that concerned with your modesty, you may use the sheet for a cover."

She did just that. "Good night then. And thank you."

He nodded and left the room, but only long enough to go downstairs and get a glass of water for her night table, and a cold wet cloth for her forehead. When he returned, she was asleep. He put the water on the table and placed the cloth on her forehead. Pulling a chair up alongside the bed, he took a seat and watched her sleep. For the first time since he had found her collapsed in his kitchen, he let himself relax.

Her face was illuminated by the moonlight which streamed through the window. Wet golden tangles of hair lay over her bare shoulders, making her look like a sea nymph. He scrubbed his hand over his face. What had come over him tonight? He had felt real panic at the thought of something happening to her, and then when he saw that she was going to be all right, he had used terms of endearment that he never used. How many times had he ridiculed Connor for such silliness? And yet it had seemed so natural to call her Angel or Princess for she was as sweet as any celestial being, and as lovely as a king's daughter.

Waves of tenderness and lust warred inside him. The lust he could handle, but the tenderness was an unwelcome intrusion in his life. After Jenny, he vowed never to fall victim to those kinds of emotions. He had spent years developing the hard-won immunity, and would not lose it. Besides, he reasoned, she was the king's daughter, and he was the peasant's son. Even if he were to let his guard fall, there could never be a life for them together.

*****

Peter sat in the chair next to the bed most of the night, watching the steady rise and fall of Bernice's chest as she slept. It would have been more appropriate for him to sleep in one of the other rooms since she was in no danger, but he needed to sit here and reassure himself that he was not reliving the past. Being careful not to disturb her sleep, he removed the cloth from her forehead and put the back of his hand against her check. To his relief, it was cool.

Early the next morning, stubble from a night's growth of beard chafed his wrists when he reached up to rub his palms over tired eyes. A shave was in order, and a hot bath would be just the thing to relieve the bodily aches from his evening vigil. Knowing that she was in no danger, and would probably sleep for a few more hours, he decided to indulge himself. In the bathing room, he removed his shirt, and was about to start shaving, when he heard the back door downstairs open and close. Not thinking to put on a fresh shirt, he headed down the steps and was wondering what he was going to tell Ivy, and then realized it was her day off. When he got to the kitchen, Connor was setting a large basket on the table.

"Sweet Jakers, you look like you got in a battle with the devil and lost. Didn't you sleep last night?" Connor asked, as he raised his brows at Peter's lack of dress. "Where's your shirt"?

Peter scratched the stubble on his chin. "I didn't get any sleep last night. As to my appearance, I was about to get cleaned up when I heard you come in. What are you doing here at this hour anyway? Don't you have things to attend to at Sara's Glen?"

"Since it is Ivy's day off and you didn't show up for breakfast this morning, Martha wanted to make sure you didn't starve. She was afraid Ivy may not have fixed anything for today."

Peter began unpacking the basket. "Ivy makes sure I

have some provisions for the days she isn't here, and I am capable of making coffee."

Connor grinned as he took a cinnamon muffin from the basket. "Then let's have some."

"I thought you brought that for me." Peter said as he went out the door to the small room off the porch that served as summer kitchen to fire up the stove and make the coffee.

When he returned, Connor nodded toward the window. "I saw Bernice's buggy outside. She comes to work early."

Peter didn't respond, but set the cups on the table instead, and then went out to the summer kitchen to get the coffee he had just made. After he poured the steaming liquid in both cups, he waited for Connor to realize the obvious.

"Where is she anyway?" Connor asked. "Is she over working in the herbal room you created for her?"

Peter looked him straight in the eyes. "She is upstairs in my room asleep."

Connor took a slow sip of his coffee and raised a brow. Peter recognized the look on his friend's face. To anyone else it would seem that he was perfectly calm, but that placid exterior could mask a cauldron of anger. "Do I need to remind you that Bernice is Rasheen's best friend, or that she is like a daughter to your mother?"

"You can stop looking like you are about to beat my carcass to a bloody pulp. When I arrived home from your place last evening, she was collapsed in my kitchen. She had come in for a glass of water after Rasheen dropped her off. She was too exhausted for me to try and drive her home. To be honest, I feared she had suffered a heat stroke, but fortunately, that was not the case. I had her take a cool bath, and put her in my room because it has the most windows. Nothing happened. I kept watch over her as a doctor treating a patient."

Connor let out a long breath. "Just the same, she will

be ruined if anyone finds out."

"No one is going to find out." Peter gave him a knowing look.

"If anyone comes by your office, they will see her vehicle." Connor rubbed his knuckles across his chin thoughtfully.

"Any patients would assume it would be here anyway, because she would be working."

"But you have a sign on the door saying you are out."

"She sometimes goes with me on house calls, so there should be no suspicions."

"I take it that means you don't want me to tell Rasheen or Martha that Bernice was ill."

"You can tell them, but they are not to show up on my doorstep. Make that crystal clear. The last thing Bernice needs right now is for those two to cluck over her like a pair of mother hens. She needs rest, and I intend to see that she gets it. I plan on letting her sleep as long as possible, and then I'll take her home this afternoon. I don't think it would be a good idea for her to try and manage a buggy by herself until she gets her strength back. She is still weak from all the time she spent nursing Jack."

Peter took a gulp of his coffee, and thought the whole damned situation was becoming more complicated than necessary. Things always did when his family got involved.

Connor nodded in the direction of Sara's Glen. "You realize I am not going to have a moment's peace until those two see Bernice again."

"You will manage." Peter gave an indifferent shrug of his shoulders.

Connor surprised him by taking the subject in a completely different direction. "Why don't you marry the girl?"

Peter glared at him, not answering. He couldn't believe how marriage had changed Connor. Now he wanted everyone married, whereas before the two of them had managed to avoid all such discussions whenever his mother or Connor's aunt broached the subject.

Connor gave him a pitying look. "Ejit. Look at you. It is obvious to everyone, but you, how much you care for her."

"I am a doctor. It is only natural that I would be concerned."

"How can you be such a horse's arse?" Connor shook his head in disbelief. "There is something between the two of you. You can't deny that."

"It doesn't matter. There is no room in my life for another person."

Connor drained his cup and left, but not without a warning. "Just make sure nothing happens to hurt Bernice if you insist on letting the past be your mistress."

*****

After Connor left, Peter checked in on Bernice and found her still asleep. He tried to be as quiet as he could, so as not to disturb her rest, while rummaging through the dresser drawers to get a fresh shirt and socks. The gasp he heard coming from the bed, proved he had been unsuccessful. When he turned around, she was huddled against the bed's headboard with the sheet pulled up to her chin, staring wide-eyed at his bare chest. He smothered his desire to chuckle with a cough as he leaned a hip on the dresser and said, "Your virtue is safe. I just came in to get a clean shirt. How are you feeling? Are you hungry?"

She kept the sheet up, but loosened her grip some. "I feel much better. Thank you for taking care of me last night. I am such a ninny."

He forgot about the shirt, and walked over to the bed. "You have no reason to apologize. If there was a fault, it was mine. I should have realized you were in a weakened state from caring for Jack. You should never have gone to the wreck site."

"In the end, I was more of a hindrance." Bernice bit her lower lip.

He ran his finger over her cheek. "A tremendous

help would be a more accurate description. You have not had anything to eat since yesterday morning. I am going downstairs to fix you a tray."

She struggled to get up, but stilled when she realized it would be impossible without dropping the sheet. "There's no need for you to go to all that bother, if you give me my clothes, I can come downstairs and get it myself."

He gave in to the urge to grin. "Stay put. Connor brought a basket of food earlier this morning. My mother thinks I will starve if she doesn't send anything on Ivy's day off. "

Bernice clenched and unclenched her finger around the edge of the sheet a worried expression on her face. "Does Connor know I spent the night here?"

"He knows what happened, and agreed that it was for the best that you were here where I could keep watch over you. He is not about to spread any gossip. You know him better than that. Close your eyes and rest for a few minutes while I get your breakfast." Before she could say anymore, he went downstairs.

When he returned, she was propped up in bed with the sheet snugly tucked behind her outlining the curves of her breasts, and exposing her shoulders and arms. He swallowed hard, and not from the smell of the food. She seemed more at ease when he set the tray in front of her. Not only that, but she invited him to join her. "I cannot possibly eat your breakfast. Please, at least share it with me."

His stomach growled reminding him that he hadn't eaten anything yet, and the tray was laden with enough muffins, bacon, fresh peaches, and cream for more than one person. He had even brought up two cups of steaming coffee, but his intention had been to drink his while soaking in the tub. He pulled the chair over close to the bed, knowing that he was only going to torture himself, and accepted a muffin from her as he removed one of the cups of coffee, and set it on the night stand. "If you are sure you cannot eat all of it, I am hungry."

"I could not possibly eat this much food." She took a forkful of the peaches and popped them into her mouth, and then took another and offered it to him. He opened his mouth, and tasted the sweetness of the fruit. There was something very intimate in the simple act, and yet it felt so natural. When a drop of juice fell on his bare chest, he thought that if he had a shred of propriety, he would at least put on a shirt, but if he had to try and eat with her tantalizing breasts just below that sheet, then she could bloody hell deal with his bare chest. He did not even offer an excuse, and she seemed to have gotten over her initial shock. She took the napkin and wiped the juice off him causing a tremor to course through him.

He finished his muffin, took a strip of bacon, and ate it before washing it all down with the remainder of his coffee. Then she fed him more of the peaches, and her fingers brushed against the stubble on his chin reminding him he needed to shave. He got up from the chair, and moved it back to the side. "I need to go get cleaned up. You finish your breakfast, and if you need anything else, I will get it for you as soon I am finished." He would have to forgo the soak in a hot tub to ease his aching muscles. Right now, he needed to get a cold bath to help get his body under control.

After he had finished shaving and taken his bath, he realized he had not brought in clean clothes. "Damn, no wonder," he muttered to himself. Throwing on his pants, he headed to his room to try once more to retrieve some clean clothes. The polished wood floor felt cool on his bare feet as he padded down the hallway.

*****

Bernice ate the remainder of the food on the tray, and set it on the night table, and then she stood up and wrapped the sheet around her. Where were her clothes? She had to get dressed before Peter returned. On the other side of the room there was a door that must be to the closet. To her surprise, it was a small dressing room. Inside, she found her clothes neatly hung except that her corset was missing. She looked about perplexed. He must have placed it somewhere in here, but where?

"You are supposed to be eating and resting." Arms folded across his chest in an accusatory manner, Peter stood in the doorway.

Her heart pounded and she felt something akin to goose bumps in her stomach. She sensed danger, a delicious danger. "I...ah... finished eating and I have had enough rest. I thought I would dress, but I cannot find my corset."

He scowled. "I disposed of it. They are unhealthy contraptions. I would not doubt that the thing probably contributed to your collapse. It is a wonder you could breathe wearing that torture device, let alone the constriction of the inner organs and pressure on your ribs it caused. Besides, with your slender build, you do not need it."

Bernice tried to keep her voice from quivering. "I know I am nothing to look at – that I don't have a full figure, but did you have to remind me?"

He dropped his arms to his sides, a stunned look on his face. "Did you think I was ridiculing your figure? On the contrary, I meant that you are slender enough that you have no need of artificial devices to improve what nature gave you."

Bernice refused to believe him. "My mother says I have a figure like a stick. She is right, of course, but it still hurts to be reminded of it."

"Your mother is wrong." His voice had an angry edge to it. In three rapid strides he crossed the room and grabbed her hand to pull her in front of the mahogany trimmed floor mirror in the corner of the dressing room. "Let me show you what I see."

When she tried to turn her head away, he took her chin

in his hand, and turned her face back toward the mirror. His body was so close to hers that she could smell the sandalwood soap on his skin. He leaned his clean-shaven face against her cheek, and caressed her bare arm with the back of his hand. With the other hand, he caught a handful of her hair and held it away from her shoulder where it was resting. "I see a silken wild mane of pure gold cascading over soft shoulders that are just begging to be kissed." Shivers ran through her as he kissed her shoulders, one, and then the other. His kisses were as light and soft as butterflies dancing on her skin.

He raised his head and let out a loud breath. "I have to get out of here before your virtue is compromised, and the little honor I have left is lost. Don't let your mother or anyone else ever make you feel you aren't beautiful."

She touched his cheek as he turned to go. "I will love you forever for saying that."

Peter kissed the top of her head. "Don't love me, Angel. Don't love anyone. The cost is too great."

"It's too late." She let the sheet drop to the floor and the last thread of Peter's honor fell along with it.

CHAPTER 14

Peter glanced up from his desk to look through the open door to the room where Bernice worked on her herbs. It was unoccupied, just as it had been all the other times he had done so this morning. He missed Bernice's presence more than he cared to admit, but she needed some rest. It had been early evening by the time he had taken her home yesterday. His original intention was to take her home early, but after their encounter in his dressing room, all other goals were abandoned. Fortunately, no patients showed up, so they were undisturbed.

His thoughts were interrupted when Mr. Winters arrived, seeking relief for his aching joints. Peter examined him and then gave him some liniment to rub on the sore areas. "That should give you some relief."

The older gentleman looked about the room, and then into the adjoining room where Bernice normally worked on her herbs. "Where's Miss Peterson?"

"She had some personal business to tend to today." Peter saw no reason to share the fact that Bernice was exhausted and needed some rest.

The man gave a disappointed frown, and winced as he stood. "She gave me some kind of herb stuff that really helped. I was hoping to get some more of it."

"Perhaps, I might be able to help." He directed the man to take a seat and went to check Bernice's books where she kept her notes. There were several books.

Some listed the herbs and what they cured, while others contained the names of patients and the herbs, she had recommended to them. He checked the latter, found the mixture he would need, and went to the shelves to pull the herbs. To his surprise, there was a shelf with nothing but bottles of herbal mixtures labeled with ailments. He found one for rheumatism and gave it to Mr. Winters. "Is this what she gave you?"

"Yep, that's the stuff." The man gave a relieved sigh.

"And you know how to take it?" Peter asked.

"Mix it in tea. It really works, doc."

A feeling of pride washed over Peter. "That doesn't surprise me. Miss Peterson is a skilled herbalist."

Mr. Winters shook his head. "Your office seems not quite right without her here. I hope you don't lose her. I like her."

Peter gave the man a puzzled look. "She is only gone for the day. She'll be here for your next visit."

"I don't know. A pretty girl like her must have lots of beaus. One of them is going to steal her away from you. What will we do then?"

"We would miss her, but manage somehow. I do have some healing powers, you know." Peter laughed, but the idea of losing Bernice was unthinkable.

"Why don't you marry her, Doc? If she was your wife, you wouldn't ever have to worry about losing her, and you wouldn't even have to pay her. That's not such a bad deal. Besides, like I said, she's awful pretty, and smart too." Mr. Winters shot Peter a between-you-and-me wink.

Peter ushered Mr. Winters out of the room. "That's one way to keep her, isn't it?" He laughed in a joking manner.

Mr. Winter's expression turned serious. "You could do a lot worse, Doc."

After Mr. Winters left, there were other patients, and Rasheen dropped by later in the day to see if Bernice was there. He assured her that Bernice was home resting. She reached up and touched his cheek in a sisterly fashion. "When are you going to realize how much she means to you?"

"I am lost without her to help me. Every one of my patients has asked about her today." He reached up and rubbed his temples with the palms of his hands. Thoughts of how he had spent the previous day with Bernice had left him with little sleep, as he tried to come to terms with the next step.

"That's not what I meant." She gave him a dubious frown, but let the matter drop. "Are you going to bring Bernice to Sara's Glen for dinner?"

Peter looked at his pocket watch and realized that dinner would be in two hours. "No. I think it would be best for her to stay home and get another good night's rest. I'm sure there is no way I will be able to keep her away from here another day."

"Then I won't go and visit her," Rasheen said as he walked her to her buggy.

Once she was gone, Peter tried to get back to his work, but too many thoughts distracted him. He put his feet up on his desk, leaned back in his chair, and put his hands behind his head. He looked around his office, through the open door to Bernice's herb room. Everything was more organized since her arrival. He missed her. Everyone was right; things were out of balance without her. He was out of balance. Yesterday was the first time he had felt truly alive in years. There had been women since Jenny, but none of them shed a light on that dark corner of his soul the way Bernice had. Once he had made love to her assuring her of the beauty she possessed, she seemed to blossom within his hands, and her touch had been like a balm to his parched soul just as it was a fire to his skin.

There was a connection with her that he had not had with the other women in his life. He never let himself get involved with anyone other than women who weren't interested in a permanent relationship. Most of them were society women who were interested in physical pleasure just as he was, but would never stoop to marriage to a mere doctor. Bernice might have been born in that class, but she was far above it in her morality and mentality.

If she stayed in his life, they could not go back to the way they were. They would have to marry. Oddly the idea of marriage wasn't as distasteful to him as it had been in the past. Mr. Winters was right. It was just a matter of time before someone snatched her away. Just because Kingsley was an idiot, didn't mean that there wouldn't be others. A jealous possessive current snaked its way through him. He couldn't bear the thought of anyone else being with her. He would convince her he was the best choice.

After all, his parents were fond of her; she was as close to Rasheen as he was to Connor. They got on well. In fact, he was lost without her in the office. All of these were good reasons for a marriage, but the most compelling one was their physical connection. A contented smile formed in his lips, as he remembered the afternoon spent in bed with her. It wouldn't be so bad having her in his bed every night. Things he had never thought about before surfaced, like children to play with Rasheen and Connor's children. It could be a good life as long as he kept his deepest emotions locked safely away so what was left of his heart remained unscathed. She said she loved him. That was dangerous territory. If he could steer her away from it, this could be a good arrangement for both of them.

He decided to go and see her this evening after she had a full day to rest. As far as he could determine, the only obstacle would be if she were opposed to marrying out of her sphere, and he knew that wasn't possible. If that were the case, she would never have agreed to his mother's suggestion that she work with him. Ladies in her social circle were far above such tasks. All of these thoughts raced through his mind as he tried to comprehend the change in his attitude regarding marriage, but in the end, none of them mattered because he had a responsibility to offer marriage after what had happened between them. He was, after all, an honorable man. He let out a sarcastic laugh at that thought. Honor wasn't what had motivated him yesterday, nor would it in the future whenever he was alone with her.

A squeak sounded from the door in the back of the dispensary. Bernice was the only one who used that door other than him. He was going to thrash her for not listening to him and staying at home resting. Why had she bothered to come so late in the day? He started to rise from the desk to do just that and froze. Dugan appeared before him, with a gun pointed at his heart.

*****

Bernice stared at her reflection in the elaborately designed rosewood mirror of her vanity, and thoughtfully touched the pulse on her neck where Peter had kissed her. Though it had been hours ago, the memory was so vivid she could almost feel his breath there; like the gentle whisper of a butterfly wing. She sighed and put down the silver hairbrush when the maid came in to help her pin up her hair. Upon completing the task, the maid then began to arrange the brush and mirror on the vanity, but Bernice instructed her to leave it as it was. The young woman gave her a worried glance before doing as she was instructed.

"Until my mother returns, we can indulge ourselves in a little less rigidity," Bernice said, realizing the maid was concerned about not following her mother's instructions. She dismissed the maid and looked about the room that was supposed to be her own private space. A large pink cabbage rose pattern, with yellow and blue ribbon trim all but hid the cream-colored background of the wallpaper. It was so unlike the plain spring green painted walls of Peter's room with their simple Irish lace curtains, which had, no doubt, been suggested by Rasheen. They were the only touch of frippery in an otherwise plain room whose furnishings were expensive, but practical.

Her room, on the other hand, had been decorated according to her mother's dictates without any considerations for Bernice's likes or dislikes. She was not even allowed to set her brush and hand mirror as she chose, but had to place it exactly the way her mother wished. Even the fluted bottles of perfume were her mother's choices, but in that respect she had her moment of defiance because she never used them, choosing instead to use her own scents made from herbs. She kept them hidden in one of the many powder boxes so that the maid wouldn't remove them per her mother's orders.

Bernice gave a discontented sigh and decided to go downstairs. She had followed Peter's instructions, and slept late in the day. She even stayed in her wrapper, and had brunch in bed. Only in the last hour had she gotten dressed, even though it was too late in the day to receive callers, not that she wished to do so. Working at the Dispensary had kept her from being her mother's substitute; a fact that no doubt Mrs. Delacourte had written to inform her mother. The thought made her realize that she could see to her correspondence before dinner. As she passed the downstairs maid, she asked her to bring the mail to the small sitting room which adjoined the music room. A few minutes later the maid came in with a silver tray bearing several envelopes. Bernice took the pile and placed it on the desk, sorting through what appeared to be mostly invitations addressed to her mother, except for the pale-yellow envelope embellished with her mother's initials. Taking the crystal handle of the letter opener firmly in hand, she tore open the envelope with more force than was needed. The letter was as she had expected it, full of praise for European society and titles. It was the last part of the missive that gave her a jolt. It said that if Bernice wasn't able to make Ambrose move more quickly on the marriage proposal, they might consider a titled suitor.

"No, mother, I have already found someone and marriage is not in the picture at the present time. Even if he were to offer it, you would never approve of such a union," Bernice whispered to the sheet of paper in her hand. He may not love her, but he had called her beautiful, and in his arms she felt like the most beautiful woman in the world. For now, she would take what he had to offer and maybe someday he would be able to return her love. She jumped up from the desk tossing her mother's letter aside. It was ridiculous, but she missed Peter. Though it was too late in the day to accomplish anything, she could at least see him and have dinner at Sara's Glen as they had been doing before the train wreck. Memories of their afternoon made her ache with a desire she hoped was mutual. There was only one way to find out. She would have to disobey the doctor's orders.

Remembering that her buggy was in Peter's barn, because he had brought her home yesterday in his vehicle, she pulled the rope to ring for the maid instructing her to have the driver bring the carriage round. During the short ride to the dispensary, her stomach fluttered nervously as she thought about seeing him. It was late enough in the afternoon that there shouldn't be any patients unless there were an emergency, but still a little early for dinner. With luck he would have left the dispensary and be in the house. She would be alone with him. How did one go about seducing a man? In the future she would ask Rasheen, but it would have to be brought up in a general sort of way so as not to give any hint as to what was happening between her and Peter.

Bernice instructed the driver to pull into the drive of the stone house and dismissed him, assuring him that she would have another ride home. She planned to drive herself home in the buggy unless she was here after dark, and then she was sure Peter would drive her. At this rate, her buggy may never leave his barn. If only she could say the same about herself and his home.

Going into the house, she discovered that Ivy had left for the day as she had hoped. She called out for Peter, but got no answer, so she decided to check upstairs in case he hadn't heard her. Upon not finding him, she descended the steps with a twinge of disappointment. He must have a late patient. Should she wait here, or go over to the dispensary? If she showed up there at this late hour the person would wonder why. She would say that she was on her way to Sara's Glen for dinner, and thought to stop by the dispensary and ride with him. It didn't sound like a good explanation, but it was the best she could come up with, she thought, as she made rapid strides across the distance from the stone house to the dispensary.

She came in the front door in case Peter was conducting an examination, because she didn't want to interrupt. The door squeaked loudly like someone in agony, reminding her that she had forgotten to tell him it needed to be fixed in all the excitement of the last two days. The door to the exam room was closed, but the door to Peter's office was open. Peter was seated at his desk talking to someone she couldn't see. "Bernice, go home," he shouted. "Now!"

Bernice froze in the middle of the room, unable to move.

"She ain't goin anywhere. Get in here missy." The voice came from Peter's office.

"Let her go, Dugan, she's done you no harm." There was more than a hint of pleading in Peter's voice.

"So's she can go warn yer friends? Get in here now lady or I shoot him, and then you."

Bernice regained her senses and scrambled into the room where Mr. Dugan stood with a gun pointed at Peter's heart. She positioned herself next to Dugan – close enough to knock the gun from his hand. Thoughts of how to do that without taking the risk of getting Peter killed raced through her brain. Peter looked at her, silently shaking his head, as if he read her thoughts. "Why are you here?" he asked. A spasm of torment and frustration crossed his features for a brief second before being replaced by the cool professional mask he normally wore.

She thought to answer that they were expected to Sara's Glen for dinner, but feared that the threat of someone else showing up might prompt Dugan to act rashly. "I needed to see you," she answered honestly. Then to the man standing next to her with the disheveled appearance and wild eyes, she asked, "Mr. Dugan, why are you pointing that gun at Doctor Schmidt?"

"He killed my girl, and now he is going to pay for it, but first he has to suffer like I have." Dugan's hand shook as tears streamed down his face.

Bernice gingerly reached out to touch his arm, but he jerked back, and swung the gun at her for a brief second before aiming it once more at its original target.

Leaving her hand outstretched, her heart thundering in her chest, she said, "He didn't harm your daughter, and I think deep in your heart you know that's true. He works very hard to save lives, not end them. Would you kill a good man to help assuage your grief? That won't help. It will only make your pain greater. Your daughter wouldn't want that."

Dugan kept the weapon aimed at Peter's heart. Bernice saw that his hand was becoming very unsteady, and she worried that the gun might go off. Behind him, she saw Connor's head pop up on the other side of the open window, a finger to his lips with one hand and a motion that he was going to the front door with the other. Panic gripped her as she remembered the loud noise it made. She nodded toward the back room. Hoping that Connor would understand, she spoke in a voice loud enough for him to hear. "Let me go in the back room and get you some water. You look thirsty." Conner nodded and disappeared.

"Don't want any water." Dugan shook his head in

torment. The gun began to slip from his fingers, but he tightened his grip on it. "I ain't ever killed anybody before."

Bernice forced a calm demeanor and stepped in closer. To her surprise, he allowed her to touch his arm in a reassuring gesture. At the very least, she thought, she would be able to divert his aim should he decide to fire the gun, if Connor wasn't able to sneak in from behind him. "You're a good man, Mr. Dugan. Do you think your daughter would want to see you acting like this? You are insulting her memory."

"Don't you understand? She's in hell. She killed her baby. God punished her. What good is her memory now?" He sobbed. "Somebody has to pay."

Remembering Sister Imelda's words to Doctor Ogden, Bernice said, "She was little more than a child herself. If anyone deserves to be punished it's the man who got her pregnant and then deserted her. I don't believe for one minute that a merciful God would condemn a girl who was so frightened that she took a tragic course. We would all do well to remember that none of us is fit to throw stones." She heard the anger in her voice as she said the words. She had seen too many of her mother's friends put themselves on pedestals they didn't deserve, all the while condemning anyone who didn't follow their dictates.

"Give me the gun before someone gets hurt," Peter rose slowly from his seat. "You don't want to do this Dugan. I wish I could have saved her. No one can imagine the pain of losing someone you love. You become the walking dead, no warmth left in you, nothing but shreds left of your heart, but you learn to go on. You manage to live somehow, and with time it gets better. Life is never the same, and the emptiness never leaves, but getting up and facing another day becomes easier."

"You talk like you've walked in my shoes." Dugan stared at Peter through tear-filled eyes. "Have you lost a child?"

Peter began to come around the desk slowly and cautiously. "No, but I lost someone I loved who was around the same age as your daughter. It was a long time ago, but I still bear the scars."

"Why did my baby girl have to die? Why did she do that? I would have taken care of her and the baby." Dugan crumbled to his knees, dropping the gun to the floor.

At that moment, Connor came in and snatched it up. "John is outside. I'll have him go get the sheriff."

Bernice knelt next to Dugan and put her arms around him, allowing him to sob on her shoulder. "This is what he needs," she said looking up at the two younger men.

John came in from the back room and was reassured everything was all right. "Can you go get the sheriff?" Connor asked.

"That won't be necessary," Peter interrupted.

"What the hell do you mean? The man just tried to kill you." Connor asked in disbelief.

"He was out of his mind with grief. Bernice is right. He'll be all right now. Take him to the hotel for the night, and ask them to send the bill to me. I'll stop by in the morning to pick him up and take him to the train station."

"All right then," Connor said as he reached out his hand to help Dugan up. "We'll see you back at Sara's Glen."

"I have to take Bernice home." Peter said. "She should not have been here in the first place." There was more than a hint of anger in his voice. His breathing seemed to be labored as well.

"Your mother and Rasheen are going to want to see you and know that you are all right. You never asked me what I was doing here, but I'll tell you anyway. Dugan showed up at Sara's Glen asking about you, and Bertie unknowingly sent him to the dispensary. When you didn't show up for dinner, she mentioned that a stranger was looking for you. When she described him, I figured it was Dugan from the time I ran into him when he was hanging around the hospital in Baltimore. Thought I should make sure you were all right, but turns out you didn't need me. All the same, you need to reassure the women you are all right. Besides, it will lift me in my wife's esteem if you bring Bernice along."

"You manage to stay in Rasheen's good graces without my help, and you can reassure them that we are all right," Peter answered in a matter of fact tone.

Bernice noticed that his breathing had slowed to normal. Perhaps if they spent some time at Sara's Glen, he would get over his irritation at her. "I wouldn't mind seeing Martha and Rasheen, and I am a little hungry."

"Very well, then, but we won't be staying long." His voice softening some, Peter took her chin in his hand and studied her eyes. "You still look a little tired to me."

"Don't leave before I get home," Connor said over his shoulder as he headed out the door with Dugan, "I need to talk to you about something."

Peter scowled. "Can't it wait until tomorrow?"

"No."

*****

"Dugan probably would not have hurt me, but Bernice showing up complicated things." Peter gave her a pointed look, and felt some satisfaction as a momentary look of discomfort crossed her face.

"There's no telling what he might have done, if she had not been there to distract him," Martha argued as she poured him another cup of coffee. They had finished eating, and were waiting for Connor and John to return from taking Dugan to the hotel.

"The two of you are safe now, and that is all that matters." Rasheen took the baby from Bernice who had been bouncing her on her lap. "I guess this little one isn't going to see her father before going to bed."

She was turning to go out of the room when Connor

and John returned from taking Dugan to the hotel. "What did you say about my daughter," he asked.

Rasheen laughed and handed him the baby. "Kiss your daughter goodnight, papa."

"Good night sweet girl," he cooed and then looked around the room as he noticed Jack's absence. "Where's the lad?"

"He is out in the barn helping to bed Midnight down for the night. He'll be along in a bit," Martha answered over her shoulder from the sink where she was helping Bertie with the dishes.

Rasheen asked Bernice, "Would you like to come up with me while I tuck Clare in for the night?"

Bernice looked over at Peter. "Do I have time?"

"I have something to discuss with him that will take a few minutes, go on up," Connor answered before Peter could respond. The questioning gaze that passed between husband and wife didn't go unnoticed by Bernice; nor did the silent "Oh" that formed on Rasheen's lips. Anxious to ask her friend what was going on, she followed her out of the room.

Once the baby was settled in her crib in the nursery, Rasheen and Bernice went quietly into the adjoining bedroom. Rasheen was about to go out the door when Bernice grabbed her arm. "What is Connor discussing with Peter? If it is a private matter that doesn't concern today's events, just tell me to mind my own affairs; but if Peter is still in danger, I need to know." Fear and uncertainty gave her voice a slight tremor.

Rasheen motioned her to take one of two chairs near the room's small window alcove and then sat in the other. "Peter isn't the one we are worried about." She gave Bernice a knowing look. "There is more to the story than you just showing up at the dispensary today."

"What do you mean?" Bernice studied Rasheen's features for some clue as to just how much she knew.

"Connor saw the two of you yesterday."

Bernice was mortified. "What did he see?"

"He saw Peter and you kissing as he helped you into the buggy."

"Is that all?"

"There's more?" Rasheen arched one amber brow.

"Yes. And no, I am not ready to talk about it, but when I do, it will be your counsel I seek."

Rasheen gave her a sympathetic smile. "He loves you. He just can't come to terms with it. Give him time, but be careful. I told you about the pleasures of love, but forgot the part about protecting yourself from …"

"I know how to prevent myself from becoming pregnant, so you can refrain from further instruction," Bernice said as she tried unsuccessfully to hide her grin.

Rasheen blushed furiously as if she were the one having sex without the benefit of marriage. "Bernice Peterson, don't you dare laugh at my embarrassment," she scolded. "I am only trying to help. There are other methods besides herbs."

"I know about such methods in spite of Mr. Comstock's laws on such practices." Bernice reached across and squeezed her friend's hand. "I'm not exactly a young girl. My mother reminds me often that I've been on the shelf a long time and could be considered a spinster in some circles."

"Your mother is an ejit!" Rasheen put her hand to her mouth, turning a deeper shade of scarlet. "I'm so sorry. Please forgive me. I just hate to see you take such criticism to heart."

Bernice's laughter broke the tension. "Don't you dare apologize. I happen to agree with you. Don't worry about me. I promise to talk with you if the need arises."

"Everything will work out – you'll see. Before the end of the year you will be a member of our family."

Bernice felt the panic rise in her chest. "Is that what Connor is discussing with Peter now?"

"Not exactly. Connor just wants reassurance from

Peter that what he witnessed yesterday will not have unfortunate consequences for you."

Bernice closed her eyes. "Please tell him not to interfere." If Connor and Rasheen intervened, she would never know Peter's true feelings.

*****

Peter seated himself in one of the soft worn brown leather chairs and accepted the Waterford Crystal glass that was half filled with good Irish whiskey from Connor. Before Connor got into whatever it was that was so important it couldn't wait another day, he had some things of his own he wanted to discuss so he plunged ahead. "Will you write a letter to Frank asking him to counsel Dugan?"

"What does Rasheen's uncle have to do with this?" Connor tugged at his hair.

"Dugan thinks his daughter is damned for all eternity because she killed her baby. Frank is the one person who can convince Dugan that she wasn't thinking clearly, and that God is not as harsh as we humans."

"If it were any other clergy member, I would disagree with you, but Frank is more forgiving than most of them would tend to be. I'll send a wire in the morning, and I'll see that Dugan knows where to reach Frank."

Peter took a slow drink of his whiskey and waited a few seconds for it to slide down his throat before speaking again. "I would imagine that Dugan has lost his job. Can you see that he gets another? Maybe in one of your warehouses?"

"Would you like me to build the man a house? Furnish it? Provide him a carriage maybe?" Connor asked

"No, just a job." Peter answered, ignoring the sarcasm.

"For your sake, I will give him a letter to take to the warehouse foreman. But I am also going to give him a warning that if he shows his face around here again, he is either going to jail, or worse."

"Fair enough. I am in your debt," Peter said.

Connor didn't answer, but swirled the amber liquid in his glass studying it as if he were looking for an answer to some unasked question. His dark brows slanted in a frown, a momentary look of discomfort crossed his face before the words finally came, slowly and deliberately, as if he were questioning someone in a court of law. "I have no desire to pry into your personal affairs, but something has come to my attention."

Peter looked him in the eye and realized that Connor knew what had happened between Bernice and him. "Obviously, you are aware of certain things that have transpired. Are we going to have to go outside and handle it like we did as boys?"

Connor shook his head. "We are grown men now, and normally I would never interfere in your private life, but we are all very fond of Bernice. I stopped by your place late in the day yesterday to bring you some dinner. Martha thought perhaps you were working late since you had taken Bernice home, but you weren't working. Bernice was still there. If you tell me nothing happened, I'll believe it."

"I won't lie to you, but this matter concerns Bernice and myself." Peter waited for Connor's reaction wondering if they were going to end up in fisticuffs.

Connor's voice, though matter of fact, held an ominous tone. "You are like a brother to me, but she is like a sister thanks to Rasheen. If you hurt her, I will be forced to... Damnit, Peter, I don't know what I'll do."

"I intend to ask her to marry me." Peter wasn't afraid of Connor even though he knew enough to take the threat serious, but he wanted to put his friend's mind at ease. The last thing in the world he needed or wanted was to have any bad feelings between them lurking in the shadows.

A wide grin crossed Connor's face as he got up, and smacked Peter on the back. "This calls for a celebration."

Before Peter could object, he poured them both another glass, and proposed a toast to Peter and Bernice's future.

Afterward, Peter asked, "Please keep it quiet until I have asked her."

Connor nodded. "Of course, she would want to be asked before everyone else knew, but there is no doubt she'll say yes. The girl adores you."

"Just keep it quiet."

"I'll stop by your place tomorrow to get the good word before I tell anyone, even Rasheen. If she ever finds out I knew and didn't tell her, I will be in a great deal of trouble. Lucky for me, I know how to get round her." Connor's expression grew more serious. "I'm happy for you. It's time you shared your life with someone, and Bernice will make you happy."

CHAPTER 15

On the drive to Bernice's house, Peter tried to formulate a way to propose that would be acceptable. He couldn't give her the hearts and flowers version that most women wanted. That didn't fit the situation, and he found it difficult to believe Bernice fit the mold of most women. Still, she was a female, and they had certain expectations, even the ones whose families arranged their marriages. The game was still played with poetic fervor. He had heard the young men at college bragging about the advantageous marriages their families had arranged, but they would still have to pretend to be the amorous suitor as if the outcome were not already known.

Bernice broke the silence before he could come up with a way to present his case. "I'm sorry for upsetting you."

Thunderstruck, Peter turned his attention from the road keeping the reins firmly in hand, and faced her. "It was more than a mere upset. You cost me years off my life today. I'll be reliving those moments in nightmares for days, maybe weeks, or even months to come. Do you realize you could have been killed, or at the very least hit by a stray shot? Why did you come after I told you to stay at home?"

Bernice flattened her palms in her lap, and squared her shoulders, but didn't look at him when she spoke. "I wanted to see you. I needed to talk about what happened yesterday."

A cold knot formed in his gut at the thought of losing her. "Are you having regrets?"

Her eyes finally met his and he knew the answer before she gave it. "On the contrary; it was the most wonderful experience of my entire life. I...wanted ...to see you." Her gloved hands twisted and untwisted until one of the gloves needed to be pulled tight once more.

"So you've said, but for what purpose?"

"Well, we will be working together and spending as much time together as we do, it is only logical that well, you know...."

Peter couldn't believe his good fortune. With a little luck, he might not even have to make his proposition, because she might just do it for him. "I see. What do you suggest we do about it?"

She let out a long breath as if she'd been holding it. "On the drive here yesterday, I was trying to think of ways to seduce you."

Peter tossed his head back and let out a peal of laughter as the tension left his body. "Bernice, you are a rare find."

"You needn't make fun of me because I'm inexperienced." There was more than a hint of irritation in her voice.

"Sweetheart, you might be inexperienced, but all I have to do is be in the same room with you and it is pure torture for me to keep my hands from you. The way you move, speak, laugh, and anything else you do sends jolts of desire through me. Believe me. I'm not making fun of you. It is a serious matter. In fact, we need to talk about it."

Furrowing her brow, she protested, "You're not going to tell me I can't work with you anymore, are you?"

"Marry me." The words came more forcefully than Peter had intended.

"Why?"

The reply wasn't what he had expected. "I would think

the fact that we are so attuned physically would be reason enough, but there is the also the fact that my family adores you and you are fond of them. You are a skilled herbalist with a talent for healing, and we make a good team. We learn from one another. My patients need you. You know I respect your skills and will do anything you want, and will provide anything to further your knowledge."

"Is that all?"

"That isn't enough? What more do you want?"

She arched her brows and lowered her head, "If you don't know the answer, we should not be discussing marriage."

"Enlighten me." He was becoming irritated.

Her voice was little more than a whisper. "What about love?"

"There are many good marriages that aren't based on that particular emotion. I thought you of all people would understand that. Isn't it the practice of your class to arrange marriages so that certain alignments are made or higher positions are attained? What would be so terrible about us marrying for the convenience of a good working relationship, family, and the physical pleasures we can give each other?"

"My parents have a union without love and trust me – there is no happiness there. I would think after witnessing the happiness Rasheen and Connor share, you would understand my feelings."

"Yes, what they have is wonderful, but if something were to happen to take one of them away, the pain will be all the greater because of that love. You don't want your heart torn to shreds. I won't forfeit what's left of mine." Peter put his free hand over hers and spoke gently as if explaining an unpleasant fact to a child. "Angel, you don't want to love. It tears out your heart, and leaves you a walking void when it leaves. In the end, someone has to be left behind. I will do everything in my power to make you happy, but I cannot give that kind of emotion to another person."

"I am not asking you to. If you can't marry me for love, then don't." She leaned toward him and placed a soft kiss on his cheek.

Keeping his eyes on the road one more, he said through gritted teeth, "I don't know how we are going to make this work."

He felt her body give a small shiver next to him. "I may be inexperienced, but I am not a fool."

She was being completely unreasonable. Somehow he had to make her come to her senses. "You could be ruined if anyone found out. What if you got pregnant? You could already be pregnant."

Bernice reached over and took one of his hands away from the reins. "It would be worth the risk."

Realizing he wasn't going to win this battle, Peter let out a resigned breath and growled, "I don't understand you at all. You will risk pregnancy or ruination rather than marry me. Would you marry me if you became pregnant?"

She brought his hand up to her lips and kissed it. "We'll discuss it if the need arises, but it won't. Don't take me home tonight."

Peter let out a long whistle. "It's too risky. Believe me, there is nothing better I would like than to sleep with you in my arms tonight, but we passed my house ten minutes ago."

"We could go back." There was hint of anticipation in her voice.

He shook his head. "Ivy will be there tomorrow morning. If you married me, we wouldn't even be having this discussion."

They rode the rest of the way in silence. Each lost in their own thoughts; Bernice thinking of future encounters, and Peter thinking of the consequences of those encounters. Then the answer stuck. Give her just enough to make her want more, but hold off until she agreed to marry him. The only problem was that she wasn't the only one who would suffer.

When they finally reached the Peterson residence, he walked her up the stairs and kissed her. She clung to him, wanting more, and he obliged by placing his hand behind her neck and deepening the kiss while caressing her back with his free hand.

She pulled him to her, but he gently pushed her away. "Before long you will beg me to marry you." He gave her a wicked grin.

"You have a devilish streak in you that I would never have thought possible, Doctor Schmidt." Her fingers trembled slightly as she touched his cheek.

"Miss Peterson, it must be your devastating charms that have bewitched me." There was a lightness in his voice that he barely recognized, because it had been gone for so long.

"I'll see you in the morning." He kissed her forehead. "Pleasant dreams."

*****

Peter ate the last of the bacon and eggs Ivy had just fixed for his breakfast and took a slow swallow of his coffee as he thought about the coming day. Somehow, he was going to get Bernice alone again and make her beg him to marry her. The sound of a vehicle rumbling up the drive drew his attention away from his thoughts. It was too early for her to be here, but then maybe her thoughts were traveling the same path. Perhaps she had reconsidered her answer. When the kitchen door opened, he was disappointed to see Connor walk in.

"Well?" Connor accepted a cup of coffee from Ivy, but refused breakfast.

Peter told Ivy she could go ahead and start cleaning upstairs. He didn't wish to discuss his personal business in front of the young woman. Connor should have known better than to ask in her presence. Once she had left the room and he could hear her ascending the stairs, he answered the question. "She turned me down."

"How can that be? She loves you. I would have imagined she would have said yes in an instant. It doesn't make sense." Connor shook his head.

Peter set his cup down and folded his arms across his chest. "It does if you consider the fact that she demands undying love as a requirement. I can't give her that emotion."

"You are just a stubborn jackarse who won't examine his own heart for fear of losing it." Connor slammed his fist down on the table so hard it moved across the floor about half an inch on his side.

Unmoved, Peter answered, "If you recall, I did that once."

His voice quieter, Connor said, "You were only a lad at the time. You have had enough years to heal. Don't be an ejit. You have a chance at happiness. Isn't it worth the risk, or do you want to spend the rest of your life alone? She won't wait forever, and it isn't fair to do this to her."

"She's the one that wants more from me than I am capable of giving."

"Rather you choose to acknowledge it or not, you are just as much in love with her as she is with you. When in the hell are you going to let go of the past?"

"It's my life, Connor. I would appreciate the same respect I have given you when it came to the women in your life. I knew Amelia was wrong for you, just as I knew Rasheen was a good match, but I refrained from voicing my concerns."

Connor gave a grudging nod of agreement. "What are you going to do?"

"Keep at it until I wear her down."

"Don't hurt her."

"That is the last thing I want, but she is going to marry me."

"And then you'll figure it out — that you love her. I think you're right."

Peter gave him a mock salute. "I am happy to have your approval."

"Now that we have covered that matter, there is something else I need to ask you." Connor gave a nervous rap on the table with his knuckles. "It seems Uncle Patrick has acquired some peafowl, and since he can't keep them in the city, he has sent them to Sara's Glen. Would you keep them for me until I can arrange to have them shipped to the zoo?"

Peter rubbed the back of his head. "How in the blazes did he do that?"

"He and Aunt Elaine were at some fancy dinner in Washington where there were several foreign dignitaries, and Patrick mentioned to the man from India that he thought they were beautiful birds. You know how full of blarney Uncle Patrick can be. The next thing he knew, he got notice that the man was sending him a pair of them, so he had them shipped to me, of course. They arrived just an hour ago and already have created havoc."

"What harm could a couple of fancy birds do?" Peter knew that any animal was capable of a lot of destruction having grown up on a farm, but couldn't resist the impulse to spur Connor on.

"No sooner had we gotten them out of their crates than the peacock went after the chickens, because they don't take well to domestic birds. Finn, in turn, went after the peahen. Your mother went after the peacock, because he was after her chickens. I was trying to contain Finn, and keep her from beheading the peacock with a shovel, when Jack finally came out and helped me get Finn inside. I have them locked in a shed for now. I tell you they are a damn nuisance. I'm running a horse farm, not a bird sanctuary."

Peter threw his head back and laughed. "I would have loved to be there to see that show."

"It isn't funny. A man can't even have a quiet breakfast. Will you keep them for me? I promise to have them out of here as soon as I can make arrangements with the zoo. It shouldn't take any more than a few days."

"I'll keep them. Why didn't Patrick have them sent to the zoo to begin with?" Peter asked.

"Good question. I think he and Aunt Elaine were only home long enough to get ready for another trip. They are in Annapolis at the moment. You know how Uncle Patrick is when it comes to politics. He is down there cooking up something with the Governor."

"Go ahead and bring them here." Peter said.

"I'll have my men bring them down as soon as I get back to Sara's Glen. Where do you want them in case you are busy with patients?"

"Just let them loose in the back yard. I haven't any chickens for them to torment, and my horses are in the back pasture. I'll let my stable hand know they are coming by, and he'll direct them."

Connor frowned. "All the same, I'll have two of my men go into town and get some materials to build a temporary pen, as soon as they finish with this morning's chores. You don't want them running around and harassing your patients."

Three hours later, Peter was seated in his office, the peafowl forgotten. It had been a busy morning. Mrs. Winslow came in with a colicky baby, one of Jake Barlow's farmhands had a nasty gash from where a saw blade slipped when he was trying to cut wood, and Billy Linton fell out of a tree and broke his arm. Thank heavens he had Bernice to help him, Peter thought, as he walked Billy and his father out the door. They had been so busy that he hadn't had time to think what he was going to do to convince her to marry him. Now that they were alone, he could at least steal a kiss. That would be a start. Anything else would be too risky, as there was no telling when someone would come in needing medical assistance.

She was in the herb room grinding up some mixture of herbs when he came in behind her, bent his face to her neck and let his lips trail as far as he could before the collar of her dress stopped him. To his surprise, she didn't start, but said, "ummm… that's nice."

Her hands came up and her fingers tangled through his hair as she pulled him closer. All he wanted to do was make love to her. His body felt a painful need to be connected to hers. Just as he was about to snap and lose all control, he pulled her hands away and ended the kiss. "I was the one who was supposed to be doing the seduction, but it would seem you have turned the tables. As much as I would like to continue, I'm afraid this won't work."

Bernice gave a frustrated sigh. "You're right of course. Perhaps it would be better if I go out and get some more Bee Balm from the garden since I've used all that I had dried in here."

"Some distance might be a good idea at the moment. If we were married, as soon as the last patient was out of here and Ivy gone for the day, I could drag you up to bed."

She gave him a sensuous smile with her lips as well as her eyes, but said nothing as she picked up her basket and went out the back door.

*****

Bernice opened the gate to the herb garden, went to the Bee Balm, and began snipping the flowers, making sure to get a good portion of the leaves with them. She had just finished filling her basket when she heard a yowling sound, almost like a child crying, coming from the corner of the garden. Walking over to where the sound came from, she found a rather large peacock and peahen. "Who said you could play in my garden?" She began to shoo the birds toward the open gate, but they screamed all the louder.

The peacock fanned its tail feathers in a magnificent display of shimmering blues and green, and crept toward her without the slightest sign of any fear. Her first reaction was that it was beautiful, but it kept coming closer, the feathers vibrating while it screamed all the louder with the female following as if they planned to attack her. Growing alarmed, she began to back away, but they kept advancing until she was pinned in the corner of the garden, at which point she pulled up her skirts and jumped up on the fence, clutching her basket of Bee Balm. The peacock was at her feet and the peahen flew up on the fence until it was only two feet from her. Frightened, she screamed for Peter.

Seconds later Peter came running into the garden, grabbed a shovel and chased the birds. The peacock screamed louder and flew up at Peter, but when he swung the shovel, it flew up onto the opposite side of the fence with the female close behind. Peter took Bernice in his arms and carried her back inside.

Once the door was closed against the sound of the screaming birds, he pried the basket from her fingers, set it on a table, and held her against his chest. "I'm sorry; I forgot to tell you about the birds. The damn things will be gone in a few days. Are you all right?"

Bernice tried to still her shaking body. "I thought a child was lost or hurt. When I went to check on the sound, I found the birds instead. They were fascinating until they came after me when I tried to shoo them from the garden."

Peter tightened his arms around her, kissing the top of her head. "The peacock was displaying himself for you in a mating ritual. The peahen may have been jealous, or she might have been trying to persuade you to join the harem."

"But there were only two birds." Bernice looked up and saw a humorous glint in his amber eyes.

"Well, a fellow has to start somewhere. You have to give him credit for having excellent taste in females." He touched his forehead to hers.

"What about you?"

"Me?"

"Do you have a harem?" Unwanted memories of the beautiful women she had seen him with in Central Park invaded her mind.

Peter chuckled. "No, you are enough for me to handle. Look at the trouble you get into when I'm not with you."

"I am embarrassed enough without your laughter, Doctor Schmidt." She slapped her hand against his chest.

Peter's expression turned more serious. "You shouldn't be. Peacocks and peahens have sharp, powerful spurs on the back of their heels known as kicking thorns. They can inflict serious damage to the face of an adversary."

"Why do you have them here?" Bernice snuggled into his chest and put her arms around his waist. It felt so safe, so natural. She decided it was time to banish thoughts of the gorgeous red head. For now, he was hers.

"Connor sent them here because they were wreaking havoc at Sara's Glen. He is going to send some of his men to build a sturdy enclosure for them until he can make arrangements to donate them to the zoo."

"How did he get them in the first place?"

"Patrick sent them, since they were a gift for which he had no use. He didn't have time to make arrangements for the zoo to take them, because he is traveling." Peter held her back a bit and studied her. "Are you sure you're all right?"

"I'm just shaken a bit." Bernice moved away from him and looked out the window and saw the peacock rummaging around her herb garden with the peahen behind him. "If I weren't concerned about my garden, I would enjoy watching him. It's amazing how long his feathers are. They were longer than his body, and the red, gold, and blue hues are exquisite. The poor female was drab in comparison."

"Females are believed to choose their mates according to the size, color and quality of the male's tail feathers. You must have destroyed his ego since you were unimpressed. I'm glad you were happier with my endowments." He gave her a look that melted her insides.

Bernice reached up and stroked his cheek, and then wound her hand around his neck to pull his mouth to hers. Before she could kiss him, his lips parted hers in a soul-reaching massage causing her knees to weaken until she was limp against him, a delightful shiver coursed through her. Half in a daze she remembered where they were and broke the kiss. "Perhaps you should lock the door in case a patient comes."

"I'm too busy at the moment." He led her over to the one chair in the room and sat her in his lap.

She knew she should be worried, but at the moment all she could do was hope no one showed up, and they could finish what they had started. Her hopes were dashed as the front door to the office opened.

"Damnit!" He quickly closed the door to the examining room so they couldn't be seen. "I swear to you that before this day is done, I am going to get you alone and convince you to marry me."

"Perhaps you should worry about whoever came through that door for now."

He donned the long white coat on a nearby hook. "This better be a serious problem."

*****

Bernice stripped the dried Feverfew, placed it in the mortar, and took the pestle in hand to crush it into a fine powder. Once that was done, she dumped it into the wide-mouthed glass Mason jar, and slowly poured the alcohol over the powder until it was completely covered, before adding two additional inches of the liquid. She labeled it and made sure the top of the vodka bottle was screwed on as tightly as possible so that its contents didn't leak or evaporate. The tincture would be used in the treatment of fevers, migraine headaches, toothaches, and for labor during childbirth.

Next, she placed it in a paper bag, and put it in the

cabinet in the far corner of the room before picking up one of the other four bags that were in the cabinet. She pushed the door closed with her hip to make sure the cabinet's contents remained in the dark. At the table, she removed the bag from the bottle, placed a towel over it just in case it might leak, and shook it as hard as she could before marking the date on the outside of the bag and placing the jar inside once more. She returned it to the cabinet to join its mates, before doing the same with the next one and on down the line until she came to the last one.

Noting that the last one had cured for almost three weeks and been through the last full moon for the added natural drawing power, she decided to bottle it. Setting the jar on the table, she pulled down a cobalt blue jar, a blank label, and then cut some cheesecloth. She poured the tincture through the cheesecloth into the bottle, squeezed the saturated herbs to extract any remaining liquid until all the drips disappeared, closed the bottle with a cap, and was just finishing the label when the dispensary door opened. Quickly finishing, she dried her hands on her apron, and went to help Peter with the next patient.

The stylishly dressed woman gave her a dismissive glace and sashayed into Peter's office without as much as a "good day." Bernice decided to go back to her lab until Peter called for her. Sometimes he spoke to his patients before taking them into the exam room, and her presence wasn't required. In fact, some cases required pre-exam conversations with the patients to put them at ease. This must not have been the case for he didn't get up to close the door, and the woman didn't seem to notice. Bernice was about to start another tincture, when the conversation in the other room caught her attention.

The woman introduced herself as Mrs. Rentzel. Bernice recognized the name from her mother's society lists, though she had never met her. Her mother thought highly of the young woman, and often held her up as an example for Bernice, since she had managed to land an esteemed husband in the demimonde. What was she doing here in North County, and why in heavens name would someone like her seek treatment from a humble country doctor? But then Peter was well known and respected in Baltimore, so perhaps that might be the reason. Bernice knew she should close the lab door and not be eavesdropping, but she was too curious to stop herself.

Though Peter spoke in a moderate tone, not overly loud or soft, his voice carried across the small distance between the two rooms. "What seems to be your ailment, Mrs. Rentzel?"

"I have suffered from a nervous disorder for some years now. When we lived in Boston, Doctor Pheltyn treated me. Now that my husband has decided he needs to be nearer his business interests in North County, we will be stuck here for some time. I require the services of a reputable physician. Is it any wonder I have a nervous disorder, considering the lack of culture in this godforsaken hamlet?"

Peter's laugh drifted across to Bernice's lab, and without seeing it, Bernice knew he was giving the woman his professional smile. Bernice felt a smug satisfaction in the realization that she had seen the smile that he rarely showed, the one that captivated and sent her pulses racing. "I think you would find there are many things here in North County that might interest you, and you are only a train ride away from Baltimore. However, if you feel you need something for your nerves until you become acclimated, Miss Peterson has some herbal cures. If you are seeking laudanum, I have to warn you, it can be addictive, and I only prescribe it for serious cases involving physical pain."

"Oh no, no, nothing like that. I don't require any medicine. Doctor Pheltyn said that my symptoms were a sign of a nervous disorder, and he treated it without the aid of any drugs."

The laughter from Peter's voice disappeared. "What were your symptoms?"

"I suffer from headaches, irritability and depression. After one of the doctor's treatments, I always felt much relieved." Mrs. Rentzel all but purred at the mention of the wonder treatment.

Intrigue kept Bernice riveted to the conversation taking place across the hall as to what this treatment could possibly be, since Mrs. Rentzel insisted, she had taken no medication. Perhaps it was a form of hypnosis, but Peter didn't use that in his practice as far as she knew.

"The correct medical term for what you are describing is Female Hysteria, and if I'm not mistaken, the doctor you refer to treated you by performing a massage of the external genitalia with a machine which resulted in a paroxysm that relieved your symptoms."

Bernice had to cover her mouth to keep from letting out a gasp. This woman was asking him to touch her in the most intimate places for things that could easily be relieved with a few herbal remedies. No wonder he had responded in such a blunt manner, because she had never heard him speak so explicitly. No doubt Mrs. Rentzel would exclaim her displeasure and storm out, but to her surprise the woman remained seated and continued to badger Peter.

There was no trace of shame or embarrassment in Mrs. Rentzel's voice when she asked, "Can you perform the treatment?"

Bernice heard the impatience in Peter's polite reply. "I don't have the machine to perform that type of treatment."

"Well, you could get one or perhaps do a manual massage. That's what my other doctor did before he obtained the machine. I am willing to pay double your fees, I am so desperate for relief," she pleaded.

"I'm sorry, Mrs. Rentzel, this is something I don't

wish to do in my practice, but if you send your husband to me, I would be happy to instruct him how to perform the treatment." Peter's voice softened a bit and held a crumb of sympathy.

Mrs. Rentzel all but screeched, "I could not possibly let you talk to Harold about such personal matters."

Bernice heard the scrape of Peter's chair as he pushed it away from the desk. "I'm afraid I can't help you. If you change your mind, send your husband to see me. Also, you might want to reflect on the fact that you would discuss the subject with a strange doctor, and not your own husband."

"If you will not help me, can you recommend someone?" Mrs. Rentzel asked as Peter walked her to the door.

"No." The next thing Bernice heard was the door slam, and then Peter was standing inside the doorframe to the lab.

"How much did you hear?" he asked.

"I'm sorry, but once she started I couldn't stop listening. Do many doctors perform the treatment? Have you ever done it?" The questions spilled out of Bernice's mouth in rapid succession.

"No and no. A few doctors do it because it is very profitable, and there is no risk of any harm to the patient."

Bernice tapped her chin with her forefinger. "I have to admit, at first I was horrified, but if it helps, why wouldn't you want to do it?"

"Because it is something her husband should be doing. With the proper instruction, he could learn to do what the doctor did and more."

"Would you show me the treatment?" Bernice felt a sudden shiver down her spine at the thought of Peter attending to her body in such a fashion.

A smoldering glint shown in his amber eyes. "Umm, I think I will devise a treatment with you in mind only, one that would have a doctor thrown out of the medical profession it would be so scandalous, but for a lover it would be exquisite. Would you like that?"

"I think I'm feeling a bit hysterical already." She blushed at the mere thought of what he would do.

"If you marry me, I will be happy to take care of that for you, but only if you marry me."

Bernice sighed. "Peter, we have already had that discussion. I will not marry without love. While all the other things you mentioned are important, what happens when you find someone and actually fall in love? I will not end up like my parents."

"And I already told you that I will never let that emotion destroy me again," Peter growled.

Their discussion was interrupted when Ambrose arrived a few seconds later. Peter looked annoyed, but politely acknowledged him before excusing himself to return to his office.

Bernice felt a jolt of satisfaction when she realized he was showing signs of jealousy. Realizing that Ambrose might have something he wished to discuss in private, she steered him out onto the small front porch of the dispensary and closed the door behind them. She hadn't forgotten how she had listened to Peter's conversation with Mrs. Rentzel, and wasn't about to have him overhear her conversation with Ambrose.

Ambrose leaned his tall, muscular frame against the porch railing, since he had removed his hat the sun shone in his auburn hair creating reddish gold threads. Bernice rested her hand on his folded forearm and looked up into his face. "Why, Ambrose, you've grown a mustache."

"I've had it for quite some time now. Of course, you wouldn't know that since I have not seen you for weeks. Every time I stop at your home, you are out." There was a slight spark of displeasure in his voice.

Bernice removed her hand and folded her arms over her midsection. "You know very well I'm working here at the dispensary and there were some serious incidents. Jack was very sick and then the railroad accident. You did read about that in the paper, didn't you?"

He raised one brow, his lips curving upward ever so slightly like he always did when he was making an effort not to smile. "And are you working at night too? I have come by several times to see if you might like to dine with me since your father is out of town, but you are never in, Miss Peterson."

"I have been dinning at Sara's Glen. Martha felt the same as you and insisted I not eat alone at home."

"I waited very late the other evening, and you never showed up. I doubt very seriously you were at Sara's Glen." His pale green eyes locked with hers, waiting for an explanation. Somehow he knew, but how?

She gave him the sternest look she could manage. "Your insinuation?"

Placing a sympathetic hand on her shoulder, he said, "Darling, I am not being critical. On the contrary, I am happy for you. Of course, this puts me in a spot."

Bernice decided to pretend ignorance. "What are you talking about?"

Ambrose wriggled his brows. "You have formed an attachment."

Bernice silently cursed her flushed face. She never blushed before, but then she didn't do a lot of things before Peter came into her life.

"Silly girl. You have the look of someone who has tasted the power a lover has over their partner. It is a look I know only too well. You have more physical allure than you realize. I am sorry I couldn't be the one to bring it out in you." Ambrose gave an exaggerated sigh. "A wedding. How delightful."

She shook her head and heard the sorrow in her voice as she said, "I will not marry him without his love."

"Don't be ridiculous. How many marriage proposals are you going to refuse? We have love and friendship. Yet, you will not marry me."

"I want passion, not brotherly love. We both know your passion lies elsewhere."

Ambrose gave a chuckle. "So am I to gather there has been a great deal of passion between you and the doctor?"

"I guess what I really meant was that I want passionate love, not just lust."

"Tch, tch, tch. Dear girl, do not discount lust. It can be quite fun."

Bernice couldn't help but smile. "I gather you know about lust."

"We are not discussing my love life." Ambrose put his hands on her shoulders and rested his chin on the top of her head. "Just wait and see. Things will work out for you."

"Perhaps in time, whatever it is that is keeping him from giving his heart will be overcome, and he will love me, I cannot marry him until then."

Ambrose leaned his head to one side, a sign that he was going to suggest something scandalous. "You know there is a way to force him to realize his own heart."

A surge of hope lightened her mood. "And what might that be?"

"Spend more time with me, and make him jealous. Withhold your favors so to speak."

She shook her head. "That is deceitful."

"I know, but think what fun we could have."

"No."

Ambrose gave her a smug smile. "From the way he has been peeking out the window and pacing back and forth, I would say he is already agitated."

Bernice started to turn around to look, but Ambrose grabbed her face and kissed her in a way he had never done before. It was more of a lover's kiss than the brotherly peck on the cheek he normally gave her.

When he finished she looked up at him stunned. "What...why...did you do that?"

"I thought it would be good to give him something to

stew over. Might make him realize if he doesn't get over whatever it is that is in the way of his love for you, he might just lose you."

"I cannot believe you just did that, considering where your affections lie. If I didn't know otherwise, and if our relationship were different, I don't know what I would have thought. I can just imagine what is going through his mind right now."

Ambrose gave her a hug that was more in line with their relationship. "My dear Bernice, no sacrifice is too great for you. I want to see you happy."

She giggled and slapped him on the arm. "What would I do without you?"

"I would say that your life would be quite dull without me, but you seem to have managed to add spice to it. Now I had better take my leave before Doctor Schmidt has a fit of apoplexy. Besides, St. Vincent is waiting for me in the carriage."

Bernice glanced at the carriage feeling a sudden case of apprehension. "Do you think he saw you kiss me?"

"I will explain everything to him." He kissed the top of her head. "He'll understand, and you know you have no need to worry about gossip coming from his lips. He is the soul of discretion."

"Yes, considering…well, yes." Bernice looked over to the carriage again and then back to the window just as Peter was turning from it. "You'd better go before Peter gets more upset."

"Think about what I just said." Ambrose turned when he was halfway down the walkway. "Things are going to work out. If anyone in the world deserves to be happy, it is you."

She stood on the porch and watched until the carriage disappeared down the road. Ambrose was the brother she had always wanted. She knew she had a chance at happiness with Peter. Ambrose could never know that happiness, she thought with regret as she opened the door to go back inside.

The door was barely opened when she noticed Peter standing just on the other side. He grabbed her hand, yanked her inside.

"Are you in love with him?"

She shook her head.

Anger blazed in his eyes. "Then why in the hell did you kiss him after what has transpired between us? You aren't the type of woman who would behave like that."

The situation was absurd. She wasn't sure rather to laugh or return his anger. "I didn't kiss him. He kissed me. It is really none of your business."

"After what has happened between us, I would say it is. I want to marry you. Has he offered marriage?"

"There are no romantic attachments between Ambrose and me. You will have to take my word, but I promise he will never kiss me like that again."

Peter let out an exasperated breath. "Marry me."

"We have had this discussion. What happens if we marry, and you find someone you love? Then we will both be miserable. I will not have a marriage like my parents."

"Bernice, you are the only living woman I have ever proposed to. Do you honestly think I could love anyone else? If I were ever to allow myself to fall into that emotional trap again, it would be with you, and only you. Why must you insist that I lose what's left of my soul?"

She felt the tears brim in her eyes and overflow in trickles down her cheeks. "You already own my heart and soul. I love you."

CHAPTER 16

Peter paced his bedroom from the bed to the window and back, again and again, until finally he stopped and stared out the window at the fireflies twinkling in the dark night sky. Guilt from his treatment of Bernice refused to allow him sleep. He took in a deep breath and then let it out slowly. Blind jealousy had come over him when he saw Kingsley kiss her.

No other woman had done what she did to him. Not even Jenny, and he had loved Jenny, but they had never made love. There was some kissing, but they were so young. If Jenny had lived, no doubt they would have not waited much longer. But she died, and when she did, she took his love with her. For a long time, he thought she took everything in him and left a hollow shell that only walked, moved, and talked. He had found solace in his studies and later in his work. It was the only time he felt alive, but he had lost the ability to enjoy life.

Other women had given him physical pleasure, but there was no friendship, no laughter, no witty banter or teasing, not like Bernice. Why was she being so stubborn? They could have a good marriage based on friendship and passion. The key was not to get their emotions entangled. He had already slipped by becoming angry when he saw her with Kingsley. If he felt that way now, what would it be like if they were caught in love's web?

"Damn her," he said out loud. They were perfect for one another. Perhaps she wasn't being honest with him about Kingsley. Maybe she planned on marrying him after she had some time with Peter as her lover. She would settle down in the type of marriage her peers would demand. They would never accept him. But he knew that was not true. There was nothing deceitful about her. He was going to have to convince her that she could be happy with him – happier than she would be in a marriage arranged by her mother.

He might not be a member of Baltimore Society, but he was wealthy and could give her a comfortable life. She could have servants, and she could work with him. They wouldn't be attending all the society events, and she would not be invited to the snobbish luncheons, but she wasn't doing that now. He doubted she would miss any of it. Why couldn't she be reasonable?

"I have to get some sleep," he muttered as he stripped off his clothes and got into bed. He studied the shadows on the ceiling for what seemed hours, turned on his right side, closed his eyes, and then turned on his left side pounding the pillow. At some point, sleep won the battle over his restless mind. At least it did until he awoke feeling he was not alone in the room. The room was getting downright crowded. The ghost of James Bartlett stood by the window along with his wife Sara and Jenny. Sara nodded her head in Peter's direction, and whispered something to Jenny.

"If I had been drinking, I would swear I was having hallucinations, but since that is not the case, this must be a dream or an apparition. I'm in no frame of mind for ghostly visits, so get the hell out of my room." He threw a pillow at his visitors, but the pillow sailed through them landing on the floor. Peter turned away from them and said, "If you don't mind, I'm trying to get some rest."

"Peter, you mustn't be afraid to love again." The voice was Jenny's. Peter couldn't help but turn to face her and sit up in the bed.

"Have you fallen in love again?"

"I carry your love with me, but I cannot be happy as long as you shut out love like you do," Jenny said. The couple standing on the other side of the room shook their heads in agreement.

"You left me a broken man, not even a man, but still a youth. You deserted me," Peter raged at the apparition.

Jenny held out her hand to him, but not far enough for him to touch it. "I had no choice in the matter, but you do. You can choose to live and love again or accept the bleakness of your existence in exchange for never risking pain. Don't you understand? What we had was a beautiful young love, but I wasn't the one to be your life's mate. You have lived in a void thinking this because of me, but that is not true. The truth is that you were waiting for her without realizing it. You can accept the gift of love that has been given to you, or you can reject it. She deserves your heart, Peter, even more than I did because she knows you as a man, all your goodness, your strengths, and your weaknesses. She loves you without any reserve. You must give her no less."

Before he could answer, she and her companions faded as if they had been nothing but the morning mist. Maybe he was dreaming, but maybe not. James Bartlett had appeared to him once before when he was a young boy hanging around the barn in the back of the stone house where he now lived. The ghost came to warn him not to go into the barn. Later, a rabid raccoon was discovered in that same barn. James Bartlett and his wife were the original owners of the stone house over a hundred years ago. They seemed to be keeping an eye on things, but what had they to do with Jenny? And he was awake when he saw Jonathan the first time, not asleep like now. Or was he asleep? Nothing was making sense anymore. Peter closed his eyes and tried to go back to sleep either for real or in the dream, either way, he just wanted to drift off to oblivion.

He wasn't sure how long he slept before sunlight shone

through the open window and rested on his closed eyelids, letting him know it was time to get up. He drew himself a hot bath, soaked for a bit, shaved, and got dressed. When he went downstairs Ivy had already fixed coffee and poured him a cup. "Good morning, Doctor Schmidt," she said as she handed it to him. "Would you like eggs and ham for breakfast this morning?"

"Good morning, Ivy. I think just coffee this morning." He wasn't hungry at the moment, at least not for food. The lack of sleep and ghostly visitors had put him in a foul mood. "I am going to make her as miserable as I am until she sees to reason," he thought. "Stubborn creature," he muttered under his breath.

"Sir?" Ivy asked.

"Nothing of importance," he said. "I may come back for some breakfast later, but for now, I'm going to get a start on the day's work." He gulped down the last bit of coffee in his cup and placed it in the sink on his way out.

As he walked across the yard to his office, he saw that the peafowl were no longer in residence. Connor had made good on his promise to remove them. Peter stopped and rested his elbows on the fence surrounding Bernice's herb garden, remembering how frightened she had been, and how he had been just as terror struck that harm might befall her. She was so strong in many ways, and yet so fragile in others. He wanted to protect her from anyone or anything that hurt her. Yet, he was the one hurting her. The garden looked empty without her tending her precious herbs. He looked around and realized how empty his world would be without her.

Taking in the summer morning, he heard a cardinal call out to its mate, the bees buzzing about on some of the flowering herbs, but in the midst of those sounds, Jenny's words came back to haunt him, "She loves you without reserve. You must give her no less." The risk was great, but his heart whispered it was worth it. He was in love with her. He could fight it and deny it, but the simple fact was that his mother was right; the heart's own truth would not be denied. "I'll be damned," he laughed. It felt good to finally admit it. Now he would have to convince her he was not just saying he loved her to get her to marry him. "I'll court her," he said to a sunflower whose head leaned over the fence facing him.

Looking up at the clouds, he said, "I hope you're happy, Jenny. Look what's happened to me. I'm talking to flowers. Still, I'm happy. Thank you. I hope you find peace now."

He went to his office, scribbled a quick note telling Bernice he had to leave for a bit, before getting Joshua to hitch up the horses to the buggy, and heading to Sara's Glen. When he got there, he jumped down from the vehicle and told the stable hand not to bother unhitching the horses since he wouldn't be staying very long. He bounded up the back steps two at a time feeling a joy he hadn't felt in a long time. If this was what life would be like with Bernice in it, he had been a fool for waiting so long to come to his senses. Of course, he was going to take a lot of teasing from Connor, but it was worth it to feel this happy. He hadn't realized he'd been whistling until he came inside, and his mother looked at him as if he were a stranger.

"Since when do you whistle?" Martha asked over her shoulder as she stood at the sink drying the dishes Bertie was washing.

"Hmm, I wasn't aware that I was whistling. I thought I might borrow your picnic basket and that you might pack me a nice lunch."

"And are you going on this picnic alone?"

"Bernice has been working hard, and that peacock Connor asked me to keep nearly scared her to death, so I thought I might make it up to her." Peter knew his mother wouldn't be satisfied with that answer, so he went on, "I noticed the peafowl were gone this morning. I guess he must have sent someone to crate them. I

216

suppose they are on the morning train to Baltimore. The zoo will be happy to have them."

"The crates were done yesterday, and they went up to your place before sunrise." She threw the dishtowel over the oven handle and came over and hugged Peter. "It is about time you spent the day doing something fun. I am happy to see you taking some time off to spend with Bernice." Then she gently pushed him away and went to get the basket, returning a few minutes later, issuing orders to Bertie to make some sandwiches, pack some of the oatmeal cookies they had made yesterday, and fill a nice jug of lemonade. When all the food was packed, along with silverware, dishes and glasses, she said, "You'll need a blanket. Bertie, run upstairs and get that old quilt on the chest in the guest bedroom."

A few minutes later, Bertie returned with the quilt which was laid on top of the basket. Peter thanked his mother and Bertie, and took his leave. After he had gone, Rasheen came down stairs. "Did I just hear Peter's voice?"

"You just missed him." Martha took Rasheen by the arm and led her out the back door. "I want to show you what that peacock did to my garden." After they were safely away from the house, she put her arm about Rasheen's waist and squeezed. "Peter is taking Bernice on a picnic."

Rasheen raised a brow. "So, there is no damage to the garden?"

"There was some damage, but it has been repaired. I didn't want to say anything in front of Bertie."

"I think you can trust her," Rasheen said.

"Perhaps, but you know how private Peter is about his life. The only thing he said to me was that Bernice was shaken by that awful bird, and he wanted to make it up to her, but it is more than that. He came into the house whistling."

"Is that such an unusual thing?" Rasheen stumbled

over a small stone and kept herself from falling by holding Martha's arm.

"Careful, my girl. We don't want to disturb the good doctor or his assistant today." Martha helped Rasheen steady herself. "It is unusual for him to whistle. Why he hasn't done that since Jenny died. You should have seen his face, Rasheen. He was happy." Tears began to trickle down Martha's ample cheeks.

Rasheen rested her head on Martha's shoulder as her own eyes filled. "Now look what you've done. All this happiness is contagious."

They rounded the corner of one of the outbuildings just in time to see Connor who was on his way up to the house for some coffee. "Is something wrong?" Alarm shadowed his face.

Rasheen ran up to him and kissed his cheek. "No, love. Everything is wonderful."

Martha told him about Peter's visit and the change in his behavior. "I think there is more going on between the two of them then they let on."

"Jaysus…" Noting the frown on his wife's face, Connor quickly changed words. "I mean Jakers Christendom. You scared the life out of me. I thought something had happened to my daughter," he growled.

Martha and Rasheen offered no apologies.

Connor gave them a stern warning. "The two of you need to mind your own business. No meddling. Let the man do his own courting, for pity sake."

*****

Bernice stared at Peter's hastily scribbled note telling her he had gone on an errand, and would return shortly. She wasn't quite sure what to make of the note that had been propped up against her marble pestle and mortar. Upon her arrival she looked in his office, but found it empty. She thought perhaps he may have been called away on an emergency, because he was generally in the office before her, unless she arrived early enough to have coffee with him before he walked over to the dispensary to begin the day's work. She couldn't imagine what type of errands he would be running at this time of the morning, but it was just as well, considering the way they had left things yesterday.

When she told him she loved him, but wouldn't marry him, he went into his office and shut the door. He stayed there the remainder of the day, except for the times he came out to see patients. When it was time to leave for the day, she knocked on the door, but he didn't open it. Instead, his muffled voice bid her good afternoon from the other side of the door.

Bernice tossed and turned most of the night wondering how she would face him today. The hurt in his eyes when she told him she wouldn't marry him, and then the pain and confusion when she told him the reason was almost more than she could bear, but she would not marry a man who didn't love her no matter what she felt.

She took the Queen Anne's Lace seeds that had been drying in the tray, and placed them into two jars – one for the lab and one for home. She would make sure to use it the future to prevent pregnancy. After yesterday, she thought, there might not be a necessity for precaution. Everything will be all right, she told herself, not really believing it.

Just as she was about to put one of the jars on the shelf, the front door opened. Before she could alight from the stepladder she had been using to reach the top shelf, Peter came into the lab whistling. Caught off guard, she stumbled and was about to fall off the ladder. In two quick strides, he snatched her off the ladder and wrapped his arms around her midsection from behind. He didn't release her, but rested his chin on her head from behind. "Sweetheart, you have to be more careful."

Bernice turned in his arms, filled with astonishment. "I never heard you whistle before." While that was true, she couldn't help but wonder how his mood could have changed so overnight. Peter was always consistent in his temperament.

He shook his head. "My mother said the same thing this morning. Why can't a man whistle if he is happy?"

First of all, he had not been happy yesterday, and secondly and more important, what was he doing at Sara's Glen this morning? "Is everything all right at Sara's Glen? You never go there before dispensary hours when Ivy is here." Everything had to be all right or he wouldn't be in such a happy frame of mind, she assured herself.

"Everything is fine." He turned her around and kissed the top of her head.

"Then why did you go there so early in the day?" She asked puzzled by his behavior. Was this the same man she left yesterday, or for that matter, the same serious doctor with whom she spent most of her days?

"Because I needed to ask a favor of my mother," he said as he took her hand and led her out of the room. "I needed to borrow a picnic basket, and while I was there I had her pack us a nice lunch to fill it."

"Is Ivy not here today? We could have just as easily gone to lunch at Sara's Glen. You should not have put Martha to all that trouble." Bernice kept her hand in his as he led her to the front door where he hung the Doctor Is Out sign. After the sign was hung, he pulled her out of the building and closed the door.

"In answer to your question, Ivy is here. As for Mother's trouble, she was very happy to pack us a nice lunch when I told her I was taking you on a picnic." He put his arm about her waist and guided her toward the buggy.

"A picnic? Whatever for?" She stood next to the buggy wondering if he had taken leave of his senses. "You have patients to see."

"I only had two patients to see today. Since their appointments were not of a critical nature, I've already sent word to them that I will not be here. Stay here a minute, while I go and tell Ivy to inform anyone who shows up seeking treatment that cannot wait until tomorrow to go see Doctor Jones in Kingsville"

*****

As they rode through the countryside, Peter continued to whistle, and although Bernice found it puzzling, she rather liked this side of him which she had never seen before, but curiosity forced her to ask, "Are you going to tell me why you are in such a pleasant mood?"

"Am I that miserable most of the time?" He kept his eyes on the road, but heaved a false sigh.

"You aren't miserable, just serious. I have never seen this kind of humor from you except on rare occasions with Connor, and given the way things were between us when I left yesterday..." She regretted bringing up the previous afternoon as soon as the words left her mouth. "I'm sorry, Peter. I don't want to bring up anything to spoil our picnic."

He took an arm and placed it around her shoulders, giving her a gentle squeeze. "I was an ass yesterday. I am sorry. No more questions. Enjoy the ride."

They spent the hour riding in companionable silence until they came to a small grove of pine trees next to a stream. Peter drove the buggy under the trees, and helped Bernice down. "It is a little too early for lunch. Shall we go for a walk?"

She took his arm and followed as he led her on a path along the stream. After they had walked about a half mile, he stopped and picked up a stone and skipped it over the water. "I bet you did that a lot when you were growing up," she said.

"Connor and I used to come here to go fishing and swimming." He looked out over the water and Bernice saw a glimpse of the boy he must have been. It was sad, she thought, that life had robbed him of the joy he was experiencing now.

"Those must have been happy times." She leaned against a wide trunked elm tree watching the sun streak through the tree leaves and glint off the water.

He put his arms on either side of her and gave her a sweet kiss. "I thought that kind of pure joy was lost to me forever, but you changed that. It feels good to simply skip a stone across the water. So many things feel good because of you."

Peter took both her hands in his. "I did a lot of thinking last night, and finally came to the realization this morning that no matter how much I fight it or try and deny it; I am in love with you. If I have to live my life without you, the shell of a man that I am will crack and fall apart. Please marry me, and save me from that fate." There was a pleading tone in his voice as he continued, "You should know me well enough by now to know that I would not say what you want to hear just to get you to marry me. If I were not deeply in love with you, I could never say the words."

"Why now?" Bernice had to ask the question.

"How much do you know about Jenny?"

"Martha told me that you loved her and never got over it when she died."

"We planned to marry when we were older, but she became ill with scarlet fever. There was nothing that could save her. Her death is the reason I became a doctor. She was only 16 when she died. I refused to eat or sleep, and wanted to die so I could be with her. Connor brought me out of it, by goading me into a fistfight of all things, but it helped spend the anger. Strange as it may seem, the pain from the beating I took at his hands made me at least feel something – that I was still living and breathing. I managed to survive, but that was all I was doing –until you came into my life. Last night when I was laying awake, I knew that knowing you were alive and I had lost you would be the worst thing that could ever happen to me. I realized that to open oneself to love is to lay oneself open for loss. It is the price we pay because the real loss is not to love. With you I am no longer a shattered man missing those pieces of my heart. All the pieces come together, and my life is complete. I love you, Bernice. You have to believe me. I wish you could know the sincerity of my heart. Please marry me."

Bernice took his face in her hands and kissed him. "I believe you."

"Then you will marry me?"

"Yes."

He gave her a lingering kiss and then held her against his chest for a few minutes before saying, "Let's go have our picnic and talk about our wedding."

When they got back to the buggy, he retrieved the basket, opened it and spread out the blanket with Bernice's help.

While they were eating their sandwiches, he asked, "Do you want a big wedding or small one?" He asked.

"Small – just family and friends."

"Good. I do not want to wait any longer than necessary."

"We probably should wait for mother to return, but she will not be happy about it, and my sister said she may be staying in Europe longer than she planned, as she has found a titled friend."

"Why don't you wire her the date? It will be up to her as to whether she comes or not. Would you be terribly upset if she was not there?"

"She would most likely only spoil the day for me, since she is not going to be happy." Bernice stroked his cheek.

"I'm sorry, love. Would it help if I wrote to her?"

She shook her head. "Most likely she would not even open your letter. Let's not let her spoil it for us."

"All right, but I want to go and see your father and ask his permission."

"He will say yes."

"You seem awfully sure about that."

"He told me he has a lot of admiration for you." Bernice rested her back against the tree and handed the one remaining cookie from their lunch to Peter. He took a bite and then held it up to her lips. She took a small bite.

"You can do better than that," he teased. She took a big bite leaving only a tiny piece in his fingers and crumbs spilling down the front of her dress as she laughed with her mouth full of cookie. A fleeting thought of what her mother's reaction to such behavior would be caused her to laugh even more. She could just see the horrified expression and hear the lecture that would follow, but for this moment in time, it didn't matter. It seemed silly. She felt silly, rather like a schoolgirl. Perhaps that was because Peter was acting like a schoolboy.

He took her hand and raised it to his lips, kissed her palm, and then turned it over and kissed the backs of her fingers. He held her hand to his heart. "Feel that. It's a healed heart that will love stronger than before with love for you and our children." He dropped her hand, lay down on the blanket and rested his head in her lap.

She stroked his hair, pushing a stray lock from his forehead. "Children?"

"Would you like to have children? I just assumed you would since you seem so comfortable with Clare."

"I have never given it much thought. Marriage and a family of my own didn't seem possible in my world. I thought I would just go on working in the dispensary with you."

"My mother would be happy to take care of our children so you could continue to work with me, if you are concerned about that." Peter seemed to be searching her face.

"Martha watching a baby would be perfect." She bent her head down and kissed him.

"Sara's Glen was a wonderful place for Connor and me when we were young boys. Our children will be happy playing with Rasheen and Connor's offspring, all the while being spoiled by my mother."

"Perhaps we should tell them we are to be married before we have them watching our children." She laughed.

He closed his eyes and said, "You have made me a very happy man."

"And you have made me a happy woman. I would say that makes us well suited." Bernice removed his head from her lap and scooted down where she could snuggle next to him. "I cannot wait to see everyone's faces at Sara's Glen when we tell them. Martha is going to be impossible since she will feel this is all her doing."

Peter yawned. "They are all going to have to wait for a bit to hear the good news because right now I am going to take a nap."

She kissed his closed eyelids, rested her head on his chest and closed her eyes. "That is an excellent idea."

CHAPTER 17

Bernice and Peter arrived at Sara's Glen just as the family was sitting down to the evening meal. He opened the door for Bernice and then took her hand as they walked into the dining room. He looked down at her and gave a conspiratorial wink as they stood there not speaking.

Martha looked up at them and then gave Rasheen an "I told you so" nod without saying anything.

There was a satisfied smile on Peter's face as he announced, "We have some news."

Connor set the forkful of food he was about to lift on his plate and asked, "Do you now, and what would that be?"

"We are going to be married." Though he spoke to those seated at the table, his gaze rested on Bernice filling her with a happiness she would never have believed possible until this moment.

"Jaysus …I mean Jakers," Connor quickly corrected his language when his wife frowned at him. He threw down his napkin and got up to give Peter a slap on the back. "It is about time you realized what a gem you have there."

Martha and Rasheen jumped up from their seats to hug the happy couple.

"Good," said Jack with his mouth full, escaping a verbal reprimand from Martha since she was busy gushing over her future daughter-in-law.

Finally, everyone sat down again, including Bernice and Peter, since they had been expected for dinner and their places were already set. John, who had been quiet up to this point, raised his glass. "To the happy couple," he said. "Bernice, we will be proud to call you daughter.

Thank you for showing my son that he can be happy again."

Martha reached across the table and patted John's hand. "Didn't I tell you?"

Peter took a sip of sweet tea before asking, "How could you have known when I just figured it out for myself?"

"Your face is gentler, your voice becomes softer when you say Bernice's name. You say her name differently than anyone else's. I know love when I see it."

"I never realized I was so transparent," Peter mused.

"You are not. At least not to others, but a mother knows her child."

"Blarney," Connor snorted. "I knew he was hooked the moment he saw Bernice on that horse when she and Rasheen returned from a riding excursion."

Bernice enjoyed watching the two men tease one another. She almost cheered Peter on when he answered, "As I recall, it was you who was smitten with Rasheen at the time."

Connor was not about to give up. "And that was how I recognized your symptoms. You do realize that Aunt Elaine and Martha have done everything imaginable to orchestrate this match. Of course, I suppose it is my duty to warn Bernice that life with you isn't going to be a living paradise."

"Your wife doesn't exactly have a bed of roses." Peter gave Rasheen a sympathetic glance.

"I do not believe my wife has any complaints about our bed or what happens thereon." Connor winked at Rasheen and asked, "Isn't that right, love?"

Her face turned a deep scarlet. "Connor Reilly, will you please behave yourself?"

"Come now, dear, we would both hate that."

Not to be outdone, Peter continued the discussion. "I can assure you; Bernice will have no regrets. In fact, she will be absolutely rapturous."

Bernice felt herself blush all the way to her toes.

"Bernice, I have never seen you blush before," Rasheen noted.

"I…it's just a bit warm in here," Bernice stammered.

"Enough of this nonsense! Let's discuss the wedding," Martha said. "I was cheated out of a wedding by these two," she said, pointing to Rasheen and Connor, referring to the fact that they had eloped. "I would suppose your family will want a big wedding with all society present."

Bernice shook her head. "Actually, we would prefer a small wedding – perhaps at the Stone House with only our close friends and family present."

Rasheen raised one dark brow. "What about your mother?"

"She most like will not even come. You know this is not part of her grand plan," Bernice said.

Rasheen gave her a sympathetic look. "I'm sorry."

Bernice shrugged. "Don't be. Martha is more of a mother to me anyway. You all have been the family I would have liked to have had growing up, and now you will be my family."

"Be careful what you are thankful for. You might not be so sure about it when you have to deal with us all the time," Rasheen laughed.

"You are forgetting all the days we were at the little school," Bernice said. "You are my dearest friend and soon to be sister, so I can think of no one else I would want to be my matron of honor. Will you do it?"

Rasheen gave her a broad smile. "Of course, I will. Have you decided on a date?"

"Peter needs to get some things in order at the dispensary and then we are going to visit my father in New York so Peter can ask his permission. We'll be picking a date after that."

Connor gave Peter a questioning look.

"Bernice tells me, that unlike my future mother-in-law, he likes me and will be happy about it," Peter reassured him.

"That is good to know."

"Are your parents planning to move to New York when your mother returns?" Martha asked.

Bernice wasn't sure how to answer. She didn't feel it was her place to reveal her parents' marital discord, but she could not lie to Martha. "Since my mother is going to be away for so long, my father took up residence in New York for his business. I honestly don't know what the future holds for them." That was the truth for the time being.

*****

Two weeks after their engagement announcement at Sara's Glen, Peter and Bernice left to visit her father in New York with a stop in Baltimore at the Reilly residence on the way. Peter wanted to visit the City Dispensary to confer with a colleague about one of his elderly patients in North County. He managed to get a promise from his mother and Rasheen not to write Elaine with the news of the upcoming wedding, as he and Bernice wanted to share the good news in person.

After dinner, Patrick took Peter into the library to go over some investments with him, and give him some papers to take back to Connor. While the men were discussing business, Bernice caught Elaine up on all the news from Sara's Glen except one upcoming event. It was almost bedtime by the time the two men joined them in the parlor. Peter sat next to Bernice on the sofa, took her hand, and grinned. "Now?"

She laughed. "I am about to burst. I thought the two of you would never finish."

Elaine and Patrick shared a warm smile between them, but kept quiet waiting for the young people to speak.

"Bernice has agreed to be my wife." Peter raised the hand he was holding to his lips and kissed it.

Patrick shook Peter's hand, hugged him and then

hugged Bernice. Elaine hugged and kissed both of them. "We could not be happier. Well done, you two. When is the happy event to take place?"

"When we leave here, we are going to New York to see Bernice's father so I can ask his permission. The wedding will be as soon as possible after that," Peter said.

"You will need at least a few months to plan a proper wedding, and Bernice's mother is still in Europe," Elaine said.

"We are going to be married when we return from New York. It is to be a simple ceremony in Peter's home with only family and friends in attendance. I plan on sending a cable to my mother informing her of the wedding and the date." Bernice felt a twinge of sadness at the thought that her mother would not wish to attend even if she were home, but more than anything, she had a sense of relief. Everything would be much easier if her mother just remained where she was and left them in peace.

Peter put his arm about her shoulders and gave a gentle squeeze. "You will have to get used to saying our home."

"The young people in this family just won't let us have a proper wedding," Elaine sighed. "But it is very romantic to be married in the home you will live in and raise your family. At least we will be present at this one."

"Dearest, you cannot blame Connor and Rasheen for eloping. Under the circumstances, they had no other choice." Patrick was referring to the fact that Connor and Rasheen had married quickly to save her reputation after they were found spending the night in his home without a chaperone, even though the circumstances were innocent.

"I am so happy for the two of you. It doesn't matter what kind of wedding you have as long as you are happy, but Bernice does need a beautiful gown. She can go to see my dressmaker tomorrow while you are at the Dispensary," Elaine said.

Bernice gave her an apologetic smile. "I am afraid I have made an appointment with Sister Imelda. We are going to meet while Peter attends to his affairs."

"When was this appointment made?" Peter arched a questioning brow.

"I wired her when I found out we would be stopping in Baltimore before visiting father." Bernice gave a sheepish grin. "I was waiting until after Sister and I finished working out the details before telling you, but everything seems to be in order so I will share the news now. You may recall awhile back my mother's aunt left me her estate which consists of a rather large house near Mount Vernon Place. I had planned to either sell it or donate it to some sort of charity that works for children. However, when I was at the Dispensary with you the last time, I got an idea that might put it to the best use. The sisters are going to operate it as a home for unwed mothers. Sister has made it possible for members of her order to help staff it."

Bernice waited anxiously for Peter's response, but he sat rubbing his chin thoughtfully. After several anxious moments, he spoke, "You amaze me. You are one of the most intelligent women I have ever met." He glanced over at Elaine. "And I have been in the company of well-informed women my entire life. Leave it to you to identify a need and be generous enough to offer the solution." He shook his head in disbelief, repeating, "You are incredible."

A flush of pleasure at his admiration washed over Bernice. "Then you are not upset with me for keeping it a secret?"

"Well, after we are married, I hope you share this sort of thing with me, but no, I am not the least upset with you." He bent down and kissed the tip of her nose. "In fact, why don't you ride to the Dispensary with me, keep your appointment with Sister Imelda, and then go see the dressmaker with Elaine? We will stay an extra day."

"That sounds perfect, if it is all right with Elaine." Bernice liked the idea of shopping for a special gown for the wedding. Everything was happening so fast she had not given her wedding dress much thought.

"Splendid! I will send word to her that we will be there tomorrow around two if that is agreeable to you." Elaine clapped her hands together. "Now if you young people will excuse me, all this excitement for one night has made me rather tired."

"It has been a long day, and besides, you young people need some time to yourselves," Patrick said as took Elaine's hand.

Peter stood and stretched. "Tomorrow is going to be a busy day. I think Bernice and I should be getting to bed also."

"You will be in your room as always, and I've put Bernice in Connor's old room this time. We are having some decorating done in the guest rooms," Elaine said over her shoulder as she walked from the room.

Peter waited for Patrick and Elaine to exit the room and then caught Bernice up in an amorous embrace. His lips slowly descended to meet hers in an intimate kiss. When he was finished, he whispered into her ear, "I will be paying a visit to your room this evening." His breath was warm on her neck.

"Do you think that is wise? Suppose someone sees you?"

He chuckled and took her hand to lead her upstairs. "No one will see me enter or leave. I promise."

Bernice felt a thrill at the idea of a secret liaison. "Give me half hour. And for heaven's sake, please be careful. I would not want Elaine and Patrick to think ill of us."

Peter gave her a wicked grin as he planted a kiss on her cheek and left her just inside her bedroom door. "Half hour."

Exactly a half hour later, Bernice was standing at her door in her robe listening for any sound that might be Peter. Hearing none, she cracked the door and peeked out. The hallway was empty. "Where are you?" She whispered.

"Right here." A voice behind her answered.

She spun around to face him. "But how did you get in here?"

"Through that door," he said pointing to a door on the other side of the room. It was the door to the dressing room that she had just used. "You probably didn't notice, but the floor length mirror is attached to another door that leads to my room. Connor and I used to share the dressing room when we stayed here. Elaine has made it very convenient for us to have a tryst."

"Then perhaps I am overly dressed," Bernice said.

Peter stood there in nothing but his trousers having disposed of his shoes, socks and shirt in his own room.

"For what I have in mind, love, we are both overly dressed." He pulled the belt on her robe loose and yanked it off her shoulders, throwing it over the vanity chair. Something fell out of the pocket and he bent to retrieve it. "What's this? Were you writing me a love letter?" He teased.

Bernice looked perplexed. "Not this time. What is it?" When he handed the paper to her and she read the first line she knew immediately what it was. "It is a letter from my mother with advice on how to properly train my husband to avoid the marriage bed. I must have shoved it in the pocket and forgotten about it." She rolled her eyes.

Peter laughed. "It cannot be that bad. May I see?"

She handed it to him. "You are not going to approve."

As he began to read, his facial expressions changed from humor to annoyance. "This is rubbish. Is there any wonder women are seeking hysteria treatments when they are fed this nonsense?"

Bernice put her arms about his waist. "You needn't worry. I won't be following mother's advice."

"Just the same, I think as your doctor, it is my duty to inform you of the proper facts," he teased, a sensual flame burning in his amber eyes.

Bernice smiled. "I am a most willing student. Please

proceed."

He read a section of the letter out loud. "Never allow your husband to see you unclothed, and under no circumstances allow him to display his naked body. The marital act should be practiced only in total darkness with only enough clothing removed to allow for the act to be completed. Be careful not to allow your husband any hint of compliance."

Peter took her hand and led her to the bed. "This information is all wrong. Let's see how I can go about correcting it."

*****

Much later, when they lay in each other's arms, she said, "Mother has it all wrong."

Soon they were both sound asleep, with Bernice's head resting on Peter's chest. They stayed that way until the next morning when a soft knocking at the door woke them. Bernice opened her eyes not certain of her surroundings at first, and then remembered where she was and who she was with. She rolled over and nudged Peter. "You better leave. The maid is here."

There was another knock at the door. "Miss Peterson?"

"Just a minute," Bernice answered.

Peter opened his eyes, kissed her, jumped out of the bed, grabbed his clothes, and fled the room.

An hour later when Bernice came downstairs, everyone was already having breakfast.

"I hope you slept well dear," Elaine said.

"Yes, very well, thank you." Bernice took her seat next to Peter, who had come down a few minutes before her, and accepted a plate of eggs, toast and bacon from the butler.

"You both looked so tired yesterday, but to be honest, you look like you were up half the night."

"I can't remember when I have had a better night," Peter said as he gave Bernice a conspiratorial smile.

"Nor I," she sighed.

*****

"What do you mean, he is no longer here?" Bernice asked the hotel clerk. She and Peter had planned to surprise her father with their visit. She knew even if he were spending most of his time with Julie, he would still keep a room at the Sturtevant for appearances sake and would have his mail sent to that address.

"He took ill last week and was taken to the hospital. He has since checked out, and his mail is being forwarded. Would you like for me to check the address?" The clerk began to sort through his card file without waiting for an answer. "I have here that his mail is going to the address of a Mrs. Boughers. Would you like me to copy it for you?"

"Thank you, but I know that address." Bernice clutched Peter's arm in panic and whispered, "Something must be terribly wrong."

He brushed a gentle kiss on her forehead. "Don't fret, love. Everything will be all right."

"Will you be checking in, Sir? The clerk asked.

"We would like adjoining rooms." Peter instructed the clerk. He signed the register, instructed the clerk to have their bags taken to their rooms, and then led Bernice toward the hotel door. Once outside on the bustling New York City street, the hotel doorman acquired a hansom cab for them, and they were on their way to Julie Boughers' home.

When they arrived at the Boughers' residence, they were escorted to the parlor where Julie and Mr. Peterson were having tea with another gentleman. The man, who appeared to be about her father's age, was distinguished looking with thick silver hair and a mustache to match. Bernice noticed a black medical bag next to his chair. Before anyone in the room could speak, she rushed over to her father and threw her arms around his neck. "Papa, Papa…" she choked out.

"There, there, child, I am all right now," her father said. "Julie should not have troubled you."

"But I did not go against your wishes," Julie protested.

Bernice straightened and walked over next to Peter. "Peter and I came for a surprise visit to share some news. I was not expecting to be the one surprised."

Julie invited them to have a seat and had the maid bring more tea. Once the maid had left the room, Mr. Peterson introduced the gentleman who had been seated next to him. "This is Doctor Wilkinson. He has taken excellent care of me, as you can see. Doctor Wilkinson, may I present my daughter, Bernice, and her friend, Doctor Schmidt."

"It is an honor to meet you," Peter said. "I worked with a colleague of yours, Doctor Leonard, when I was at University Hospital."

"He is a good man, as are you, Schmidt. Thanks to your efforts to have Lister's method of antiseptic surgery promoted, a great many of my patients are living today who most likely would not have been otherwise," Doctor Wilkinson said.

"It is gaining acceptance, but it has been a herculean struggle." The two doctors continued talking medicine while Bernice, Julie, and her father sat in silence, each anxious about the discussion that would follow when Doctor Wilkinson departed.

Doctor Wilkinson rose from his seat. "Mrs. Boughers. I will take my leave now, and allow you to have a family visit."

Mr. Peterson rose to see him to the door, but Peter interrupted. "If you would allow me, I would like to discuss your case with Doctor Wilkinson."

After Mr. Peterson gave his permission, Doctor Wilkinson retrieved his bag, and the two doctors disappeared into the hallway where their soft voices were heard.

Julie steepled her fingers and touched them to her lips

several times as if trying to make a decision. She studied Bernice for a few seconds and then finally spoke. "There is something different about the two of you."

"That is not important at the moment." Bernice gave her father a stern look. "Why did you keep your illness from me?" She was not going to let Julie escape a chastisement either. "And you should have wired me, no matter what he said."

Julie gave her a contrite smile. "You have every reason to be upset with us, and I, for one, promise that I will never keep anything regarding your father's health from you again, no matter what he asks of me."

Bernice swallowed the lump of fear that had been in her throat. "All right then. I suppose I have no choice but to forgive you."

"And tell us your news," Julie said.

When Peter stepped into the room from the hall, Bernice walked over to him and took his hand. "Peter has something he wishes to ask Papa."

A wide grin crossed Mr. Peterson's face. "I'll be damned."

Julie and Bernice both chided him, but Peter laughed and asked, "Does that mean you will give your consent to my marrying your daughter?"

"You have my consent and my blessing." Mr. Peterson rose from his chair, and shook Peter's hand.

Julie whispered to Bernice. "I knew something was different. I am so happy for both of you."

The next several minutes were spent discussing Bernice and Peter's future plans. After they informed Mr. Peterson and Julie of their intention to marry as quickly as possible, Julie gave Mr. Peterson a worried look. "You have to tell them."

Bernice ran over and knelt at her father's feet. "What is it Papa?"

He stroked her hair. "Your mother is unhappy with your lack of progress with regards to Mr. Kingsley. She sent me a threatening letter with a Post Script for you."

"How could mother possible threaten you?" Bernice asked before realizing the obvious answer.

"Oh," she said as she watched the exchange between her father and Julie. "She knows, but how?"

Julie answered before Mr. Peterson could continue. "One of her friends saw us together in Central Park and wrote to her. She hired a private investigator."

"She has threatened to ruin Julie with a very public divorce unless I persuade you to hasten your progress in fulfilling her wishes," Mr. Peterson said.

"And I told him that he was not to worry you with any of that," Julie added.

"But there is more," Mr. Peterson leaned over and kissed Bernice's forehead. "That same person has informed her that you were seen in the company of Doctor Schmidt on several occasions, and an attachment seemed to be forming. In her message to you, she says you are to cut off all contact with him at once and if she does not receive a copy of the Sun Paper Society page with your engagement notice to Ambrose Kingsley by the end of the month, she will see that Doctor Schmidt is ruined."

Peter shrugged. "I doubt she could hurt me."

Mr. Peterson held up his hand palm outward. "Do not discount her. Her friends have husbands in high places. A word here and there and you would find yourself without patients because they were afraid of the consequences from their employers, bankers, landlords, etc."

"I don't understand." Bernice shook her head, brows drawn together. "She would be cut off from her society friends should she divorce."

"She says she will wait until after you and Kingsley marry and then seek a quiet divorce if you do as she wishes," Mr. Peterson said. "From her letter, I gather she plans to remain in Europe."

"Then why is she so concerned with a marriage between Ambrose and me?" Bernice wondered.

"Because she thinks that is in your best interest. That is what she has raised you for – a successful marriage. She has no idea of the happiness you will have with Peter," Julie said.

"I still cannot believe she would risk harming her standing in society, and why on earth would she want to remain in Europe, unless…"

"Unless what?" Peter snapped.

"Unless it has something to do with my sister's letter." Bernice rubbed her temples with her fingers to try and relieve the tension that gripped her like a vise.

Peter began to massage her shoulders. "What was in the letter?"

"Something about a titled aristocrat. She is his guest, and apparently acting as his hostess since he is a widower."

"Connor has people who find information for him. Perhaps he can see what this is all about," Peter said. "I will have him look into it for us as soon as we return home."

"But this is in Europe," Bernice cautioned.

"It doesn't matter. Connor knows people that can find information, and I think Patrick might have friends in Scotland Yard." Peter squeezed her shoulders and ceased his massage. "Better?"

"Much, thank you." Bernice gave a long sigh. "We will have to wait until this is settled before we marry."

"Rubbish," Julie protested. "You will do no such thing. Your father and I will be fine, and so will Peter."

"Julie and I will be all right. It is Doctor Schmidt that I am worried about." Bernice's father moved in his chair to get more comfortable and winced.

"Doctor Wilkinson has given me some pain medicine if you need it." Peter removed the bottle from his pocket and handed it to Julie.

"No, nothing like before. It was just a slight twinge from moving. And if you are to be my son-in-law, I think we can dispense with the formalities. My name is

Charles."

"Very well then, Charles, follow Doctor Wilkinson's instructions and you will be back to your normal activities in a week or so."

*****

Bernice rested her head on Peter's bare chest and breathed a contented sigh. They had refused Julie's offer to come and stay with her and Bernice's father, insisting that he needed his rest. Peter acknowledged to Bernice while that was true, he had the selfish motive of getting her back to the hotel where he could sneak into her room. He had done just that and continued her education as to the proper way for a wife to respond to her husband. The instruction had proven satisfactory to both parties. Now as she lay in his arms, worry snaked its way into her mind, crawling over her happiness.

"Peter, you don't think Doctor Wilkinson kept anything from us regarding Papa's illness, do you?" Her intelligence told her otherwise, but her fear refused to be reasonable.

He brushed a strand of hair from her cheek. "Your father and Julie rented a boat and he did the rowing himself. Apparently he pulled a muscle in his chest and the pain was so intense that he thought he was having a heart attack. It was nothing as serious as that, but he needs to rest a bit. Doctor Wilkinson is one of the finest doctors in the country, and he says there is no danger."

"Still, perhaps we should wait to get married. At least until he is fully recovered." Bernice ran her hand over his chest. "None of this makes sense. My mother only likes scandal when it applies to someone else. There has never been any in our family. This has to have something to do with her titled friend."

Peter took her hand and placed it over his heart. "Connor will find out."

"I really would like to wait until my father is fully recovered to get married." Bernice felt the steady beat of his heart, the rhythm constant like the man beside her.

"That should be in about two or three weeks at the most. There is no need for us to change our plans."

The apprehensions regarding her mother lingered. Even with an ocean between them, her mother was still controlling her life. *Only if you allow it*, a small voice whispered.

CHAPTER 18

Ambrose swirled the brandy in his glass, gazing into it as if it were a crystal ball about to give him an answer. When it did not, he tossed it down, and then refilled his glass from the decanter that rested on the ebony cabinet. Once more, he stared into the amber liquid, but this time he spoke. "Let me get this straight. You want me to get my friend at the Sun Paper to have an engagement notice printed, and that notice is to announce our coming nuptials? Darling, while I am not averse to a marriage of convenience with you, what about Doctor Schmidt? I thought things were going rather well between the two of you."

Bernice paced in front of the large parlor window, once to the right, then to the left, and back again before turning, folding her hands and touching them to her lips thoughtfully. When she brought them back to her sides, she said, "They are. Peter has asked me to marry him. We are engaged."

Ambrose chocked on the brandy he had just swallowed. When he finally got himself under control he said, "Don't you think he might object?"

Bernice waved her hands. "No, well, I mean he would not be happy about it if he knew, but there is no need for him to find out."

"Bernice, you can't put a notice in the Society Column that you are marrying another man, and not expect your fiancée to find out about it."

"I don't want you to have the notice actually printed in the paper, just a fake copy that we could send to my mother." Suddenly realizing she had not told Ambrose about her visit to her father and all that had transpired, she perched on the edge of the sofa and explained her reasons for the request. "I just want Mother to leave things be until Papa is fully recovered."

"What did the doctors say?"

"Doctor Wilkinson says it was an injured chest muscle, and Peter says that he was probably already recovered, but they wanted him to rest for another few days as a precaution."

"Then why are you going to all this bother?"

Bernice knew that Peter and Doctor Wilkinson were right, but she wasn't ready to face her mother's wrath. And even though Peter had said she could not harm him, she was afraid for him. What if her father was right about her using her position in society to influence people that could destroy him? And what of Julie? "I need more time. Peter said Connor knows people who might be able to find a way around her."

"But how?" Ambrose rubbed the back of his neck.

"I have no idea, but something is peculiar. My mother is threatening to divorce my father and create a scandal. Can you see her doing that?"

"Perhaps it is an idle threat," Ambrose said.

"But she also said she will divorce him quietly if I do as she wishes, and she plans on living in Europe, Ambrose. None of it makes any sense. My mother's world is here. She pictures herself the queen of North County, and aspires to be the ruling Society Matron in Baltimore. Why would she stay in Europe where she is unknown?"

"It is a mystery to me." Ambrose shook his head. "I will get your copy for you, but are you certain you want to keep this from Peter?"

Bernice leaned back into the sofa. "He would never approve, even though it is something that no one will ever see other than my mother. Maybe we can get through this without him ever knowing." A cold chill in her heart told her that was impossible and the small voice inside her reminded, "*An ocean separates you, yet you give her control.*"

Ambrose put his drink down and knelt in front of her, taking her hand in his, and looked deep into her eyes with an expression she would almost believe if she did not know how well he was schooled in masking his true feelings. "My Dear Miss Peterson, by now I am certain you must be aware of my high regard for you. Will you do me the honor of pretending to marry me?"

Bernice burst into a fit of giggles, "But Mr. Kingsley, I do not see a ring for my finger."

In a stern voice, he said, "I am willing to wager you did not giggle when the good doctor asked for your hand. And come to think of it, I do not see a ring on your finger either."

Bernice tried to speak in between the giggles. "We are having a special ring made. It will be a wide gold band with inlaid crushed gems around the border. I wanted something that would be practical for when I am working with my herbs and plants, and he wanted something which he said befitted my beauty."

"Since you will not be working after you are married, what difference does it make?"

Bernice gently slapped his hand with her free hand. "I most certainly will continue to work after I am married. Peter not only approves, but insists."

"How can you marry such a brute, when I am offering you my undying love?"

"You are not offering me that kind of love." The laughter bubbling up inside her chest was making it difficult for Bernice to speak.

Ambrose sprung to his feet and sat next to her on the sofa. "Ummm… now my dear girl, you are going to have to explain what you mean by that kind of love."

"We are not that close," Bernice said with a shake of

her head.

Ambrose took her hand in his, and said in a more serious tone, "Even though our relationship has been deceitful where your mother is concerned, I don't think you should involve the good doctor in any deception. Are you certain you want to do this?"

Bernice chewed on her lower lip as she thought a minute. "Maybe it isn't such a good idea. I am never confident with my actions when it comes to my mother."

"I know, but this is your chance at happiness. Don't let her spoil it. You love him. He loves you. Your father supports you in this. No matter what your mother threatens, he is the more powerful of the two. Trust him." Ambrose brushed a kiss on her forehead.

She stood and took his hands. "You're right. I don't want to do this. What would I do without you to give me courage?"

"Yes, you are a fortunate woman to have two men love you." Ambrose waggled his brows.

"Your humility is the thing I admire the most about you." Bernice rolled her eyes. "Now you have to leave." Peter will be here in a few minutes." Bernice rang for the butler who retrieved Ambrose's hat and gloves.

He gave her a forlorn sigh that was anything but sincere. "Now I am regulated to becoming the other man in your life."

*****

Peter checked to make sure the cotton bandages were comfortable and secure before he reached over to grab a strip of Plaster of Paris soaked linen from Bernice. He then wrapped it around the bandages on Ben Hart's broken arm. She had prepared the plaster solution, while he worked on Ben's arm and explained to him what they were going to do and how long it would take to heal. It still amazed him how Bernice was completely in tune with him as he worked, knowing exactly what he needed and when he needed it.

Ben was one of Connor's workers, a young man of about eighteen, who was learning how to train the horses under John's guidance. He had been thrown by a horse earlier in the day and now was worried about not being able to work. "How long is this going to take to heal, Doc?" He asked anxiously.

"About six weeks. In the meantime, do not get the cast wet. You will probably experience some itching under the cast, but there is nothing we can do for that. If you feel any burning or pain, come in and let me check on it. Just make sure you stay off the horses until that arm is completely healed. In fact, it would be best if you stayed away from them entirely. No sense in taking any chances."

"Doc, I can't afford to do that. Mr. Reilly is not going to keep me if I am not able to pull my weight." The young man jumped off the table and reached for his hat which was hanging on a peg on the wall.

"Mr. Reilly will find something for you," Peter assured him.

Bernice removed the unused linens and plaster solution. After she finished that task, she wiped down the table where they had been working on the patient. She didn't say anything, but nodded in agreement.

Connor arrived a few seconds later to check on Ben. "How's the patient?"

"He's worried about his job. I told him he is to stay away from the horses until that arm is healed," Peter said.

"No need to worry, Ben. We'll find something for you. There is plenty to be done and when you are healed, you can go back to work with the horses. John tells me you have the makings of a first-rate horse trainer," Connor assured him. "I would not want to lose you."

"Thank you, Mr. Reilly." Ben gave the cast a dubious look. "How do you get this thing off anyway, Doc?"

"We will try using scissors, and if they prove too difficult we will soak it in a vinegar and water solution and then unroll it. Unfortunately, both are time consuming and frustrating for patient and doctor, but we will get through it."

Connor offered to take Ben home, and on the way out told Bernice and Peter he would see them at dinner at Sara's Glen later.

After the two men had gone, Peter went into his office to go through his mail and do some paper work. Bernice went to work in her herb room. About an hour or so later, he called her into his office. He tossed a letter onto the desk and chuckled. "That is from my cousin, Violet. She is very upset with me for not visiting her when we were in New York. It seems my mother has written her about our engagement and she is anxious to meet the woman who finally captured my heart. She and I were very close before my parents moved to Sara's Glen. Violet is like a sister to me. Her parents sent her to visit our farm during the summers when we were youngsters. You might say she was my best friend before Connor came along."

Peter held up the letter which Bernice noticed was signed, Your Affectionate Bo Peep.

"Why Bo Peep?" More importantly, there had never been another woman. Rasheen had been right.

"On one of her visits, it was time to shear the sheep. Violet thought it would hurt them so she opened the pen and let them loose. My brothers and I had to get them all back inside again. After that we called her Bo Peep like in the nursery rhyme because she had lost the sheep."

Bernice rested her hand on his shoulder. "I hope she approves of me."

"She will love you. In fact, she and her husband are coming to Baltimore to set up some kind of business arrangement with Alex Brown and Sons." He put his hand over hers as he continued. "Violet is a financial wizard. Gilbert and she are opening an investment firm in New York. She will choose the stocks and he'll do the trading since women aren't allowed on the stock floor. They have invested their own funds and made enough profit that they can afford to open the firm. In fact, Connor and I are going to be among their first clients."

"How does she know which ones to choose?"

Peter shrugged. "She has always had a knack for figures and can predict the chances of a business's success when given the right information. I would trust her with my money any day. In fact, Patrick and Connor use her insight for a good portion of our investments and she has done very well by us. I can't wait for her to meet you and Rasheen. The three of you are very much alike."

Peter reached across the desk and retrieved another letter. "Almost forgot, this one's for you."

She took it from him and sat in the chair next to his desk and opened it. The letter was from Sister Imelda.

Peter finished what he was working on and looked over at her as she bent over the letter reading intently. Her brow wrinkled in a little frown, and her lips pursed. "Bad news?"

"Sister is having problems acquiring the services of a doctor for our home. It seems Doctor Ogden is blocking her efforts."

"I can get around Doctor Ogden."

Bernice gave him an appreciative smile. "I think I know a midwife who would be willing to help us on a permanent basis, but we still would need a doctor for the more serious cases. It would be helpful if you could persuade Doctor Ogden to stop being an obstructionist."

"Anything for you." Peter slid his chair back from the desk and reached out his hand. "Come here." Once she was in front of him, her hand in his, he sat her on his lap and placed her arm around his neck. She nuzzled her face into his neck.

"Has Ivy left for the day?"

"I would have to check my pocket watch and at the moment, I am unable to do so."

She gave him a wicked grin, as she slid off his lap. "It wouldn't set well if someone were to come in and discover us here. I thought if Ivy were gone, we might walk over to the house."

"When we are married, we can go over to the damn house any time we want," he growled, keenly feeling her absence from his lap.

"Never mind that now. Can we take that walk or not?" She said as she leaned down and nibbled his ear.

He took out his watch and checked the time. "Ivy is gone, but we have to leave for Sara's Glen, or we will be late for dinner. Wouldn't do for us to be in the middle of making passionate love and have Connor stroll in with our dinner."

She gave a disappointed sigh. "No, I suppose not."

"After dinner we are going to discuss our wedding plans. I am going to get the license tomorrow. I cannot take any more of this sneaking around. Pick a date and make it soon."

"What about my father?"

"You have been assured by two doctors that he is all right. Stop worrying."

"But the business with my mother?" She bit her lower lip.

"We stick with the original plan."

"But, Peter, even if I write her and she wanted to come to the wedding, a month is not enough time."

"My point, exactly. Do you really want your mother here? She will just spoil it for you."

Peter stood up behind her and placed his arms about her waist. "Pick a date and make it soon."

"We agreed to next month."

"Too long."

"I need to go to Baltimore to get my dress and even though our wedding will be small, we still need to make some arrangements."

"Next month – no later." He drew her up against him, placing his lips on her neck.

"Next month," she sighed.

"Thank you. You have just made me a very happy man."

CHAPTER 19

Bernice finished the remainder of her breakfast, and sipped her coffee, thinking of her conversation with Peter the previous evening about setting a wedding date. Peter was right. There was no reason for them to delay their marriage plans. Her father and Julie had both assured her they would be fine, and they did not care about being cut by society. Julie was not part of Mrs. Astor's 400 anyway. She traveled in the art set and was a bit bohemian.

Peter was safe from any harm her mother might try to inflict. She doubted that her mother's friends would go to the trouble of having their husbands put pressure on Peter's patients. Half of his patients worked for Connor Reilly anyway. Besides, he didn't need the income from patients, not that there was much. Most of them were poor working men. Connor's Uncle Patrick had seen to it that Peter was well invested and wealthy on his own without the necessity of his medical practice. If he lost patients for a while, he had assured her he would merely concentrate on his research, and perhaps put in more time at the City Dispensary. In fact, they were going to the city tomorrow so that Peter could meet with one of his former colleagues to discuss a project they were working on. While he did that, she was going to interview a housekeeper for the home for unwed mothers while he attended to his medical business. The woman was a friend from her days at her former boarding school. In addition to being the housekeeper, she was a skilled herbalist and could also function as a midwife if the occasion arose.

Bernice tapped her finger to her lips thoughtfully. Peter was right about not having her mother present at the wedding. Tonight, she was going to write her mother telling her of her engagement to Peter, or better yet, she would wait until after they were married and send her mother the announcement of the marriage of Miss Bernice Peterson to Doctor Peter Schmidt. She could just see her mother going into apoplexy when she read it. A sense of strength came to her as she grew more determined to grasp the happiness that was hers. Only one thing was required – take back control of her life from her mother. When she thought of how much she loved Peter, the task was a simple one. Why had it taken her entire life to get to this point? Because she had never been in love before, she thought.

She walked over to the Italian walnut sideboard and poured herself another cup of coffee from the ornate silver pot. She grinned at the idea of performing such a breach of etiquette in her mother's house. Obviously, the butler was none too pleased with her action as he entered the room, just as she finished pouring the coffee. "Miss Peterson, please allow me," he said as he took the cup from her and placed it on the table, pulling her chair out and seating her properly. He then handed her the morning paper and asked if she required anything else.

"That will do, thank you, Samuel." No need to argue with the poor man. When her mother returned, things would be just as always in the Peterson household, with one exception – Bernice would no longer live there and she would no longer be Miss Peterson. Warmth surged within her at the thought of being Mrs. Peter Schmidt and the future that would be shared by the happy couple.

*****

Peter looked up from the paper he was writing and watched Bernice through the open door to the workroom. She was using the pestle to crush some lavender and the scent drifted into his office making him feel far too relaxed for the task at hand. Next to the pile of lavender she was working on sat sage and yarrow. There were some bottles on the table and some liquid to mix a tincture. He enjoyed watching her work. Her forehead had a slight furrow and her lips were drawn in as she seemed to be deep in thought.

The office door opened, and the excited voice of Jimmy Fitzgerald pulled him out of his thoughts. "Doctor Schmidt, Pa says you have to come. Ma is in labor and it ain't going too good."

Peter rose from his chair and walked around the desk to put his arm on the boy's shoulder. "What seems to be the trouble?"

"Don't know. She's not been so good all night, and Pa says the baby should be here by now. Mrs. Knott's there helping and she's real good at birthing babies, but even she is worried."

Peter nodded. "All right, let's see if we can get your sibling born. Do you need to ride back home with me?"

"No sir, I rode the plow horse."

"Okay, then you get home and tell them I am on my way."

By this time Bernice was standing in the doorway. Peter looked over at her and asked, "Would you like to go along and assist me? I can't say how this is going to turn out. Mrs. Knott's experienced in these matters. If she is worried enough to send for me, it doesn't look promising."

"I have never been present for a birth. I would like to come along."

"Let's hope all goes well and it is a happy experience." Peter began packing his bag with things he would need, and then told her to bring any of her herbal remedies that she thought might be helpful.

*****

It took them a little over an hour to get to the

Fitzgerald farm. A small farmhouse resembling a cabin sat at the end of the rutted dirt drive off of the main road. There was a nice sized porch on which sat a roughly made wooden chair and a bench. Mr. Fitzgerald greeted them anxiously at the door and led them into the bedroom where Mrs. Knott was rubbing his wife's back as she worked through a contraction. He ran his hand through his thick red hair. "It's been like this all night, and I suspect yesterday, but she never said anything until later in the day when she asked me to send for Mrs. Knott."

Peter knew better than to give any false hope. "Let me confer with Mrs. Knott and examine your wife. For now, you and Jimmy can sit on the porch or find something to do to keep you occupied. She is going to need you when this is over and it won't do any good if you are just as worn out as she will be."

Mrs. Fitzgerald thrashed her head from side to side as she struggled through another contraction. Her dark hair was braided in one long braid that hung off to the side of the pillow. The braid kept the hair from getting in the way had it been loose. After talking to Mrs. Knott and examining his patient, Peter pulled the sheet back and said, "The baby is breach. I am going to have to turn it."

By this time Mrs. Fitzgerald was in a semi-conscious state, and Peter was worried that she might not survive what he was going to have to do, but if he didn't turn the baby, both the mother and child would be lost.

He went into the kitchen and pumped some water from the hand pump into the sink and then poured some water from one of the four pots that Mrs. Knott had put on the stove to boil. Then he rolled up his shirtsleeves and washed his forearms and hands with soap before using some of the solution from a bottle that he had brought to sterilize them. When he returned to his patient, he pulled the sheet covering Mrs. Fitzgerald up to her chest. He instructed Mrs. Knott and Bernice to stand on either side of the bed and pull her legs up and hold them apart as wide as they could.

"This is going to hurt, but you can't push – no matter how bad it gets." Mrs. Fitzgerald screamed as another contraction ripped through her body just as he invaded it with his hand. He gently grasped the unborn infant's foot. Mrs. Knott and Bernice spoke softly to Mrs. Fitzgerald trying to talk her through the pain as Peter found the baby's thighs and guided the second foot down into the birth passage. He looked up just as the mother gave a whimper and then went limp and silent. "Don't give up on me now. Stay with us."

Bernice reassured him. "She is still breathing."

"Hold her open, it's almost over." Peter struggled to keep the infant's feet together and guide them out. He withdrew his hand as another contraction struck her. Almost immediately, tiny feet appeared. "We've got two feet showing," he said quietly, beginning to hope for the best.

Mrs. Fitzgerald stirred, pain fluttering across her features as she regained consciousness.

"You can push now. It's coming," Peter grasped tiny feet slippery with blood, then felt something give as the thighs appeared. A moment later, a torso and two tightly crossed arms slid into his writing hands.

"A daughter," he said.

A loud cry wrenched from Mrs. Fitzgerald's chest as the baby's head appeared in a gush of blood and fluid. Peter was holding a perfectly formed little girl, covered with patches of white vernix and blood. The baby was very much alive, relieving his fears of a stillborn.

He wiped the infant's face with a clean cloth, then turned her over and patted her back. A wad of mucus came from the baby's mouth and then she was squalling like any other newborn. It was the most beautiful sound he had ever heard. He laid the baby on her mother's stomach, looped the umbilical cord, tied it off, and then cut it.

Mrs. Knott picked the baby up, wrapped her in a towel and carried her over to the washbasin for her first bath.

Bernice held Mrs. Fitzgerald's legs open while Peter delivered the placenta and placed it in a bowl to be buried later. Then she helped him clean their patient and assisted while he sewed up the torn tissue. He said a silent prayer of thanks that there was no hemorrhaging, just the normal bleeding and placed a thick cloth pad between her thighs and lowered her legs.

"Dry gown for the new mother," he said handing the garment to Bernice. "Perhaps you might give her a quick sponge bath first. It will make her feel a little better." He turned and crossed over to check on the newborn.

She was perfect - tiny, wizened face, ten fingers and toes. By the sound of that first cry, she possessed a healthy set of lungs. He wrapped the baby in a swaddling blanket and exchanged a relieved, happy grin with Bernice. Mrs. Knott carried the newborn over to her mother, who settled her in the crook of her arm. Immediately the tiny mouth began to root searching for her mother's breast.

Once their patient was made comfortable, Peter told Mrs. Knott she could bring in Mr. Fitzgerald and Jimmy.

Bernice, Peter and Mrs. Knott left the room so the little family could have some privacy. "Only for a few minutes though, he cautioned. Your wife has had a rough time of it and needs rest." Mr. Fitzgerald nodded and thanked them.

Once the three of them were in the kitchen, Bernice poured them all some coffee and sliced some bread that was sitting on the table. "Thank you. I didn't realize I was hungry. I haven't eaten since yesterday," Mrs. Knott said. Suddenly her eyes filled with tears. "If you had not come, Doctor Schmidt, I would never have been able to save her or the baby. We would have lost them both."

Peter let out a long breath. "I had my doubts in the beginning. Don't belittle yourself. I could not have gotten that baby out without the two of you holding her and helping. We all did a good job today."

Mr. Fitzgerald came out of the bedroom holding the baby. "My wife fell asleep while the baby was still nursing. I held her at the breast until she was finished. Is that all right?"

Peter laughed. "It's fine."

"Miss Peters, would you mind tending to the baby, while I toss the dirty linens in the washtub outside?" Mrs. Knott asked.

Bernice took the baby from her father. "It would be my pleasure." The infant was beginning to close her eyes. "I think this little one is ready for a little rest just like her mama."

"Perhaps you better put her in the cradle." Peter motioned for her to go back into the bedroom with him. Once there he checked on Mrs. Fitzgerald to make sure she was resting comfortably. He looked over at Bernice, and she still held the baby as she stood over the cradle, gazing awestruck at the new life she had just helped bring into the world. Her mouth formed an angelic smile, as she whispered something to the newborn. His chest tightened and his eyes felt full. This couldn't possibly be tears – could it? A fleeting image of her like that with his child in her arms floated in his mind. That was all within his reach now, but on some level, it still terrified him. Life was a very fragile gift.

*****

On the beginning of their ride home they were both silent, each in their own thoughts. A while later, Bernice put her hand through the bend in his arm and leaned into his side. "That was….I can't even find the words. A whole new person just came into the world and you made it possible."

Peter chuckled. "Umm, well no, that would have been her parents."

"You know what I mean; if you hadn't been there the outcome may have been very different."

He frowned. "It still could have turned out bad."

"But it didn't. Thank you for allowing me to be there."

"You were, as always, a help beyond measure. I'm glad I got to share this with you. It is a miracle every single time - one of the best things about being a doctor. You looked pretty content holding her. What were you whispering?"

"She is so perfect and beautiful, I thought of something I read in one of the psalms – I thank you God that I am fearfully and wonderfully made."

There was that pressure in his eyes again. "That is a perfect description."

She nodded. "One can't do better than the Almighty."

He placed a gentle kiss on her cheek. "Our children will be blessed to have you as their mother."

She wrinkled her brow. "I didn't expect to ever marry, or have a family."

"And now?"

She heaved a contented sigh. "Everything has changed."

CHAPTER 20

On the train ride to Baltimore, Bernice held Peter's hand and didn't care who might see them and report the impropriety to her mother. They could all go to the devil as far as she was concerned. She was too happy to care.

Before long, they arrived at Camden Station and headed to the Dispensary. Once there, Peter checked in with the old woman who sat at the front desk at the hospital entrance and asked her to locate Sister Imelda for Bernice. They had agreed that she would confer with Sister about her plans for the home for unwed mothers, and then leave to interview the person she wanted to hire, while he attended to his business. If they had time later, they would try and make a surprise visit to Patrick and Elaine before catching the last train back to Baltimore. A few minutes later, the old woman returned with Sister, and Bernice and Peter each went their separate ways.

Peter checked in with some of his friends and waited for his colleague to arrive. He noted the changes at the Dispensary since his departure. There was a new addition with a surgical room. He was pleased to see the progress, and itched to perform an operation there using the latest techniques.

A short time later, he received a note telling him that his friend had been delayed and would not arrive until later in the day. That meant they would miss the last train to North County and would end up spending the night at

Patrick and Elaine's. A slight glitch in plans, but he knew Bernice wouldn't mind. Sister Imelda passed him in the hallway as he was walking, "Doctor Schmidt, I understand congratulations are in order. You look content. I am so pleased and happy for you. Bernice is a rare young woman."

"Thank you, Sister. I have to agree with you. Has she left for her aunt's place?" Peter looked down the hall to check even as he asked.

"I am afraid so, and her aunt's place is now called Joseph's House. Bernice and I decided that would be a good name as we are asking St. Joseph to protect these young women and their babies just as he protected Mary and her baby. Aren't you supposed to be meeting with Doctor Hendler?"

"Unfortunately, he has been delayed and that is going to change our plans. I have a few hours before he arrives, and thought I might take Bernice to lunch, if she finishes her interview early. If you will excuse me, I am going to see if she is agreeable to that."

Sister smiled. "I don't think it will take much persuasion on your part. Have a pleasant lunch, Doctor."

*****

"Then it is settled, you will take the job and teach the sisters all that you know about herbs." Bernice had met the woman sitting across from her during her time at Oldfield's Boarding school for girls. In addition to working as the cook at Oldfield's, Mrs. Murphy had been the community mid-wife when needed and was also a source of infinite knowledge when it came to herbal cures.

"It is a blessing. After my husband passed away last year, I decided to move to the city to escape the memories. But ever since Charlotte Eagerston started those rumors, no reputable family will hire me as their cook." Mrs. Murphy placed her cup in the saucer, and nodded when Bernice asked her if she wanted another cup.

The older woman took her hand and squeezed it.

"You are an angel."

"I am just happy you are willing to take the position. It is one less problem for me to worry about."

Bernice was in the middle of a sentence explaining her plans for the home when the maid came and announced Peter's arrival.

Before she could ask Peter the reason for his surprise appearance, something in his expression caught her attention. He was staring at Mrs. Murphy as if he had seen the devil himself.

"What is it?" she asked.

His voice had the edge of a sharp blade and cut just as deeply. "Do you have any idea who this woman is or what she does?" He jerked his head toward Mrs. Murphy whose jaw dropped open. "Surely, you read the newspaper."

"I have known Mrs. Murphy since my school days. She is the one who first taught me about herbal cures."

"You can't have her here with these women after what you witnessed with that poor girl in the Dispensary, surely you understand."

Bernice shook her head. "I understand that you would feel as you do, if Mrs. Murphy was guilty of your accusations, but she is not."

"You may not want to acknowledge that she is an abortionist because of your past association with her, but that does not change the story in the paper. She was charged with performing at least one and who knows how many others?" Peter folded his arms in front of him, unyielding.

Bernice mimicked his posture. "The girl who accused her lied, and she was proven innocent. However, the papers never bothered printing that story, nor would they use the girl's name as she comes from a wealthy family. She ruined this poor woman all because she thought she might be pregnant and came to Mrs. Murphy to rid her of the pregnancy. As it turned out, she was not, but she wanted to punish Mrs. Murphy for refusing her."

Peter dropped his arms to his side. "Then I apologize, but surely you understand my reaction."

Bernice lowered her brows and said in a stern voice, "Yes, I understand better than you know. It is perfectly all right for the male gender to use women's bodies and hearts and then discard them like broken toys. Men like your esteemed Doctor Ogden sit in judgment while not doing a thing to make things easier for these poor women. The self-righteous Anthony Comstock and his laws make it so a woman can't even space the conception of her children without the risk of going to jail for using any method other than abstinence and how many men are willing to abide by that? No, it all falls on the poor woman. What about the maids and working women? They are helpless against the predatory sexual behavior of powerful men. Society's double standard punishes them for the sins of men. And yet when I try to do one small thing to help, you climb up on that pedestal with the rest of your gender." The words poured out of her much to her surprise.

Peter held his hands up in surrender. "Everything you say is true, but you know I do not think like that. Would you hold me accountable for other men's actions when you know otherwise?"

Realizing that he spoke the truth, she shook her head. "No, you don't. Mrs. Murphy is special to me. I guess I'm still angry about her treatment, and you bore the brunt of that anger."

Peter walked over and kissed her on the forehead. "Bernice, I do believe you have a fierce temper, and I never want to be on the receiving side of it. Now how would you and Mrs. Murphy like to have lunch with me?"

"What about your meeting?"

"Doctor Hendler was delayed. It looks like we will be staying with Elaine and Patrick tonight."

Bernice smiled up at him. "I really am sorry, Peter."

Turning to Mrs. Murphy she asked if the older woman would like to join them, but Mrs. Murphy said she had things to settle in order to make her move to Joseph House and that the young people needed some time on their own.

*****

Doctor Hendler had been responsible for the use of the carbolized surgical environment at Presbyterian Hospital just as Peter had been responsible for introducing it to the Baltimore Dispensary. When Doctor Hendler had returned to Presbyterian Hospital after a Medical Conference, he had risked losing his hospital appointment when he challenged one of the attending surgeons.

A 14-year-old boy was hit by a slow moving train, and sustained multiple rib and pelvic fractures as well as a deep laceration of the knee that appeared to enter the joint. The surgeon was about to explore the knee wound with his unwashed; bare little finger, as was the custom before proceeding with amputation. Doctor Hendler made strenuous objection, incurring the wrath of the surgeon who withdrew from the involvement with the patient. Using knowledge he gained at the Medical Conference, Doctor Hendler took over the case. First he irrigated the wound with a carbolic acid solution. Next, he sealed it with a collodion dressing which was made by dissolving a mixture of nitrate and sulfuric acid on cotton in ether and alcohol. The dressing dried instantly, forming an artificial scab that prevented air from reaching the damaged tissue. The wound healed without infection, and amputation was avoided. The patient recovered with no loss of function or wound problem. After that, Lister's sterilization methods were routinely used.

"How are things at Presbyterian?" Peter asked.

"Things are going very well." Doctor Hendler seated himself opposite Peter in the small meeting room. "How about here at the Dispensary?"

"It has been slow going trying to get the staff here to

use Lister's methods, but we are finally making progress." Peter offered Doctor Hendler a glass of water from the pitcher on the table, before pouring himself one. "I still have some influence, but not as much now that I no longer practice here."

"Why didn't you accept the Director's position? I always imagined you as Head Surgeon here, or at one of the more prestigious institutions."

Peter shrugged. "I grew weary of all the patients coming in from the factories and railroad with injuries that could have been avoided. It was exciting at first, but then it just never seemed to end. I like being back home with my family, and find that I have more time for research and reading as a country doctor."

"Hmmm … and I believe there is a young lady in your life. I heard you were engaged." Doctor Hendler smiled.

"I am." Peter returned the smile.

Doctor Hendler gave his congratulations and then changed the subject. "Are you using the sterilized dressings as well?"

"We are. The sisters were making them for us, but it is much easier now that a company has been formed that manufactures them." Before the sisters had begun sterilizing the dressings by using the carbolized acid solution, the doctors had simply used leftover floor droppings from the cotton mills to pack wounds. Surgeons never even bothered to wash their hands, and often operated or treated wounds in their frock coats with an apron for protection from blood splatters. The aprons were rarely, if ever, washed. Peter could hardly believe the improvements that had occurred in the last few years, many of which were due to doctors like himself and Doctor Hendler who were not afraid to battle the status quo.

CHAPTER 21

"Not too much longer and you will simply come home with me," Peter said as he brought her bags inside. Since they had arrived home later than expected, Bernice had dinner at Sara's Glen and then he dropped her at the Peterson residence.

Bernice put her arms around his neck and said, "I am looking forward to starting our new life together. I never thought I could be this happy."

"Oh, I plan on making you a very happy woman, but it is best I leave before we get ourselves into trouble." He reluctantly pushed her away and bounded down the stairs.

She stood in the doorway smiling as she watched him drive away. In her entire life, she never expected to experience so much happiness.

Once she had settled in for the evening, she picked up the pile of mail from the silver tray that was on the entrance hall table. She would go over it before retiring just to make sure there was nothing urgent. Most of the envelopes were invitations for her mother and a few calling cards had been left. She frowned when she spotted one from Mrs. Delacourte and tossed it in the waste can next to her writing desk. At the bottom of the pile there was a letter from her mother. With a confidence she had never felt before, she picked up the letter opener and tore it open. "Whatever you have to say won't spoil my happiness," she said, but her defiance quickly changed when she read the words on the single page.

It has come to my attention that you are behaving in a scandalous fashion, so I am taking matters in hand. I know what has been going on with you and that farmer's son. You will cease at once. I have instructed your father to speak to Mr. Kingsley and settle your future. If he is not successful, you are to book the next passage to Europe. I have made connections here that will assure you a marriage that will give you a title. This may be even greater than my previous expectations.

If you disobey me in this, there will be consequences. When Mrs. Delacourte informed me of your actions since my absence, I acquired the services of a Private Investigator. It seems that there was a rumor that Doctor Schmidt was involved in an abortion that resulted in a young girl's death. We have this on the anonymous information from one of the doctors at the hospital where he worked. If you do as I say, I will not disclose the information. If you do not, I shall have it printed on the front page of the Sun Paper. If you recall, Arunah Abell is married to my cousin, Mary Fox. One word from me, and all of his papers will print the story.

As for your father and his mistress, that will also be in the New York papers. I no longer care about the scandal as I have decided not to return to the U.S. I will be expecting the news of your engagement to Mr. Kingsley immediately, or a letter informing me that you will join me here. Otherwise, I shall be contacting Mary and the New York papers.

Bernice dropped the letter on the desk and felt her mother's cold shadow even as it reached across an ocean spreading numbness throughout her body, chasing the happiness she had felt just a moment ago.

She didn't know how long she had remained in this frozen state when the maid appeared to turn down the bed. After the young woman set out her nightclothes, Bernice dismissed her for the evening. Only after she heard the maid's footsteps fade down the hallway did she give way to hysterical sobbing as the anguish overcame her fragile control.

Before long there was a soft knock at the door, "Miss

Peterson, are you all right?" asked the voice on the other side.

Bernice took a breath, and said in as calm a voice as she could manage, "Yes, please just leave me be."

She got up from the bed, went to the far corner by the room, and once more yielded to the compulsive sobs that shook her, muffling them with her balled up handkerchief so no one would hear. Evening's gloom came and drove the last vestiges of twilight before she quieted for a bit, only to dissolve into tears again. She had never shed tears before. Such unseemly behavior was forbidden by her mother. Proper young women never revealed their emotions. Now she could not control them. Spasms of nausea overtook her as she broke down again and again, until dawn's light washed over the garden below her window. There were no more tears to shed now. She stared out the window. The sun was up. A new day was beginning, but there would be no joy in it for her.

She pulled the cord to summon her maid and had some coffee brought up to her room before dressing in a wrapper.

"Will that be all, Miss, or would you like me to bring up some breakfast?" the maid asked.

"Just have some more coffee brought to the breakfast room. I'll be down in a few minutes."

*****

"Darling, whatever has happened?" The question came from Ambrose who quickly strolled across the room and knelt in front of her, his voice soft and caring.

"Ambrose, please, just leave me alone." She turned away from him.

He put his hand under her chin, and turned her head, forcing her to look at him. A soft, loving smile touched his lips as he spoke to her. "Just look at you. That beautiful face is scarlet and swollen from crying. Something horrible had to have happened to cause this."

"How did you get past Samuel, and why weren't you

announced? I would have told him I didn't want to see anyone, not even you."

Ambrose shrugged. "I have my ways to get around servants, but the truth is that I think your maid told Samuel to let me come to you unannounced for the very reason you just mentioned."

Her voice a lifeless monotone, Bernice said, "She should have minded her own business. If I were mother, I would fire her."

"But you are not your mother, and your maid would not have acted so, if she were not worried about you. Tell me what happened. I gather it has something to do with the good doctor."

Bernice heaved a weary sigh and tried to look at him through her swollen eyelids. "I do not wish to talk about it."

"I am not leaving until you do." Ambrose sat on the floor, cross-legged with his arms folded in front of his chest in an undignified manner. Under different circumstances, she would have found it amusing.

"Ambrose... mother has won. She always gets her way. Why did I think it would be different this time?" She handed him the letter.

"Poor baby," he said when he finished reading it. "You aren't going to let this stop you, are you? You deserve to be happy."

"She will ruin him. I love him too much for that. If he can't practice medicine, he will be miserable. I won't destroy him like that. I won't be responsible for the people of this community losing their doctor." More tears. "Mother will drag me to Europe, and I will have to keep trying to avoid her matchmaking efforts."

"Darling, you are an adult. Your mother cannot drag you anywhere you choose not to go." Ambrose wagged his finger at her. "Please try and remember that."

"I do, I did, I mean I had made my mind up to marry Peter, and let her have her apoplexy in Europe, where I would not have to suffer it."

Ambrose heaved an exaggerated sigh. "We will figure this out."

"There is nothing to figure out."

"True love never runs smooth." He closed his eyes and winced as if in great pain. "Now look what you have done. I never use clichés."

The sound of horseshoes hitting the drive ended their discussion. Ambrose rose and walked to the window. "The good doctor is about to ring your bell. I think it would be wise for me to leave the two of you alone, so I will sneak out the delivery entrance."

"Ambrose, please, I cannot do this now," she pleaded.

"Then get yourself upstairs, and I will protect you from the poor devil, but only for today. Tomorrow, you deal with this like the sensible woman I know and love."

She kissed his cheek and fled up the stairs.

Ambrose shook his head and sighed. "Our marriage of convenience would have been much simpler than all this."

*****

Peter took out his pocket watch and checked the time once more. Where was she? It was already past noon. If she was going to be late or not come to the Dispensary, she would have sent word. Since there were no patients, he decided to close the office and ride out to the Peterson residence. He stopped by the stable and asked Joshua to ready a vehicle on his way inside the house to let Ivy know where he would be in case anyone showed up needing emergency treatment. When he went into the library and scribbled a note to tack onto the Dispensary door, he saw the stack of unread mail and noticed the fancy blue envelop with the unfamiliar handwriting. Mrs. Peterson's name was at the top of the missive. "This should be interesting," he mused to himself as he tore it open.

The letter instructed him to have no further contact with Bernice. Surely, he could understand how different their stations in life were and that he was ruining any chance Bernice might have with Mr. Kingsley. She went on to say that Kingsley was going to make his intentions known in the next few days. Bernice was to cut ties with him immediately. If he did not respect her mother's wishes, it would be a ruinous calculation on his part.

He crumpled the blue sheet of paper into a tight ball and tossed it into the waste bin. "Don't threaten me, woman. I'm not your daughter," he said as he stormed out of the room. No doubt Bernice had received a similar missive and that was the reason for her absence this morning. If her mother thought that he would let her marry anyone other than him, she was very much mistaken.

When he reached the Peterson house, Peter ran up the steps and forcefully pumped the bronze lion head doorknocker several times. To his surprise, the door was not opened by the Peterson butler, but Ambrose Kingsley. "What are you doing here? Where is Bernice?"

Ambrose did not answer the first question. "She is resting at the moment."

"Like hell she is. Get out of my way, Kingsley." Peter tried to push past him, but Ambrose did not budge so Peter took a swing at him only to have it blocked. Before he could get another one in, he felt a hard fist hit his jaw, sending him down the steps and sprawled on his backside.

Kingsley stood at the top of the porch steps.

Peter started up the steps. "I have to see her. You will have to kill me to stop me."

"Stop being so dramatic." Ambrose rolled his eyes as he opened the door, and let Peter pass in front of him. Once inside, Peter saw that Bernice was nowhere in sight. Ambrose explained the state she was in, and told him about the letter she had received from her mother.

Peter could see that Kingsley was worried about her. He could not stop himself from asking the question that was driving him into a jealous rage. "Are you in love with her? Do you wish to marry her?"

"She is in love with you." Ambrose poured them both a drink.

Peter took the glass from him and drank it down, feeling the burn in his throat. "Not enough to stand up to her mother."

"Give her time to gather her courage again. She'll overcome her fears of her mother. She is afraid for you and her father. In case you haven't noticed, Bernice always puts the interests of those she loves first."

"Do you love her?" Peter asked once more.

"Not the way you do. I cannot love any woman that way." Ambrose swirled the last drops of liquid in his glass. "Bernice and I worked out a plan where we pretended to be on the verge of an engagement. Such an arrangement worked well for both of us.

"What will you do now?" Peter asked.

"I have no idea. For what it is worth, Schmidt, I am on your side. She loves you, and I believe you can make her happy. She deserves that and more."

"Where did you learn to fight like that?" Peter rubbed his throbbing jaw. At least it didn't feel as if it were broken. In a short time, the side of his face would be swollen and purple.

"St. Vincent and I were on the boxing team in college, and I have kept up with the skill by working with a professional trainer at the gym on Keman's Corner"

Peter felt his chest tighten and his breath become labored at the thought of what might happen. "I cannot lose her."

Ambrose gave him a sympathetic slap on the shoulder. "You won't."

*****

The clock on the night table said ten past three. Peter jabbed at the pillow in an effort to reconfigure it to cradle his head better. Sleep came grudgingly, only to torment him with nightmares. In one he was going to see Jenny, but her father came to the door shaking his head. Inside the shadows of the room, her mother was wrenched with sobs. Then the dream changed, and the focus was on Bernice - how she had given him back hopes and desires long since abandoned. Happiness flooded his soul at the thought of the warmth and tenderness from her that transformed his life. Bernice's mother appeared in a black mist and snatched her from his arms, screaming that she would never allow her daughter to marry him. In the darkest hours before dawn, a dull empty ache gnawed at his soul as he twisted in the bed sheet until it became tightly wrapped around his legs as if it were a rope. The next morning he woke exhausted and determined to set things right with Bernice.

A few hours later, he stood at the Peterson front door, hand above the knocker. He inhaled sharply and pulled the knocker. To his relief, the butler answered, and he soon found himself in her parlor waiting and wondering if she would see him. If she declined, he would come back tomorrow, and the next day, and the next. He would not give up however long it took. His determined thoughts were interrupted when she walked into the room. She did not take a seat, or invite him to do so. She was dressed in an ivory colored dress with pale green stripes. The ivory color made her pale complexion appear even more translucent, and her lovely blue eyes were rimmed in red with dark shadows beneath them.

She stood there in ghostly silence.

Now he was getting nervous. "Say something."

She remained silent, but he saw the defeat in her eyes.

He would tear out his heart to remove it. "Bernice, don't let your mother do this to us.

Finally, she spoke. "Mother always gets her way. I should have known better than to try and get around her. I will not let her destroy you or my father."

Peter grabbed her shoulders. "Your father has assured you he will be all right, and I am not afraid of your mother."

"You say that now, but you would be miserable if you couldn't practice medicine. I won't be the one to destroy your life. I love you too much."

He grabbed her arm pulling her back. "You're a coward. Don't you know I will be destroyed without you?"

"Peter, please...." The remainder of her sentence was left unsaid. It hung in the air between them for a moment before she turned and walked away, leaving him standing in the middle of the room alone.

He knew it was futile to try and stop her. The finality in her voice made his stomach contract into a tight ball. He was already feeling her loss growing like a cancer, destroying his soul.

*****

An hour later, Peter stood in front of the crystal whiskey decanter in his study. He poured a full glass, tossed it back, and then poured another and drank that down. He stood there pouring and drinking three more glasses until the decanter was empty. "Hell," he said to the empty room as he grabbed a fresh bottle of whiskey from the nearby cabinet and set it and his glass on a small table next to a leather wing chair. He sank down into the chair and poured more alcohol into his glass, drinking it slower now. It was not helping to dull the ache that had settled in his chest.

Memories of Bernice would haunt him for the rest of his life. There had never been another woman like her, not even Jenny. He had been able to subdue the pain and banish it after Jenny, but it was back with a vengeance. Somehow he knew this time it would never leave, because as hard as he had fought against it, he had fallen in love with Bernice. She loved him, and now he had lost her.

He would drink all night if that's what it took to escape this pain. An unfamiliar trickle ran down his cheek, and he realized he was crying – something he had not done since Jenny died. In the blur of his tears, he saw Jenny, but she remained mute, a sad look on her face. "Tell me what to do now, damn you," he screamed. She faded away leaving him alone in his misery. He reached for the bottle, not bothering to pour any of the amber liquid into the glass this time, but rather put the rim straight to his lips gulping down what he hoped would help him get drunk enough to bring forth another image of Jenny so she could tell him what to do to make things right. She did not reappear, but at least he accomplished the feat of drinking himself into oblivion.

*****

"What in blazes is going on?"

The words thundered in Peter's ears as he struggled to remain in the comatose state he had finally reached in the middle of the night. A pair of strong hands shook him and sharp pains jolted through his head like someone was using it for target practice. "Answer me, for the love of God and all the saints, man."

"Leave me be," Peter mumbled. The words felt like dry clay coming out of his mouth.

"I will not." The voice got louder. "What happened?"

Peter forced his eyelids open and saw a blurred face not more than two inches from his own. Was he hallucinating again? It wasn't Jenny, and the voice was too loud. He closed his eyes again hoping it would go away, but it got louder and the hands began shaking him again.

"Open your eyes and look at me." The voice was familiar. Peter opened his eyes again and tried to make sense of the blurred image. After a few seconds of concentrated effort, he recognized Connor's face frowning at him.

"Go away, Connor."

"I guess we will have to sober you up first." Connor departed the room leaving Peter in peace once more, but now his head hurt, and he could not get back to his previous state of oblivion. He cursed Connor to hell and back.

A few minutes later Connor returned with a glass in his hand. "Here, drink this."

Peter accepted it, hoping the concoction might help slow down the herd of horses that were stampeding in his head. "Smells like manure," he croaked.

"Not supposed to smell good. In a few minutes it will do the job it was meant to do." Connor pulled him up out of the chair.

"What are you doing?" Peter tried to sit again.

"You are going to want to be beside the toilet when this stuff works." Connor dragged him upstairs to the bathroom just in time for the contents of his stomach to empty.

"Bloody hell! Are you trying to kill me?" he asked in between vomiting and catching his breath after each retching episode.

When it finally subsided, Connor drew him a hot bath and instructed him to get cleaned up and come downstairs. By this time his head hurt, his stomach hurt, and the pain he had drunk himself into oblivion to escape was back with a vengeance, so he saw no reason to argue, but did as instructed.

Ivy and Connor were in the kitchen when he came downstairs. "Ivy, would you please fix some eggs for Doctor Schmidt?"

"Nothing to eat for me this morning," Peter protested.

"Fix him the eggs." Connor insisted and then handed Peter the coffee he had just poured.

Peter drank it down in a quick gulp, the hot liquid burning his throat. "Hot," he yelped.

Connor rolled his eyes and looked upward. "Of course it is hot, you ejit."

Peter took some more, but a slow sip this time. The coffee was not helping his head, and his stomach thrashed. When Ivy put the plate of eggs and toast in front of him, he thought he would be sick again, but he could see

Connor was not going to let him be until he ate the damn things. Fine, then Connor could be the one to clean up after him when the contents of his gut came up again, because he was not going to do it, and Ivy was not hired to do that type of task. To his surprise, his stomach actually felt better once he got past the first few bites. Connor gave him a smug smile. "Doctors do not have the cure for everything. Sometimes the old remedies work better."

"And when did you ever have occasion to use this remedy?" Peter asked, his voice growing stronger.

"I got into a few situations while you were away studying medicine. One of my drinking mates taught me the cure. My life is such these days that I have no use for it, thankfully." Noting that Peter had finished eating, Connor rose from the table, grabbed his coffee, and motioned for Peter to do the same. "Ivy, we will be in the study and are not to be disturbed unless there is a medical emergency."

When they reached the study, Connor closed the door behind them. "Now tell me what happened to make you resort to such drastic behavior. You can start with how you got that bruise on your face."

"Kingsley gave it to me. It is over between Bernice and me." Peter relayed everything that had transpired the previous day while Connor drank his coffee listening intently.

"Kingsley is right. You need to give her time. She loves you. She will come round, but for now, you have patients to see and work to do. Keep busy for the next week and then try with her again," Connor assured. "She isn't planning on going to Europe right away, is she?"

Peter rose from his seat, his head once more reminding him of his overindulgence of the previous evening. "I doubt that she will rush to her mother, but I do think she will give in to Mrs. Peterson's demands."

Connor patted him on the back. "Beg, plead, throw her over your shoulder and kidnap her, do whatever it takes. The two of you would be miserable without one another."

*****

Peter opened the door to Bernice's workroom and went to retrieve one of her remedies for his head. Once more he was amazed at her organization as he found what he needed immediately. A pang of loss washed over him at her absence. How was he going to get through the day knowing she may never use this room again?

The day progressed with several patients, nothing major that would have required Bernice's assistance, but he missed her, and so did the patients. Everyone that came into the dispensary was concerned over her absence. Not wishing to expose their personal affairs, he gave the excuse that she had some personal business to attend to and was not sure how long it would take. He knew that sooner or later the truth would come out, but not today.

When the day finally ended, he sat at his desk remembering how she would come in at the end of the day, sit in the chair next to his desk, and talk. Before going home, he stopped at Sara's Glen for dinner. He wasn't hungry, but by now Connor would have told Rasheen and his mother what had happened between Bernice and him.

As he walked across the porch, he saw that Boots reclined near the threshold. Peter went to grab the screen door handle and the cat hissed at him. He stomped his foot. "Get out of my way you miserable feline, or I will kick you to Hades and back again." The cat blinked at him, stood and stretched, and then rubbed against his pant leg. "If I had known that was all it took to win you over, I would have threatened you sooner." Peter stooped down and rubbed the cat behind its ear.

"So, you have won over her pet. What about the lady?" The question came from Connor who was standing on the other side of the screen door.

Peter shook his head. He gently opened the door so as not to hurt Boots. The cat got up and came inside with him, all the while rubbing against his leg.

Dinner was quiet with no one mentioning Bernice. He imagined Connor had spoken to Rasheen and Martha. For once they were keeping their suggestions to themselves. He ate quickly, and excused himself saying he had work to do at home. Mercifully, no one argued with him.

When he was leaving, Martha asked, "Would you mind dropping by the Merryweather's place on your way home? Old Mrs. Merryweather took a fall and broke her wrist. The doctor over in Harford County set it, but she cannot fix meals, so we have been sending them something."

Less than half an hour later Peter was on his horse with the basket of food resting in front of him. By the time he got to the Merryweather's there was a light rain falling. He stayed and chatted with them as they ate their dinner. When he finally was able to leave, the rain had begun to pour down hard. The Merryweather's tried to persuade him to wait it out, but he used the excuse he had given his mother about having work to do at home, and there was no telling when the rain would let up again. By the time he got on his horse he was already drenched.

*****

Bernice sat in the gazebo watching a pair of blue birds picking about for bugs in the perennial garden which surrounded the structure. She always found peace here. It was one of her favorite places to come to escape, since her mother never used the garden because she said it aggravated her allergies. As far as her mother was concerned, the garden was merely for show. It was a shame for such a beautiful spot to be ignored. The garden was laid out in four rectangular beds with the daylily garden circling the gazebo in the center. The beds consisted of roses, shrubs, cutting flowers, annuals, and perennials. The blooms began with the blue, white and lavender crocus in early spring and ended with the scarlet and gold mums in the fall. Even with the gray sky threatening to send the rains all day, this was still her refuge.

The sound of footsteps on the stone pathway caught her attention. She looked around to see her father approaching. "I received a threatening letter from your mother," he said as he stepped inside the gazebo.

Bernice heaved a weary sigh. "I'm sorry. This is my fault. I should have known better than to try and deceive her. If I hadn't, you wouldn't be included in her threats."

"My dear girl, there is nothing to worry about."

The tears welled in Bernice's eyes. "There is everything to worry about. She is getting what she wants. She always gets her way. I will not see her destroy you and Peter just so I can be happy. She knows that."

Her father put his arms around her and held her against his chest stroking her hair. "Bernice, your mother is insane if she thinks Arunah Abell is going to run any story regarding me or Peter. He may be married to her cousin, but my bank holds his mortgage, plus he has several loans against his businesses. Not only is he heavily indebted to me, he is also an old friend from my college days."

"That won't stop her from getting her story in the New York papers to discredit you and Julie."

Her father gave snort. "Let her try. Whitelaw Reid is an old friend of Julie's husband and godfather to Matthew. He controls the news industry in New York. Your mother is not the only one with connections."

Bernice pulled away and looked up at her father feeling like a small child who had just been rescued from danger. "Father, are you sure?"

"Before I caught the train here, I checked with Whitelaw and I stopped at Abell's office on my way to North County. Both men assured me that they would not involve themselves in your mother's affairs or mine. Now I believe you have a young doctor that you need to visit."

"But what about you? You just got here."

"You go and see Peter. I will spend the night here and be on the first train back to New York tomorrow. Julie is going to be waiting for me and not have a moment's peace until she knows you and Peter are going to go ahead with your wedding plans."

*****

Since Joshua had left for the day, Peter took care of unsaddling his horse and feeding it before going inside to take care of his own needs. Once in the house, he shed his coat and draped it over a kitchen chair. The rain had soaked clear through to his shirt which clung uncomfortably to his skin. He was about to dash up the stairs when he noticed that the lamp in the parlor was lit. Ivy would not have lit it, because she left before darkness set in. A bit uneasily, he stepped away from the stairs, and headed towards the parlor.

Bernice stood up from the chair next to the lamp, and walked to him without waiting for him to come through the door.

He opened his arms and she stepped into them.

She gave him a tender kiss and then noticing the wet spot forming on her bodice where she had leaned into him. "You are soaked. We have to get you out of those clothes before you get a chill."

Peter swept her up in his arms and started up the stairs. "Excellent idea. Care to join me?"

She snuggled safely against his chest in silent reply.

*****

"Why aren't you up yet?" The voice crashed through Peter's dream of Bernice in his arms all night. He smiled when he opened his eyes and realized it was not a dream. The shouting was in the hallway now and getting closer.

Peter jumped out of bed and pulled on his pants just as Connor came through the bedroom door.

"You better not ...." Connor stopped just inside the doorway. "Bernice?"

Bernice pulled the sheet up to her chin. "Good morning, Connor." She shrugged a shoulder at Peter. "I guess we should share our news."

"It had better concern a marriage between the two of you," Connor warned.

"The wedding will take place next week," Bernice announced calmly.

"Next week?" Both men said in unison.

Bernice reached a hand to Peter. "If you can arrange it, I see no reason to wait."

"No problem, but are you sure?" Peter took her hand and sat on the bed next to her.

Bernice gave him a radiant smile. "I have never been more certain of anything."

"I think Martha and Rasheen will be fine with moving the wedding up a week. Now I will leave the two of you alone. Perhaps it would be best if I tell Ivy she has the day off," Connor suggested.

Bernice shook her head. "I trust Ivy to be discrete should she arrive before I get myself together. Besides, we have patients to see and work to do."

"You are definitely the right woman for Peter," Connor laughed as he left them.

Putting his arm around Bernice, Peter said, "Connor, in the future I would appreciate it if you do not barge into my bedroom."

Connor grinned. "Understood."

CHAPTER 22

Six Months Later

"Did you know you had letters from Ambrose and Julie?" Peter asked as he handed Bernice an envelope. She was sitting in her favorite chair in their parlor. It sat facing the fireplace, with a window at her back so she had good light to read by during the day.

"I saw them when we got home, but we were late to dinner and then after Ivy left, you had other plans that did not involve the parlor. Remember?"

He remembered. After all, it had only been an hour ago. "Ummm, perhaps we might make use of the parlor for something other than sitting and reading."

She giggled. "I would like to read my letters, if you don't mind."

He winked. "Later, my dear."

She waved her hand in mock dismissal, tore open her letter and began to read.

Peter plopped down in the chair across from her, and picked up the newspaper. In the last six months they had settled into married life easily.

Bernice held up a newspaper clipping Ambrose had sent her and read aloud. "After he was jilted by a certain young socialite, a prominent gentleman left Baltimore and is touring Europe with his business associate to heal his broken heart." She tossed it on the small table next to her and fished a sheet of paper out of the envelope. "Ambrose writes that he and St. Vincent plan to reside some place in France."

Peter let his paper drop to his lap. "I never thought I would say this, but I am going to miss him." Once he had learned the true nature of Bernice's relationship with Ambrose, and no longer saw him as a threat, they had become good friends.

"I am glad the two of you got to know one another." Bernice sat the letter aside and opened the one from Julie. "She does not give a flying fig about propriety when it suits her purpose."

Peter looked up from the newspaper, a surprised expression on his face. "Are you talking about Julie?"

Bernice shook her head. "I was referring to my mother. She is marrying the elderly nobleman she befriended. She has petitioned my father for a divorce. As soon as it is final, Julie and Papa will be married in a quiet ceremony, but they want us to be there and stand up for them. At least now they can all be happy."

"I am surprised the aristocrat will marry your mother. Surely, they will be outcasts among his peers." Peter folded his paper and tossed it over on the table next to Ambrose's letter.

"This man is very powerful, and he has no heirs. His nephew stands to inherit, so he is also pushing for acceptance of her. Better mother than a young woman who might provide another heir." Bernice set the letter down, and looked up at the portrait over the mantel admiring it just as she had every day since its arrival last month. Julie had them sit for a portrait when they had visited New York shortly after their wedding.

Peter got up and went over to her chair, pulled her up and put his arm around her waist as they both gazed up at the painting. "They look happy. "

"They are. Julie said painting this picture gave her so much joy, because now your smile reaches your eyes."
"That is because I am looking at you."

ABOUT THE AUTHOR

Alice and her husband, Drew, live in Harford County, Maryland. She worked for several decades as an administrative assistant for various professionals including lawyers, engineers, educators, and even the clergy. In between jobs, she received her AA degree with honors from Essex Community College where she took every writing class offered

Alice's first novel was "By Fortitude and Prudence" that introduces the story of Peter and Bernice.

When not writing, she enjoys reading anything from the colonial period to the Gilded Age. Her other favorite pastime is baking, especially cookies.

She and her husband have traveled all over the United States, and parts of Canada and Ireland. Favorite places these days are Colonial Williamsburg, Seneca Lake in upstate New York, and Cape May, NJ.

Alice can be contacted at: alicebonthron@gmail.com.

Made in the USA
Middletown, DE
12 November 2019